THE TIME TRAVELERS

A SCIENCE FICTION QUARTET

Edited by
Robert Silverberg
and
Martin H. Greenberg

DONALD I. FINE, INC.
New York

Library of Congress Catalogue Card Number: 84-73521
ISBN: 0-917657-66-7

Manufactured in the United States of America

10 9 8 7 6 5 4 3 2 1

This book is printed on acid free paper. The paper in this book
meets the guidelines for permanence and durability of the Committee on
Production Guidelines for Book Longevity of the Council on Library
Resources.

CONTENTS

INTRODUCTION

For me there is no more satisfying kind of science-fiction story than the one that involves travel in time. From my first encounter with the theme, when I stumbled upon H. G. Wells's *The Time Machine* at the age of ten and came away transformed and inspired, time-travel stories have seemed to me to deliver most intensely that special astonishment that science fiction provides. To rove freely through the eons—to spy on the dinosaurs, or to look upon the beings that will inhabit our planet when the sun is old and dim, or even to go back for dinner at one's great-great-grandparents' house— I have always found profound pleasure in that sort of story, both as reader and as writer. And I feel particularly rewarded when the story is of the intermediate length that is usually termed a "novella."

The novella—a story of 20,000 to 40,000 words, too long to be considered a short story, too short to be regarded as a true novel—is unusually well fitted for science fiction. A short story, by its very nature, can provide no more than a glimpse of its setting: the short story turns on a single intersection of conflict and character, and there is little room in it for an elaborate depiction of background detail. A novel, of course, has scope for any amount of such detail; but in science fiction, at least, the development of the central idea often exhausts itself in the first fifty or hundred pages of a book and the remaining space is given over to the spinning out and resolution of the plot. But the novella seems just right to me: it offers space enough for rich depiction of scene, character, and idea, without involving itself in the intricacies of a full-length plot. When the novella deals with the wonders and paradoxes of travel in time, it is, I think, the perfect convergence of theme and structure.

H. G. Wells's pioneering *The Time Machine* was itself a novella. So too was Robert A. Heinlein's startling and oft-reprinted *By His Bootstraps,* which is probably the definitive time-paradox story. I have found the novella length congenial myself for any number of time-travel stories—*Hawksbill Station, Homefaring,* and *In Entropy's Jaws* are the first of many that come to mind. Hardly any science-fiction writer worth his Hugos has failed to tackle this immensely fertile and challenging theme.

In the present volume Martin Harry Greenberg and I have brought together four of our favorite time-travel novellas for your amazement and delight. Here we have Henry Kuttner and C. L. Moore's *Vintage Season,* that lovely and haunting tale of tourists from the future roaming our unhappy century; *Sidewise in Time,* by the veteran science fictionist Murray

Leinster, which introduced the concept of parallel time-tracks to s-f; John Wyndham's elegant *Consider Her Ways*, in which a woman of our time visits an era where men are obsolete; and Isaac Asimov's gentle, warm-hearted *The Ugly Little Boy*, that unforgettable piece about a little Neanderthal brought forward into the modern world. I think they demonstrate quite adequately the wondrous power of this most liberating of science-fictional themes.

—*Robert Silverberg*
Oakland, California

THE UGLY LITTLE BOY
by
Isaac Asimov

Time travel depends upon one's point of view. To the traveler, he may be going into the future. But from the viewpoint of those at the time of arrival, the traveler may be coming from the past. However, what happens when the traveler has no choice in the matter? What then? The masterful Isaac Asimov gives us one possibility in "The Ugly Little Boy," one of the most moving stories in the history of science fiction.

Edith Fellowes smoothed her working smock as she always did before opening the elaborately locked door and stepping across the invisible dividing line between the *is* and the *is not*. She carried her notebook and her pen although she no longer took notes except when she felt the absolute need for some report.

This time she also carried a suitcase. ("Games for the boy," she had said, smiling, to the guard—who had long since stopped even thinking of questioning her and who waved her on.)

And, as always, the ugly little boy knew that she had entered and came running to her, crying, "Miss Fellowes—Miss Fellowes—" in his soft, slurring way.

"Timmie," she said, and passed her hand over the shaggy

brown hair on his misshapen little head. "What's wrong?"

He said, "Will Jerry be back to play again? I'm sorry about what happened."

"Never mind that now, Timmie. Is that why you've been crying?"

He looked away. "Not just about that, Miss Fellowes. I dreamed again."

"The same dream?" Miss Fellowes's lips set. Of course, the Jerry affair would bring back the dream.

He nodded. His too-large teeth showed as he tried to smile and the lips of his forward-thrusting mouth stretched wide. "When will I be big enough to go out there, Miss Fellowes?"

"Soon," she said softly, feeling her heart break. "Soon."

Miss Fellowes let him take her hand and enjoyed the warm touch of the thick dry skin of his palm. He led her through the three rooms that made up the whole of Stasis Section One—comfortable enough, yes, but an eternal prison for the ugly little boy all the seven (was it seven?) years of his life.

He led her to the one window, looking out onto a scrubby woodland section of the world of *is* (now hidden by night), where a fence and painted instructions allowed no men to wander without permission.

He pressed his nose against the window. "Out there, Miss Fellowes?"

"Better places. Nicer places," she said sadly as she looked at his poor little imprisoned face outlined in profile against the window. The forehead retreated flatly and his hair lay down in tufts upon it. The back of his skull bulged and seemed to make the head overheavy so that it sagged and bent forward, forcing the whole body into a stoop. Already, bony ridges were beginning to bulge the skin above his eyes. His wide mouth thrust forward more prominently than did his wide and flattened nose and he had no chin to speak of, only a jawbone that curved smoothly down and back. He was small for his years and his stumpy legs were bowed.

He was a very ugly little boy and Edith Fellowes loved him dearly.

Her own face was behind his line of vision, so she allowed her lips the luxury of a tremor.

They would *not* kill him. She would do anything to prevent it. Anything. She opened the suitcase and began taking out the clothes it contained.

Edith Fellowes had crossed the threshold of Stasis, Inc. for the first time just a little over three years before. She hadn't, at that time, the slightest idea as to what Stasis meant or what the place did. No one did then, except those who worked there. In fact, it was only the day after she arrived that the news broke upon the world.

At the time, it was just that they had advertised for a woman with knowledge of physiology, experience with clinical chemistry, and a love for children. Edith Fellowes had been a nurse in a maternity ward and believed she fulfilled those qualifications.

Gerald Hoskins, whose name plate on the desk included a Ph.D. after the name, scratched his cheek with his thumb and looked at her steadily.

Miss Fellowes automatically stiffened and felt her face (with its slightly asymmetric nose and its a-trifle-too-heavy eyebrows) twitch.

He's no dreamboat himself, she thought resentfully. He's

getting fat and bald and he's got a sullen mouth. But the salary mentioned had been considerably higher than she had expected, so she waited.

Hoskins said, "Now do you really love children?"

"I wouldn't say I did if I didn't."

"Or do you just love pretty children? Nice chubby children with cute little button noses and gurgly ways?"

Miss Fellowes said, "Children are children, Dr. Hoskins, and the ones that aren't pretty are just the ones who may happen to need help most."

"Then suppose we take you on..."

"You mean you're offering me the job now?"

He smiled briefly, and for a moment, his broad face had an absentminded charm about it. He said, "I make quick decisions. So far the offer is tentative, however. I may make as quick a decision to let you go. Are you ready to take the chance?"

Miss Fellowes clutched at her purse and calculated just as swiftly as she could, then ignored calculations and followed impulse. "All right."

"Fine. We're going to form the Stasis tonight and I think you had better be there to take over at once. That will be at 8 P.M. and I'd appreciate it if you could be here at 7:30."

"But what..."

"Fine. Fine. That will be all now." On signal, a smiling secretary came in to usher her out.

Miss Fellowes stared back at Dr. Hoskins's closed door for a moment. What was Stasis? What had this large barn of a building—with its badged employees, its makeshift corridors, and its unmistakable air of engineering—to do with children?

She wondered if she should go back that evening or stay away and teach that arrogant man a lesson. But she knew she would be back if only out of sheer frustration. She would have to find out about the children.

She came back at 7:30 and did not have to announce herself. One after another, men and women seemed to know her and to know her function. She found herself all but placed on skids as she was moved inward.

Dr. Hoskins was there, but he only looked at her distantly and murmured, "Miss Fellowes."

He did not even suggest that she take a seat, but she drew one calmly up to the railing and sat down.

They were on a balcony, looking down into a large pit, filled with instruments that looked like a cross between the control panel of a spaceship and the working face of a computer. On one side were partitions that seemed to make up an unceilinged apartment, a giant dollhouse into the rooms of which she could look from above.

She could see an electronic cooker and a freeze-space unit in one room and a washroom arrangement off another. And surely the object she made out in another room could only be part of a bed, a small bed.

Hoskins was speaking to another man and, with Miss Fellowes, they made up the total occupancy of the balcony. Hoskins did not offer to introduce the other man, and Miss Fellowes eyed him surreptitiously. He was thin and quite fine-looking in a middle-aged way. He had a small mustache and keen eyes that seemed to busy themselves with everything.

He was saying, "I won't pretend for one moment that I understand all this, Dr. Hoskins; I mean, except as a layman, a reasonably intelligent layman, may be expected to understand it. Still, if there's one part I understand less than another, it's this matter of selectivity. You can only reach out so far; that seems sensible; things get dimmer the further you go; it takes more energy. But then, you can only reach out so near. That's the puzzling part."

"I can make it seem less paradoxical, Deveney, if you will allow me to use an analogy."

(Miss Fellowes placed the new man the moment she heard his name, and despite herself was impressed. This was obviously Candide Deveney, the science writer of the Telenews, who was notoriously at the scene of every major scientific breakthrough. She even recognized his face as one she saw on the news-plate when the landing on Mars had been announced. So Dr. Hoskins must have something important here.

"By all means use an analogy," said Deveney ruefully, "if you think it will help."

"Well, then, you can't read a book with ordinary-sized print if it is held six feet from your eyes, but you can read it if you hold it one foot from your eyes. So far, the closer the better. If you bring the book to within one inch of your eyes, however, you've lost it again. There is such a thing as being too close, you see."

"Hmm," said Deveney.

"Or take another example. Your right shoulder is about thirty inches from the tip of your right forefinger and you can place your right forefinger on your right shoulder. Your right elbow is only half the distance from the tip of your right forefinger; it should by all ordinary logic be easier to reach, and yet you cannot place your right finger on your right elbow. Again, there is such a thing as being too close."

Deveney said, "May I use these analogies in my story?"

"Well, of course. Only too glad. I've been waiting long

enough for someone like you to have a story. I'll give you anything else you want. It is time, finally, that we want the world looking over our shoulder. They'll see something."

(Miss Fellowes found herself admiring his calm certainty despite herself. There was strength there.)

Deveney said, "How far out will you reach?"

"Forty thousand years."

Miss Fellowes drew in her breath sharply.

Years?

There was tension in the air. The men at the controls scarcely moved. One man at a microphone spoke into it in a soft monotone, in short phrases that made no sense to Miss Fellowes.

Deveney, leaning over the balcony railing with an intent stare, said, "Will we see anything, Dr. Hoskins?"

"What? No. Nothing till the job is done. We detect indirectly, something on the principle of radar, except that we use mesons rather than radiation. Mesons reach backward under the proper conditions. Some are reflected and we must analyze the reflections."

"That sounds difficult."

Hoskins smiled again, briefly as always. "It is the end product of fifty years of research; forty years of it before I entered the field. Yes, it's difficult."

The man at the microphone raised one hand.

Hoskins said, "We've had the fix on one particular moment in time for weeks; breaking it, remaking it after calculating our own movements in time; making certain that we could handle time-flow with sufficient precision. This must work now."

But his forehead glistened.

Edith Fellowes found herself out of her seat and at the balcony railing, but there was nothing to see.

The man at the microphone said quietly, "Now."

There was a space of silence sufficient for one breath and then the sound of a terrified little boy's scream from the doll-house rooms. Terror! Piercing terror!

Miss Fellowes's head twisted in the direction of the cry. A child was involved. She had forgotten.

And Hoskins's fist pounded on the railing and he said in a tight voice, trembling with triumph, "*Did* it."

Miss Fellowes was urged down the short, spiral flight of steps by the hard press of Hoskins's palm between her shoulder blades. He did not speak to her.

The men who had been at the controls were standing about now, smiling, smoking, watching the three as they entered on the main floor. A very soft buzz sounded from the direction of the dollhouse.

Hoskins said to Deveney, "It's perfectly safe to enter Stasis. I've done it a thousand times. There's a queer sensation which is momentary and means nothing."

He stepped through an open door in mute demonstration, and Deveney, smiling stiffly and drawing an obviously deep breath, followed him.

Hoskins said, "Miss Fellowes! Please!" He crooked his fore-finger impatiently.

Miss Fellowes nodded and stepped stiffly through. It was as though a ripple went through her, an internal tickle.

But once inside all seemed normal. There was the smell of the fresh wood of the dollhouse and—of—of soil somehow.

There was silence now, no voice at least, but there was the dry shuffling of feet, a scrabbling as of a hand over wood—then a low moan.

"Where is it?" asked Miss Fellowes in distress. Didn't these fool men *care?*

The boy was in the bedroom; at least the room with the bed in it.

It was standing naked, with its small, dirt-smeared chest heaving raggedly. A bushel of dirt and coarse grass spread over the floor at his bare brown feet. The smell of soil came from it and a touch of something fetid.

Hoskins followed her horrified glance and said with annoyance, "You can't pluck a boy cleanly out of time, Miss Fellowes. We had to take some of the surroundings with it for safety. Or would you have preferred to have it arrive here minus a leg or with only half a head?"

"Please!" said Miss Fellowes, in an agony of revulsion. "Are we just to stand here? The poor child is frightened. And it's *filthy.*"

She was quite correct. It was smeared with encrusted dirt and grease and had a scratch on its thigh that looked red and sore.

As Hoskins approached him, the boy, who seemed to be something over three years in age, hunched low and backed away rapidly. He lifted his upper lip and snarled in a hissing fashion like a cat. With a rapid gesture, Hoskins seized both the child's arms and lifted him, writhing and screaming, from the floor.

Miss Fellowes said, "Hold him, now. He needs a warm bath first. He needs to be cleaned. Have you the equipment? If so, have it brought here, and I'll need to have help in handling him just at first. Then, too, for heaven's sake, have all this trash and filth removed."

She was giving the orders now and she felt perfectly good about that. And because now she was an efficient nurse, rather than a confused spectator, she looked at the child with a clinical eye—and hesitated for one shocked moment. She saw past the dirt and shrieking, past the thrashing of limbs and useless twisting. She saw the boy himself.

It was the ugliest little boy she had ever seen. It was horribly ugly from misshapen head to bandy legs.

She got the boy cleaned with three men helping her and with others milling about in their efforts to clean the room. She worked in silence and with a sense of outrage, annoyed by the continued strugglings and outcries of the boy and by the undignified drenchings of soapy water to which she was subjected.

Dr. Hoskins had hinted that the child would not be pretty, but that was far from stating that it would be repulsively deformed. And there was a stench about the boy that soap and water was only alleviating little by little.

She had the strong desire to thrust the boy, soaped as he was, into Hoskins' arms and walk out; but there was the pride of profession. She had accepted an assignment after all. And there would be the look in his eyes. A cold look that would read: Only pretty children, Miss Fellowes?

He was standing apart from them, watching coolly from a distance with a half-smile on his face when he caught her eye, as though amused at her outrage.

She decided she would wait a while before quitting. To do so now would only demean her.

Then, when the boy was a bearable pink and smelled of scented soap, she felt better anyway. His cries changed to whimpers of exhaustion as he watched carefully, eyes moving in quick frightened suspicion from one to another of those in the room. His cleanness accentuated his thin nakedness as he shivered with cold after his bath.

Miss Fellowes said sharply, "Bring me a nightgown for the child!"

A nightgown appeared at once. It was as though everything were ready and yet nothing were ready unless she gave orders; as though they were deliberately leaving this in her charge without help, to test her.

The newsman, Deveney, approached and said, "I'll hold him, Miss. You won't get it on yourself."

"Thank you," said Miss Fellowes. And it was a battle indeed, but the nightgown went on, and when the boy made as though to rip it off, she slapped his hand sharply.

The boy reddened, but did not cry. He stared at her and the splayed fingers of one hand moved slowly across the flannel of the nightgown, feeling the strangeness of it.

Miss Fellowes thought desperately: Well, what next?

Everyone seemed in suspended animation, waiting for her—even the ugly little boy.

Miss Fellowes said sharply, "Have you provided food? Milk?"

They had. A mobile unit was wheeled in, with its refrigeration compartment containing three quarts of milk, with a warming unit and a supply of fortifications in the form of vitamin drops, copper-cobalt-iron syrup and others she had no time to be concerned with. There was a variety of canned self-warming junior foods.

She used milk, simply milk, to begin with. The radar unit heated the milk to a set temperature in a matter of ten seconds and clicked off, and she put some in a saucer. She had a certainty about the boy's savagery. He wouldn't know how to handle a cup.

Miss Fellowes nodded and said to the boy, "Drink. Drink." She made a gesture as though to raise the milk to her mouth. The boy's eyes followed but he made no move.

Suddenly, the nurse resorted to direct measures. She seized the boy's upper arm in one hand and dipped the other in the milk. She dashed the milk across his lips, so that it dripped down cheeks and receding chin.

For a moment, the child uttered a high-pitched cry, then his tongue moved over his wetted lips. Miss Fellowes stepped back.

The boy approached the saucer, bent toward it, then looked up and behind sharply as though expecting a crouching enemy; bent again and licked at the milk eagerly, like a cat. He made a slurping noise. He did not use his hands to lift the saucer.

Miss Fellowes allowed a bit of the revulsion she felt show on her face. She couldn't help it.

Deveney caught that, perhaps. He said, "Does the nurse know, Dr. Hoskins?"

"Know what?" demanded Miss Fellowes.

Deveney hesitated, but Hoskins (again that look of detached amusement on his face) said, "Well, tell her."

Deveney addressed Miss Fellowes. "You may not suspect it, Miss, but you happen to be the first civilized woman in history ever to be taking care of a Neanderthal youngster."

She turned on Hoskins with a kind of controlled ferocity. "You might have told me, Doctor."

"Why? What difference does it make?"

"You said a child."

"Isn't that a child? Have you ever had a puppy or a kitten, Miss Fellowes? Are those closer to the human? If that were a baby chimpanzee, would you be repelled? You're a nurse, Miss Fellowes. Your record places you in a maternity ward for three years. Have you ever refused to take care of a deformed infant?"

Miss Fellowes felt her case slipping away. She said, with much less decision, "You might have told me."

"And you would have refused the position? Well, do you refuse it now?" He gazed at her coolly, while Deveney watched from the other side of the room, and the Neanderthal child, having finished the milk and licked the plate, looked up at her with a wet face and wide, longing eyes.

The boy pointed to the milk and suddenly burst out in a short series of sounds repeated over and over; sounds made up of gutturals and elaborate tongue-clickings.

Miss Fellowes said, in surprise, "Why, he talks."

"Of course," said Hoskins. "Homo neanderthalensis is not a truly separate species, but rather a subspecies of Homo sapiens. Why shouldn't he talk? He's probably asking for more milk."

Automatically, Miss Fellowes reached for the bottle of milk, but Hoskins seized her wrist. "Now, Miss Fellowes, before we go any further, are you staying on the job?"

Miss Fellowes shook free in annoyance, "Won't you feed him if I don't? I'll stay with him . . . for a while."

She poured the milk.

Hoskins said, "We are going to leave you with the boy, Miss Fellowes. This is the only door to Stasis Number One and it is elaborately locked and guarded. I'll want you to learn the details of the lock which will, of course, be keyed to your fingerprints as they are already keyed to mine. The spaces overhead" (he looked upward to the open ceilings of the doll-house) "are also guarded and we will be warned if anything untoward takes place in here."

Miss Fellowes said indignantly, "You mean I'll be under view." She thought suddenly of her own survey of the room interiors from the balcony.

"No, no," said Hoskins seriously, "your privacy will be respected completely. The view will consist of electronic symbolism only, which only a computer will deal with. Now you will stay with him tonight, Miss Fellowes, and every night until further notice. You will be relieved during the day according to some schedule you will find convenient. We will allow you to arrange that."

Miss Fellowes looked about the dollhouse with a puzzled expression. "But why all this, Dr. Hoskins? Is the boy dangerous?"

"It's a matter of energy, Miss Fellowes. He must never be allowed to leave these rooms. Never. Not for an instant. Not for any reason. Not to save his life. Not even to save *your* life, Miss Fellowes. Is that clear?"

Miss Fellowes raised her chin. "I understand the orders, Dr. Hoskins, and the nursing profession is accustomed to placing its duties ahead of self-preservation."

"Good. You can always signal if you need anyone." And the two men left.

Miss Fellowes turned to the boy. He was watching her and there was still milk in the saucer. Laboriously, she tried to show him how to lift the saucer and place it to his lips. He resisted, but let her touch him without crying out.

Always, his frightened eyes were on her, watching, watching for the one false move. She found herself soothing him, trying to move her hand very slowly toward his hair, letting him see it every inch of the way, see there was no harm in it.

And she succeeded in stroking his hair for an instant.

She said, "I'm going to have to show you how to use the bathroom. Do you think you can learn?"

She spoke quietly, kindly, knowing he would not understand the words but hoping he would respond to the calmness of the tone.

The boy launched into a clicking phrase again.

She said, "May I take your hand?"

She held out hers and the boy looked at it. She left it outstretched and waited. The boy's own hand crept forward toward hers.

"That's right," she said.

It approached within an inch of hers and then the boy's courage failed him. He snatched it back.

"Well," said Miss Fellowes calmly, "we'll try again later. Would you like to sit down here?" She patted the mattress of the bed.

The hours passed slowly and progress was minute. She did not succeed either with bathroom or with the bed. In fact, after the child had given unmistakable signs of sleepiness he lay down on the bare ground and then, with a quick movement, rolled beneath the bed.

She bent to look at him and his eyes gleamed out at her as he tongue-clicked at her.

"All right," she said, "if you feel safer there, you sleep there."

She closed the door to the bedroom and retired to the cot that had been placed for her use in the largest room. At her insistence, a makeshift canopy had been stretched over it. She thought: Those stupid men will have to place a mirror in this room and a larger chest of drawers and a separate washroom if they expect me to spend nights here.

It was difficult to sleep. She found herself straining to hear possible sounds in the next room. He couldn't get out, could he? The walls were sheer and impossibly high but suppose the child could climb like a monkey? Well, Hoskins said there were observational devices watching through the ceiling.

Suddenly she thought: Can he be dangerous? Physically dangerous?

Surely, Hoskins couldn't have meant that. Surely, he would not have left her here alone, if...

She tried to laugh at herself. He was only a three- or four-year-old child. Still, she had not succeeded in cutting his nails. If he should attack her with nails and teeth while she slept!

Her breath came quickly. Oh, ridiculous, and yet...

She listened with painful attentiveness, and this time she heard the sound.

The boy was crying.

Not shrieking in fear or anger; not yelling or screaming. It was crying softly, and the cry was the heartbroken sobbing of a lonely, lonely child.

For the first time, Miss Fellowes thought with a pang: Poor thing!

Of course, it was a child; what did the shape of its head matter? It was a child that had been orphaned as no child had ever been orphaned before. Not only its mother and father were gone, but all its species. Snatched callously out of time, it was now the only creature of its kind in the world. The last. The only.

She felt pity for it strengthen, and with it shame at her own callousness. Tucking her own nightgown carefully about her calves (incongruously, she thought: Tomorrow I'll have to bring in a bathrobe) she got out of bed and went into the boy's room.

"Little boy," she called in a whisper. "Little boy."

She was about to reach under the bed, but she thought of a possible bite and did not. Instead, she turned on the night light and moved the bed.

The poor thing was huddled in the corner, knees up against his chin, looking up at her with blurred and apprehensive eyes.

In the dim light, she was not aware of his repulsiveness.

"Poor boy," she said, "poor boy." She felt him stiffen as she stroked his hair, then relax. "Poor boy. May I hold you?"

She sat down on the floor next to him and slowly and rhythmically stroked his hair, his cheek, his arm. Softly, she began to sing a slow and gentle song.

He lifted his head at that, staring at her mouth in the dimness, as though wondering at the sound.

She maneuvered him closer while he listened to her. Slowly, she pressed gently against the side of his head, until it rested on her shoulder. She put her arm under his thighs and with a smooth and unhurried motion lifted him into her lap.

She continued singing, the same simple verse over and over, while she rocked back and forth, back and forth.

He stopped crying, and after a while the smooth blur of his breathing showed he was asleep.

With infinite care, she pushed his bed back against the wall and laid him down. She covered him and stared down. His face looked so peaceful and little-boy as he slept. It didn't matter so much that it was so ugly. Really.

She began to tiptoe out, then thought: If he wakes up?

She came back, battled irresolutely with herself, then sighed and slowly got into bed with the child.

It was too small for her. She was cramped and uneasy at

the lack of canopy, but the child's hand crept into hers and, somehow, she fell asleep in that position.

She awoke with a start and a wild impulse to scream. The latter she just managed to suppress into a gurgle. The boy was looking at her, wide-eyed. It took her a long moment to remember getting into bed with him, and now, slowly, without unfixing her eyes from his, she stretched one leg carefully and let it touch the floor, then the other one.

She cast a quick and apprehensive glance toward the open ceiling, then tensed her muscles for quick disengagement.

But at that moment, the boy's stubby fingers reached out and touched her lips. He said something.

She shrank at the touch. He was terribly ugly in the light of day.

The boy spoke again. He opened his own mouth and gestured with his hand as though something were coming out.

Miss Fellowes guessed at the meaning and said tremulously, "Do you want me to sing?"

The boy said nothing but stared at her mouth.

In a voice slightly off key with tension, Miss Fellowes began the little song she had sung the night before and the ugly little boy smiled. He swayed clumsily in rough time to the music and made a little gurgly sound that might have been the beginnings of a laugh.

Miss Fellowes sighed inwardly. Music hath charms to soothe the savage beast. It might help...

She said, "You wait. Let me get myself fixed up. It will just take a minute. Then I'll make breakfast for you."

She worked rapidly, conscious of the lack of ceiling at all times. The boy remained in bed, watching her when she was in view. She smiled at him at those times and waved. At the end, he waved back, and she found herself being charmed by that.

Finally, she said, "Would you like oatmeal with milk?" It took a moment to prepare, and then she beckoned to him.

Whether he understood the gesture or followed the aroma, Miss Fellowes did not know, but he got out of bed.

She tried to show him how to use a spoon but he shrank away from it in fright. (Time enough, she thought.) She compromised on insisting that he lift the bowl in his hands. He did it clumsily enough and it was incredibly messy but most of it did get into him.

She tried the drinking milk in a glass this time, and the little boy whined when he found the opening too small for him to get his face into conveniently. She held his hand, forcing it around the glass, making him tip it, forcing his mouth to the rim.

Again a mess but again most went into him, and she was used to messes.

The washroom, to her surprise and relief, was a less frustrating matter. He understood what it was she expected him to do.

She found herself patting his head, saying, "Good boy. Smart boy."

And to Miss Fellowes's exceeding pleasure, the boy smiled at that.

She thought: When he smiles, he's quite bearable. Really.

Later in the day, the gentlemen of the press arrived.

She held the boy in her arms and he clung to her wildly while across the open door they set cameras to work. The commotion frightened the boy and he began to cry, but it was ten minutes before Miss Fellowes was allowed to retreat and put the boy in the next room.

She emerged again, flushed with indignation, walked out of the apartment (for the first time in eighteen hours) and closed the door behind her. "I think you've had enough. It will take me a while to quiet him. Go away."

"Sure, sure," said the gentleman from the *Times-Herald*. "But is that really a Neanderthal or is this some kind of gag?"

"I assure you," said Hoskins's voice, suddenly, from the background, "that this is no gag. The child is authentic Homo neanderthalensis."

"Is it a boy or a girl?"

"Boy," said Miss Fellowes briefly.

"Ape-boy," said the gentleman from the *News*. "That's what we've got here. Ape-boy. How does he act, Nurse?"

"He acts exactly like a little boy," snapped Miss Fellowes, annoyed into the defensive, "and he is not an ape-boy. His name is—is Timothy, Timmie—and he is perfectly normal in his behavior."

She had chosen the name Timothy at a venture. It was the first that had occurred to her.

"Timmie the Ape-boy," said the gentleman from the *News* and, as it turned out, Timmie the Ape-boy was the name under which the child became known to the world.

The gentleman from the *Globe* turned to Hoskins and said, "Doc, what do you expect to do with the ape-boy?"

Hoskins shrugged. "My original plan was completed when I proved it possible to bring him here. However, the anthropologists will be very interested, I imagine, and the physiologists. We have here, after all, a creature which is at the edge of being human. We should learn a great deal about ourselves and our ancestry from him."

"How long will you keep him?"

"Until such a time as we need the space more than we need him. Quite a while, perhaps."

The gentleman from the *News* said, "Can you bring it out into the open so we can set up sub-etheric equipment and put on a real show?"

"I'm sorry, but the child cannot be removed from Stasis."

"Exactly what is Stasis?"

"Ah." Hoskins permitted himself one of his short smiles. "That would take a great deal of explanation, gentlemen. In Stasis, time as we know it doesn't exist. Those rooms are inside an invisible bubble that is not exactly part of our Universe. That is why the child could be plucked out of time as it was."

"Well, wait now," said the gentleman from the *News* discontentedly, "what are you giving us? The nurse goes into the room and out of it."

"And so can any of you," said Hoskins matter-of-factly. "You would be moving parallel to the lines of temporal force and no great energy gain or loss would be involved. The child, however, was taken from the far past. It moved across the lines and gained temporal potential. To move it into the Universe and into our own time would absorb enough energy to burn out every line in the place and probably blank out all power in the city of Washington. We had to store trash brought with him on the premises and will have to remove it little by little."

The newsmen were writing down sentences busily as Hoskins spoke to them. They did not understand and they were sure their readers would not, but it sounded scientific and that was what counted.

The gentleman from the *Times-Herald* said, "Would you be available for an all-circuit interview tonight?"

"I think so," said Hoskins at once, and they all moved off.

Miss Fellowes looked after them. She understood all this about Stasis and temporal force as little as the newsmen but she managed to get this much. Timmie's imprisonment (she found herself suddenly thinking of the little boy as Timmie) was a real one and not one imposed by the arbitrary fiat of Hoskins. Apparently, it was impossible to let him out of Stasis at all, ever.

Poor child. Poor child.

She was suddenly aware of his crying and she hastened in to console him.

Miss Fellowes did not have a chance to see Hoskins on the all-circuit hookup, and though his interview was beamed to every part of the world and even to the outpost on the Moon, it did not penetrate the apartment in which Miss Fellowes and the ugly little boy lived.

But he was down the next morning, radiant and joyful.

Miss Fellowes said, "Did the interview go well?"

"Extremely. And how is—Timmie?"

Miss Fellowes found herself pleased at the use of the name. "Doing quite well. Now come out here, Timmie, the nice gentleman will not hurt you."

But Timmie stayed in the other room, with a lock of his matted hair showing behind the barrier of the door and, occasionally the corner of an eye.

"Actually," said Miss Fellowes, "he is settling down amazingly. He is quite intelligent."

"Are you surprised?"

She hesitated just a moment, then said, "Yes, I am. I suppose I thought he was an ape-boy."

"Well, ape-boy or not, he's done a great deal for us. He's put Stasis, Inc. on the map. We're in, Miss Fellowes, we're in." It was as though he had to express his triumph to someone, even if only to Miss Fellowes.

"Oh?" She let him talk.

He put his hands in his pockets and said, "We've been working on a shoestring for ten years, scrounging funds a penny at a time wherever we could. We had to shoot the works on one big show. It was everything, or nothing. And when I say the works, I mean it. This attempt to bring in a Neanderthal took every cent we could borrow or steal, and some of it *was* stolen—funds for other projects, used for this one without permission. If that experiment hadn't succeeded, I'd have been through."

Miss Fellowes said abruptly, "Is that why there are no ceilings?"

"Eh?" Hoskins looked up.

"Was there no money for ceilings?"

"Oh. Well, that wasn't the only reason. We didn't really know in advance how old the Neanderthal might be exactly. We can detect only dimly in time, and he might have been large and savage. It was possible we might have had to deal with him from a distance, like a caged animal."

"But since that hasn't turned out to be so, I suppose you can build a ceiling now."

"Now, yes. We have plenty of money, now. Funds have been promised from every source. This is all wonderful, Miss Fellowes." His broad face gleamed with a smile that lasted and when he left, even his back seemed to be smiling.

Miss Fellowes thought: He's quite a nice man when he's off guard and forgets about being scientific.

She wondered for an idle moment if he was married, then dismissed the thought in self-embarrassment.

"Timmie," she called. "Come here, Timmie."

In the months that passed, Miss Fellowes felt herself grow to be an integral part of Stasis, Inc. She was given a small office of her own with her name on the door, an office quite close to the dollhouse (as she never stopped calling Timmie's Stasis bubble). She was given a substantial raise. The dollhouse was covered by a ceiling; its furnishings were elaborated and improved; a second washroom was added—and even so, she gained an apartment of her own on the institute grounds and, on occasion, did not stay with Timmie during the night. An intercom was set up between the dollhouse and her apartment and Timmie learned how to use it.

Miss Fellowes got used to Timmie. She even grew less conscious of his ugliness. One day she found herself staring at an ordinary boy in the street and finding something bulgy and unattractive in his high-domed forehead and jutting chin. She had to shake herself to break the spell.

It was more pleasant to grow used to Hoskins's occasional visits. It was obvious he welcomed escape from his increasingly harried role as head of Stasis, Inc., and that he took a sentimental interest in the child who had started it all, but it seemed to Miss Fellowes that he also enjoyed talking to her.

(She had learned some facts about Hoskins, too. He had invented the method of analyzing the reflection of the past-penetrating mesonic beam; he had invented the method of establishing Stasis; his coldness was only an effort to hide a kindly nature; and, oh yes, he *was* married.)

What Miss Fellowes could *not* get used to was the fact that she was engaged in a scientific experiment. Despite all she

could do, she found herself getting personally involved to the
point of quarreling with the physiologists.

On one occasion, Hoskins came down and found her in the
midst of a hot urge to kill. They had no right; they had no
right... Even if he *was* a Neanderthal, he still wasn't an animal.

She was staring after them in a blind fury; staring out the
open door and listening to Timmie's sobbing, when she noticed Hoskins standing before her. He might have been there
for minutes.

He said, "May I come in?"

She nodded curtly, then hurried to Timmie, who clung to
her, curling his little bandy legs—still thin, so thin—about
her.

Hoskins watched, then said gravely, "He seems quite unhappy."

Miss Fellowes said, "I don't blame him. They're at him
every day now with their blood samples and their probings.
They keep him on synthetic diets that I wouldn't feed a pig."

"It's the sort of thing they can't try on a human, you know."

"And they can't try it on Timmie, either. Dr. Hoskins, I
insist. You told me it was Timmie's coming that put Stasis,
Inc. on the map. If you have any gratitude for that at all,
you've *got* to keep them away from the poor thing at least
until he's old enough to understand a little more. After he's
had a bad session with them, he has nightmares, he can't
sleep. Now I warn you" (she reached a sudden peak of fury),
"I'm not letting them in here any more."

(She realized that she had screamed that, but she couldn't
help it.)

She said more quietly, "I know he's Neanderthal but there's
a great deal we don't appreciate about Neanderthals. I've read

up on them. They had a culture of their own. Some of the greatest human inventions arose in Neanderthal times. The domestication of animals, for instance; the wheel; various techniques in grinding stone. They even had spiritual yearnings. They buried their dead and buried possessions with the body, showing they believed in a life after death. It amounts to the fact that they invented religion. Doesn't that mean Timmie has a right to human treatment?"

She patted the little boy gently on his buttocks and sent him off into his playroom. As the door was opened, Hoskins smiled briefly at the display of toys that could be seen.

Miss Fellowes said defensively, "The poor child deserves his toys. It's all he has and he earns them with what he goes through."

"No, no. No objections, I assure you. I was just thinking how you've changed since the first day, when you were quite angry I had foisted a Neanderthal on you."

Miss Fellowes said in a low voice, "I suppose I didn't..." and faded off.

Hoskins changed the subject, "How old would you say he is, Miss Fellowes?"

She said, "I can't say, since we don't know how Neanderthals develop. In size, he'd only be three but Neanderthals are smaller generally and with all the tampering they do with him, he probably isn't growing. The way he's learning English, though, I'd say he was well over four."

"Really? I haven't noticed anything about learning English in the reports."

"He won't speak to anyone but me. For now, anyway. He's terribly afraid of others, and no wonder. But he can ask for an article of food; he can indicate any need practically; and he understands almost anything I say. Of course" (she watched him shrewdly, trying to estimate if this was the time), "his development may not continue."

"Why not?"

"Any child needs stimulation and this one lives a life of solitary confinement. I do what I can, but I'm not with him all the time and I'm not all he needs. What I mean, Dr. Hoskins, is that he needs another boy to play with."

Hoskins nodded slowly. "Unfortunately, there's only one of him, isn't there? Poor child."

Miss Fellowes warmed to him at once. She said, "You do like Timmie, don't you?" It was so nice to have someone else feel like that.

"Oh, yes," said Hoskins, and with his guard down, she could see the weariness in his eyes.

Miss Fellowes dropped her plans to push the matter at once. She said, with real concern, "You look worn out, Dr. Hoskins."

"Do I, Miss Fellowes? I'll have to practice looking more lifelike then."

"I suppose Stasis, Inc. is very busy and that that keeps you very busy."

Hoskins shrugged. "You suppose right. It's a matter of animal, vegetable, and mineral in equal parts, Miss Fellowes. But then, I suppose you haven't ever seen our displays."

"Actually, I haven't. But it's not because I'm not interested. It's just that I've been so busy."

"Well, you're not all that busy right now," he said with impulsive decision. "I'll call for you tomorrow at eleven and give you a personal tour. How's that?"

She smiled happily. "I'd love it."

He nodded and smiled in his turn and left.

Miss Fellowes hummed at intervals for the rest of the day.

Really—to think so was ridiculous, of course—but really, it was almost like—like making a date.

He was quite on time the next day, smiling and pleasant. She had replaced her nurse's uniform with a dress. One of conservative cut, to be sure, but she hadn't felt so feminine in years.

He complimented her on her appearance with staid formality and she accepted with equally formal grace. It was really a perfect prelude, she thought. And then the additional thought came, prelude to what?

She shut that off by hastening to say good-by to Timmie and to assure him she would be back soon. She made sure he knew all about what and where lunch was.

Hoskins took her into the new wing, into which she had never yet gone. It still had the odor of newness about it and the sound of construction, softly heard, was indication enough thet it was still being extended.

"Animal, vegetable, and mineral," said Hoskins, as he had the day before. "Animal right there; our most spectacular exhibits."

The space was divided into many rooms, each a separate Stasis bubble. Hoskins brought her to the view-glass of one and she looked in. What she saw impressed her first as a scaled, tailed chicken. Skittering on two thin legs it ran from wall to wall with its delicate birdlike head, surmounted by a bony keel like the comb of a rooster, looking this way and that. The paws on its small forelimbs clenched and unclenched constantly.

Hoskins said, "It's our dinosaur. We've had it for months. I don't know when we'll be able to let go of it."

"Dinosaur?"

"Did you expect a giant?"

She dimpled. "One does, I suppose. I know some of them are small."

"A small one is all we aimed for, believe me. Generally, it's under investigation, but this seems to be an open hour. Some interesting things have been discovered. For instance, it is not entirely cold-blooded. It has an imperfect method of maintaining internal temperatures higher than that of its environment. Unfortunately, it's a male. Ever since we brought it in we've been trying to get a fix on another that may be female, but we've had no luck yet."

"Why female?"

He looked at her quizzically. "So that we might have a fighting chance to obtain fertile eggs, and baby dinosaurs."

"Of course."

He led her to the trilobite section. "That's Professor Dwayne of Washington University," he said. "He's a nuclear chemist. If I recall correctly, he's taking an isotope ratio on the oxygen of the water."

"Why?"

"It's primeval water; at least half a billion years old. The isotope ratio gives the temperature of the ocean at that time. He himself happens to ignore the trilobites, but others are chiefly concerned in dissecting them. They're the lucky ones because all they need are scalpels and microscopes. Dwayne has to set up a mass spectrograph each time he conducts an experiment."

"Why's that? Can't he . . ."

"No, he can't. He can't take anything out of the room as far as can be helped."

There were samples of primordial plant life too and chunks of rock formations. Those were the vegetable and mineral.

And every specimen had its investigator. It was like a museum; a museum brought to life and serving as a superactive center of research.

"And you have to supervise all of this, Dr. Hoskins?"

"Only indirectly, Miss Fellowes. I have subordinates, thank heaven. My own interest is entirely in the theoretical aspects of the matter: the nature of Time, the technique of mesonic intertemporal detection and so on. I would exchange all this for a method of detecting objects closer in Time than ten thousand years ago. If we could get into historical times..."

He was interrupted by a commotion at one of the distant booths, a thin voice raised querulously. He frowned, muttered hastily, "Excuse me," and hastened off.

Miss Fellowes followed as best she could without actually running.

An elderly man, thinly bearded and red faced, was saying, "I had vital aspects of my investigations to complete. Don't you understand that?"

A uniformed technician with the interwoven SI monogram (for Stasis, Inc.) on his lab coat, said, "Dr. Hoskins, it was arranged with Professor Ademewski at the beginning that the specimen could only remain here two weeks."

"I did not know then how long my investigations would take. I'm not a prophet," said Ademewski heatedly.

Dr. Hoskins said, "You understand, Professor, we have limited space; we must keep specimens rotating. That piece of chalcopyrite must go back; there are men waiting for the next specimen."

"Why can't I have it for myself, then? Let me take it out of there."

"You know you can't have it."

"A piece of chalcopyrite; a miserable five-kilogram piece? Why not?"

"We can't afford the energy expense!" said Hoskins brusquely. "You know that."

The technician interrupted. "The point is, Dr. Hoskins, that he tried to remove the rock against the rules and I almost punctured Stasis while he was in there, not knowing he was in there."

There was a short silence and Dr. Hoskins turned on the investigator with a cold formality. "Is that so, Professor?"

Professor Ademewski coughed. "I saw no harm..."

Hoskins reached up to a hand-pull dangling just within reach, outside the specimen room in question. He pulled it.

Miss Fellowes, who had been peering in, looking at the totally undistinguished sample of rock that occasioned the dispute, drew in her breath sharply as its existence flickered out. The room was empty.

Hoskins said, "Professor, your permit to investigate matters in Stasis will be permanently voided. I am sorry."

"But wait..."

"I am sorry. You have violated one of the stringent rules."

"I will appeal to the International Association..."

"Appeal away. In a case like this, you will find I can't be overruled."

He turned away deliberately, leaving the professor still protesting and said to Miss Fellowes (his face still white with anger), "Would you care to have lunch with me, Miss Fellowes?"

He took her into the small administration alcove of the cafeteria. He greeted others and introduced Miss Fellowes with complete ease, although she herself felt painfully self-conscious.

What must they think, she thought, and tried desperately to appear businesslike.

She said, "Do you have that kind of trouble often, Dr. Hoskins? I mean like that you just had with the professor?" She took her fork in hand and began eating.

"No," said Hoskins forcefully. "That was the first time. Of course I'm always having to argue men out of removing specimens but this is the first time one actually tried to *do* it."

"I remember you once talked about the energy it would consume."

"That's right. Of course, we've tried to take it into account. Accidents will happen and so we've got special power sources designed to stand the drain of accidental removal from Stasis, but that doesn't mean we want to see a year's supply of energy gone in half a second—or can afford to without having our plans of expansion delayed for years. Besides, imagine the professor's being in the room while Stasis was about to be punctured."

"What would have happened to him if it had been?"

"Well, we've experimented with inanimate objects and with mice and they've disappeared. Presumably they've traveled back in time; carried along, so to speak, by the pull of the object simultaneously snapping back into its natural time. For that reason, we have to anchor objects within Stasis that we don't want to move and that's a complicated procedure. The professor would not have been anchored and he would have gone back to the Pliocene at the moment when we abstracted the rock—plus, of course, the two weeks it had remained here in the present."

"How dreadful it would have been."

"Not on account of the professor, I assure you. If he were fool enough to do what he did, it would serve him right. But imagine the effect it would have on the public if the fact came out. All people would need is to become aware of the dangers involved and funds could be choked off like that." He snapped his fingers and played moodily with his food.

Miss Fellowes said, "Couldn't you get him back? The way you got the rock in the first place?"

"No, because once an object is returned, the original fix is lost unless we deliberately plan to retain it and there was no reason to do that in this case. There never is. Finding the professor again would mean relocating a specific fix and that would be like dropping a line into the oceanic abyss for the purpose of dredging up a particular fish. My God, when I think of the precautions we take to prevent accidents, it makes me mad. We have every individual Stasis unit set up with its own puncturing device—we have to, since each unit has its separate fix and must be collapsible independently. The point is, though, none of the puncturing devices is ever activated until the last minute. And then we deliberately make activation impossible except by the pull of a rope carefully led outside the Stasis. The pull is a gross mechanical motion that requires a strong effort, not something that is likely to be done accidentally."

Miss Fellowes said, "But doesn't it—change history to move something in and out of Time?"

Hoskins shrugged. "Theoretically, yes; actually, except in nusual cases, no. We move objects out of Stasis all the time. Air molecules. Bacteria. Dust. About ten percent of our energy consumption goes to make up micro-losses of that nature. But moving even large objects in Time sets up changes that damp out. Take that chalcopyrite from the Pliocene. Because of its absence for two weeks some insect doesn't find the shelter it might have found and is killed. That could initiate a whole series of changes, but the mathematics of Stasis indicates that this is a converging series. The amount of change diminishes with time and then things are as before."

"You mean, reality heals itself?"

"In a manner of speaking. Abstract a human from Time or send one back, and you make a larger wound. If the individual is an ordinary one, that wound still heals itself. Of course, there are a great many people who write to us each day and want us to bring Abraham Lincoln into the present, or Mohammed, or Lenin. *That* can't be done, of course. Even if we could find them, the change in reality in moving one of the history molders would be too great to be healed. There are ways of calculating when a change is likely to be too great and we avoid even approaching that limit."

Miss Fellowes said, "Then, Timmie..."

"No, he presents no problem in that direction. Reality is safe. But..." He gave her a quick, sharp glance, then went on, "But never mind. Yesterday you said Timmie needed companionship."

"Yes," Miss Fellowes smiled her delight. "I didn't think you paid that any attention."

"Of course I did. I'm fond of the child. I appreciate your feelings for him and I was concerned enough to want to explain to you. Now I have; you've seen what we do; you've gotten some insight into the difficulties involved; so you know why, with the best will in the world, we can't supply companionship for Timmie."

"You can't?" said Miss Fellowes, with sudden dismay.

"But I've just explained. We couldn't possibly expect to find another Neanderthal his age without incredible luck, and if we could, it wouldn't be fair to multiply risks by having another human being in Stasis."

Miss Fellowes put down her spoon and said energetically, "But, Dr. Hoskins, that is not at all what I meant. I don't want you to bring another Neanderthal into the present. I know that's impossible. But it isn't impossible to bring another child to play with Timmie."

Hoskins stared at her in concern. "A *human* child?"

"*Another* child," said Miss Fellowes, completely hostile now. "Timmie is human."

"I couldn't dream of such a thing."

"Why not? Why couldn't you? What is wrong with the notion? You pulled that child out of Time and made him an eternal prisoner. Don't you owe him something? Dr. Hoskins, if there is any man who, in this world, is that child's father in every sense but the biological, it is you. Why can't you do this little thing for him?"

Hoskins said, "His *father*?" He rose, somewhat unsteadily, to his feet. "Miss Fellowes, I think I'll take you back now, if you don't mind."

They returned to the dollhouse in a complete silence that neither broke.

It was a long time after that before she saw Hoskins again, except for an occasional glimpse in passing. She was sorry about that at times; then, at other times, when Timmie was more than usually woebegone or when he spent silent hours at the window with its prospect of little more than nothing, she thought, fiercely: Stupid man.

Timmie's speech grew better and more precise each day. It never entirely lost a certain soft slurriness that Miss Fellowes found rather endearing. In times of excitement, he fell back into tongue-clicking but those times were becoming fewer. He must be forgetting the days before he came into the present—except for dreams.

As he grew older, the physiologists grew less interested and the psychologists more so. Miss Fellowes was not sure that she did not like the new group even less than the first. The needles were gone; the injections and withdrawals of fluid; the special diets. But now Timmie was made to overcome barriers to reach food and water. He had to lift panels, move bars, reach for cords. And the mild electric shocks made him cry and drove Miss Fellowes to distraction.

She did not wish to appeal to Hoskins; she did not wish to have to go to him; for each time she thought of him, she thought of his face over the luncheon table that last time. Her eyes moistened and she thought: Stupid, *stupid* man.

And then one day Hoskins's voice sounded unexpectedly, calling into the dollhouse, "Miss Fellowes."

She came out coldly, smoothing her nurse's uniform, then stopped in confusion at finding herself in the presence of a pale woman, slender and of middle height. The woman's fair hair and complexion gave her an appearance of fragility. Standing behind her and clutching at her skirt was a round-faced, large-eyed child of four.

Hoskins said, "Dear, this is Miss Fellowes, the nurse in charge of the boy. Miss Fellowes, this is my wife."

(Was this his wife? She was not as Miss Fellowes had imagined her to be. But then, why not? A man like Hoskins would choose a weak thing to be his foil. If that was what he wanted...)

She forced a matter-of-fact greeting. "Good afternoon, Mrs. Hoskins. Is this your—your little boy?"

(*That* was a surprise. She had thought of Hoskins as a husband, but not as a father, except, of course... She suddenly caught Hoskins' grave eyes and flushed.)

Hoskins said, "Yes, this is my boy, Jerry. Say hello to Miss Fellowes, Jerry."

(Had he stressed the word "this" just a bit? Was he saying *this* was his son and not...)

Jerry receded a bit further into the folds of the maternal skirt and muttered his hello. Mrs. Hoskins's eyes were searching over Miss Fellowes's shoulders, peering into the room, looking for something.

Hoskins said, "Well, let's go in. Come, dear. There's a trifling discomfort at the threshold, but it passes."

Miss Fellowes said, "Do you want Jerry to come in, too?"

"Of course. He is to be Timmie's playmate. You said that Timmie needed a playmate. Or have you forgotten?"

"But..." She looked at him with a colossal, surprised wonder. "*Your* boy?"

He said peevishly, "Well, whose boy, then? Isn't this what you want? Come on in, dear. Come on in."

Mrs. Hoskins lifted Jerry into her arms with a distinct effort and, hesitantly, stepped over the threshold. Jerry squirmed as she did so, disliking the sensation.

Mrs. Hoskins said in a thin voice, "Is the creature here? I don't see him."

Miss Fellowes called, "Timmie. Come out."

Timmie peered around the edge of the door, staring up at the little boy who was visiting him. The muscles in Mrs. Hoskins' arms tensed visibly.

She said to her husband, "Gerald, are you sure it's safe?"

Miss Fellowes said at once, "If you mean is Timmie safe, why, of course he is. He's a gentle little boy."

"But he's a sa—savage."

(The ape-boy stories in the newspapers!) Miss Fellowes said emphatically, "He is not a savage. He is just as quiet and reasonable as you can possibly expect a five-and-a-half-year-old to be. It is very generous of you, Mrs. Hoskins, to agree to allow your boy to play with Timmie but please have no fears about it."

Mrs. Hoskins said with mild heat, "I'm not sure that I agree."

"We've had it out, dear," said Hoskins. "Let's not bring up the matter for new argument. Put Jerry down."

Mrs. Hoskins did so and the boy backed against her, staring at the pair of eyes which were staring back at him from the next room.

"Come here, Timmie," said Miss Fellowes. "Don't be afraid."

Slowly, Timmie stepped into the room. Hoskins bent to disengage Jerry's fingers from his mother's skirt. "Step back, dear. Give the children a chance."

The youngsters faced one another. Although the younger, Jerry was nevertheless an inch taller, and in the presence of his straightness and his high-held, well-proportioned head, Timmie's grotesqueries were suddenly almost as pronounced as they had been in the first days.

Miss Fellowes' lips quivered.

It was the little Neanderthal who spoke first, in childish treble. "What's your name?" And Timmie thrust his face suddenly forward as though to inspect the other's features more closely.

Startled, Jerry responded with a vigorous shove that sent Timmie tumbling. Both began crying loudly and Mrs. Hoskins snatched up her child, while Miss Fellowes, flushed with repressed anger, lifted Timmie and comforted him.

Mrs. Hoskins said, "They just instinctively don't like one another."

"No more instinctively," said her husband wearily, "than any two children dislike each other. Now put Jerry down and let him get used to the situation. In fact, we had better leave. Miss Fellowes can bring Jerry to my office after a while and I'll have him taken home."

The two children spent the next hour very aware of each other. Jerry cried for his mother, struck out at Miss Fellowes and, finally, allowed himself to be comforted with a lollipop. Timmie sucked at another, and at the end of an hour, Miss Fellowes had them playing with the same set of blocks, though at opposite ends of the room.

She found herself almost maudlinly grateful to Hoskins when she brought Jerry to him.

She searched for ways to thank him but his very formality was a rebuff. Perhaps he could not forgive her for making him feel like a cruel father. Perhaps the bringing of his own child was an attempt, after all, to prove himself both a kind father to Timmie and, also, not his father at all. Both at the same time!

So all she could say was, "Thank you. Thank you very much."

And all he could say was, "It's all right. Don't mention it."

It became a settled routine. Twice a week, Jerry was brought in for an hour's play, later extended to two hour's play. The children learned each others' names and ways and played together.

And yet, after the first rush of gratitude, Miss Fellowes found herself disliking Jerry. He was larger and heavier and in all things dominant, forcing Timmie into a completely secondary role. All that reconciled her to the situation was the fact that, despite difficulties, Timmie looked forward with more and more delight to the periodic appearances of his playfellow.

It was all he had, she mourned to herself.

And once, as she watched them, she thought: Hoskins's two children, one by his wife and one by Stasis.

While she herself...

Heavens, she thought, putting her fists to her temples and feeling ashamed: I'm jealous!

"Miss Fellowes," said Timmie (carefully, she had never allowed him to call her anything else) "when will I go to school?"

She looked down at those eager brown eyes turned up to hers and passed her hand softly through his thick, curly hair. It was the most disheveled portion of his appearance, for she cut his hair herself while he sat restlessly under the scissors. She did not ask for professional help, for the very clumsiness of the cut served to mask the retreating fore part of the skull and the bulging hinder part.

She said, "Where did you hear about school?"

"Jerry goes to school. Kin-der-gar-ten." He said it carefully. "There are lots of places he goes. Outside. When can I go outside, Miss Fellowes?"

A small pain centered in Miss Fellowes' heart. Of course, she saw, there would be no way of avoiding the inevitability of Timmie's hearing more and more of the outer world he could never enter.

She said, with an attempt at gaiety, "Why, whatever would you do in kindergarten, Timmie?"

"Jerry says they play games, they have picture tapes. He says there are lots of children. He says—he says—" A thought, then a triumphant upholding of both small hands with the fingers splayed apart. "He says this many."

Miss Fellowes said, "Would you like picture tapes? I can get you picture tapes. Very nice ones. And music tapes, too."

So that Timmie was temporarily comforted.

He pored over the picture tapes in Jerry's absence and Miss Fellowes read to him out of ordinary books by the hour.

There was so much to explain in even the simplest story, so much that was outside the perspective of his three rooms. Timmie took to having his dreams more often now that the outside was being introduced to him.

They were always the same, about the outside. He tried haltingly to describe them to Miss Fellowes. In his dreams, he was outside, an empty outside, but very large, with children and queer indescribable objects half-digested in his thought out of bookish descriptions half-understood, or out of distant Neanderthal memories half-recalled.

But the children and objects ignored him and though he was in the world, he was never part of it, but was as alone as though he were in his own room—and would wake up crying.

Miss Fellowes tried to laugh at the dreams, but there were nights in her own apartment when she cried, too.

One day, as Miss Fellowes read, Timmie put his hand under her chin and lifted it gently so that her eyes left the book and met his.

He said, "How do you know what to say, Miss Fellowes?"

She said, "You see these marks? They tell me what to say. These marks make words."

He stared at them long and curiously, taking the book out of her hands. "Some of these marks are the same."

She laughed with pleasure at this sign of his shrewdness

and said, "So they are. Would you like to have me show you how to make the marks?"

"All right. That would be a nice game."

It did not occur to her that he could learn to read. Up to the very moment that he read a book to her, it did not occur to her that he could learn to read.

Then, weeks later, the enormity of what had been done struck her. Timmie sat in her lap, following word by word the printing in a child's book, reading to her. He was reading to her!

She struggled to her feet in amazement and said, "Now Timmie, I'll be back later. I want to see Dr. Hoskins."

Excited nearly to frenzy, it seemed to her she might have an answer to Timmie's unhappiness. If Timmie could not leave to enter the world, the world must be brought into those three rooms to Timmie—the whole world in books and film and sound. He must be educated to his full capacity. So much the world owed him.

She found Hoskins in a mood that was oddly analogous to her own; a kind of triumph and glory. His offices were unusually busy, and for a moment, she thought she would not get to see him, as she stood abashed in the anteroom.

But he saw her, and a smile spread over his broad face. "Miss Fellowes, come here."

He spoke rapidly into the intercom, then shut it off. "Have you heard? No, of course, you couldn't have. We've done it. We've actually done it. We have intertemporal detection at close range."

"You mean," she tried to detach her thought from her own good news for a moment, "that you can get a person from historical times into the present?"

"That's just what I mean. We have a fix on a fourteenth-century individual right now. Imagine. *Imagine!* If you could only know how glad I'll be to shift from the eternal concentration on the Mesozoic, replace the paleontologists with the historians—but there's something you wish to say to me, eh? Well, go ahead; go ahead. You find me in a good mood. Anything you want you can have."

Miss Fellowes smiled. "I'm glad. Because I wonder if we might not establish a system of instruction for Timmie?"

"Instruction? In what?"

"Well, in everything. A school. So that he might learn."

"But *can* he learn?"

"Certainly, he *is* learning. He can read. I've taught him so much myself."

Hoskins sat there, seeming suddenly depressed. "I don't know, Miss Fellowes."

She said, "You just said that anything I wanted..."

"I know and I should not have. You see, Miss Fellowes, I'm sure you must realize that we cannot maintain the Timmie experiment forever."

She stared at him with sudden horror, not really understanding what he had said. How did he mean "cannot maintain"? With an agonizing flash of recollection, she recalled Professor Ademewski and his mineral specimen that was taken away after two weeks. She said, "But you're talking about a boy. Not about a rock..."

Dr. Hoskins said uneasily, "Even a boy can't be given undue importance, Miss Fellowes. Now that we expect individuals out of historical time, we will need Stasis space, all we can get."

She didn't grasp it. "But you can't. Timmie—Timmie—"

"Now, Miss Fellowes, please don't upset yourself. Timmie

won't go right away; perhaps not for months. Meanwhile we'll do what we can."

She was still staring at him.

"Let me get you something, Miss Fellowes."

"No," she whispered. "I don't need anything." She arose in a kind of nightmare and left.

Timmie, she thought, you will *not* die. You will *not* die.

It was all very well to hold tensely to the thought that Timmie must not die, but how was that to be arranged? In the first weeks, Miss Fellowes clung only to the hope that the attempt to bring forward a man from the fourteenth century would fail completely. Hoskins' theories might be wrong or his practice defective. Then things could go on as before.

Certainly, that was not the hope of the rest of the world and, irrationally, Miss Fellowes hated the world for it. "Project Middle Ages" reached a climax of white-hot publicity. The press and the public had hungered for something like this. Stasis, Inc. had lacked the necessary sensation for a long time now. A new rock or another ancient fish failed to stir them. But *this* was *it*.

A historical human; an adult speaking a known language; someone who could open a new page of history to the scholar.

Zero-time was coming and this time it was not a question of three onlookers from a balcony. This time there would be a worldwide audience. This time the technicians of Stasis, Inc. would play their role before nearly all of mankind.

Miss Fellowes was herself all but savage with waiting. When young Jerry Hoskins showed up for his scheduled playtime with Timmie, she scarcely recognized him. He was not the one she was waiting for.

(The secretary who brought him left hurriedly after the

barest nod for Miss Fellowes. She was rushing for a good place from which to watch the climax of Project Middle Ages. And so ought Miss Fellowes with far better reason, she thought bitterly, if only that stupid girl would arrive.)

Jerry Hoskins sidled toward her, embarrassed. "Miss Fellowes?" He took the reproduction of a news-strip out of his pocket.

"Yes? What is it, Jerry?"

"Is this a picture of Timmie?"

Miss Fellowes stared at him, then snatched the strip from Jerry's hand. The excitement of Project Middle Ages had brought about a pale revival of interest in Timmie on the part of the press.

Jerry watched her narrowly, then said, "It says Timmie is an ape-boy. What does that mean?"

Miss Fellowes caught the youngster's wrist and repressed the impulse to shake him "Never say that, Jerry. Never, do you understand? It is a nasty word and you mustn't use it."

Jerry struggled out of her grip, frightened.

Miss Fellowes tore up the news-strip with a vicious twist of the wrist. "Now go inside and play with Timmie. He's got a new book to show you."

And then, finally, the girl appeared. Miss Fellowes did not know her. None of the usual stand-ins she had used when business took her elsewhere was available now, not with Project Middle Ages at climax, but Hoskins's secretary had promised to find *someone* and this must be the girl.

Miss Fellowes tried to keep querulousness out of her voice. "Are you the girl assigned to Stasis Section One?"

"Yes, I'm Mandy Terris. You're Miss Fellowes, aren't you?"

"That's right."

"I'm sorry I'm late. There's just so much excitement."

"I know. Now I want you..."

Mandy said, "You'll be watching, I suppose." Her thin, vacuously pretty face filled with envy.

"Never mind that. Now I want you to come inside and meet Timmie and Jerry. They will be playing for the next two hours so they'll be giving you no trouble. They've got milk handy and plenty of toys. In fact, it will be better if you leave them alone as much as possible. Now I'll show you where everything is located and..."

"Is it Timmie that's the ape-b—"

"Timmie is the Stasis subject," said Miss Fellowes firmly.

"I mean, he's the one who's not supposed to get out, is that right?"

"Yes. Now, come in. There isn't much time."

And when she finally left, Mandy Terris called after her shrilly, "I hope you get a good seat and, golly, I sure hope it works."

Miss Fellowes did not trust herself to make a reasonable response. She hurried on without looking back.

But the delay meant she did *not* get a good seat. She got no nearer than the wall viewing-plate in the assembly hall. Bitterly, she regretted that. If she could have been on the spot; if she could somehow have reached out for some sensitive portion of the instrumentations; if she were in some way able to wreck the experiment...

She found the strength to beat down her madness. Simple destruction would have done no good. They would have rebuilt and reconstructed and made the effort again. And she would never be allowed to return to Timmie.

Nothing would help. Nothing but that the experiment itself fail; that it break down irretrievably.

So she waited through the countdown, watching every move

on the giant screen, scanning the faces of the technicians as the focus shifted from one to the other, watching for the look of worry and uncertainty that would mark something going unexpectedly wrong; watching, watching...

There was no such look. The count reached zero, and very quietly, very unassumingly, the experiment succeeded!

In the new Stasis that had been established there stood a bearded, stoop-shouldered peasant of indeterminate age, in ragged dirty clothing and wooden shoes, staring in dull horror at the sudden mad change that had flung itself over him.

And while the world went mad with jubilation, Miss Fellowes stood frozen in sorrow, jostled and pushed, all but trampled; surrounded by triumph while bowed down with defeat.

And when the loudspeaker called her name with strident force, it sounded it three times before she responded.

"Miss Fellowes. Miss Fellowes. You are wanted in Stasis Section One immediately. Miss Fellowes. Miss Fell..."

"Let me through!" she cried breathlessly, while the loudspeaker continued its repititions without pause. She forced her way through the crowds with wild energy, beating at it, striking out with closed fists, flailing, moving toward the door in a nightmare slowness.

Mandy Terris was in tears. "I don't know how it happened. I just went down to the edge of the corridor to watch a pocket viewing-plate they had put up. Just for a minute. And then before I could move or do anything..." She cried out in sudden accusation, "You said they would make no trouble; you *said* to leave them alone..."

Miss Fellowes, disheveled and trembling uncontrollably, glared at her. "Where's Timmie?"

A nurse was swabbing the arm of a wailing Jerry with disinfectant and another was preparing an antitetanus shot. There was blood on Jerry's clothes.

"He bit me, Miss Fellowes," Jerry cried in rage. "He *bit* me."

But Miss Fellowes didn't even see him.

"What did you do with Timmie?" she cried out.

"I locked him in the bathroom," said Mandy. "I just threw the little monster in there and locked him in."

Miss Fellowes ran into the dollhouse. She fumbled at the bathroom door. It took an eternity to get it open and to find the ugly little boy cowering in the corner.

"Don't whip me, Miss Fellowes," he whispered. His eyes were red. His lips were quivering. "I didn't mean to do it."

"Oh, Timmie, who told you about whips?" She caught him to her, hugging him wildly.

He said tremulously, "She said, with a long rope. She said you would hit me and hit me."

"You won't be. She was wicked to say so. But what happened? What happened?"

"He called me an ape-boy. He said I wasn't a real boy. He said I was an animal." Timmie dissolved in a flood of tears. "He said he wasn't going to play with a monkey anymore. I said I wasn't a monkey; I *wasn't* a monkey. He said I was all funny-looking. He said I was horrible ugly. He kept saying and saying and I bit him."

They were both crying now. Miss Fellowes sobbed, "But it isn't true. You know that, Timmie. You're a real boy. You're a dear real boy and the best boy in the world. And no one, *no* one will ever take you away from me."

It was easy to make up her mind, now; easy to know what to do. Only it had to be done quickly. Hoskins wouldn't wait much longer, with his own son mangled...

No, it would have to be done this night, *this* night; with the place four-fifths asleep and the remaining fifth intellectually drunk over Project Middle Ages.

It would be an unusual time for her to return but not an unheard of one. The guard knew her well and would not dream of questioning her. He would think nothing of her carrying a suitcase. She rehearsed the noncommittal phrase, "Games for the boy," and the calm smile.

Why shouldn't he believe that?

He did. When she entered the dollhouse again, Timmie was still awake, and she maintained a desperate normality to avoid frightening him. She talked about his dreams with him and listened to him ask wistfully after Jerry.

There would be few to see her afterward, none to question the bundle she would be carrying. Timmie would be very quiet and then it would be a *fait accompli*. It would be done and what would be the use of trying to undo it. They would leave her be. They would leave them both be.

She opened the suitcase, took out the overcoat, the woolen cap with the earflaps and the rest.

Timmie said, with the beginning of alarm, "Why are you putting all these clothes on me, Miss Fellowes?"

She said, "I am going to take you outside, Timmie. To where your dreams are."

"My dreams?" His face twisted in sudden yearning, yet fear was there, too.

"You won't be afraid. You'll be with me. You won't be afraid if you're with me, will you, Timmie?"

"No, Miss Fellowes." He buried his little misshapen head against her side, and under her enclosing arm she could feel his small heart thud.

It was midnight and she lifted him into her arms. She disconnected the alarm and opened the door softly.

And she screamed, for facing her across the open door was Hoskins!

There were two men with him and he stared at her, as astonished as she.

Miss Fellowes recovered first by a second and made a quick attempt to push past him; but even with the second's delay he had time. He caught her roughly and hurled her back against a chest of drawers. He waved the men in and confronted her, blocking the door.

"I didn't expect this. Are you completely insane?"

She had managed to interpose her shoulder so that it, rather than Timmie, had struck the chest. She said pleadingly, "What harm can it do if I take him, Dr. Hoskins? You can't put energy loss ahead of a human life?"

Firmly, Hoskins took Timmie out of her arms. "An energy loss this size would mean millions of dollars lost out of the pockets of investors. It would mean a terrible setback for Stasis, Inc. It would mean eventual publicity about a sentimental nurse destroying all that for the sake of an ape-boy."

"*Ape-boy!*" said Miss Fellowes, in helpless fury.

"That's what the reporters would call him," said Hoskins.

One of the men emerged now, looping a nylon rope through eyelets along the upper portion of the wall.

Miss Fellowes remembered the rope that Hoskins had pulled outside the room containing Professor Ademewski's rock specimen so long ago.

She cried out, "No!"

But Hoskins put Timmie down and gently removed the overcoat he was wearing. "You stay here, Timmie. Nothing will happen to you. We're just going outside for a moment. All right?"

Timmie, white and wordless, managed to nod.

Hoskins steered Miss Fellowes out of the dollhouse ahead of himself. For the moment, Miss Fellowes was beyond resistance. Dully, she noticed the hand-pull being adjusted outside the dollhouse.

"I'm sorry, Miss Fellowes," said Hoskins. "I would have spared you this. I planned it for the night so that you would know only when it was over."

She said in a weary whisper, "Because your son was hurt. Because he tormented this child into striking out at him."

"No. Believe me. I understand about the incident today and I know it was Jerry's fault. But the story has leaked out. It would have to with the press surrounding us on this day of all days. I can't risk having a distorted story about negligence and savage Neanderthalers, so-called, distract from the success of Project Middle Ages. Timmie has to go soon anyway; he might as well go now and give the sensationalists as small a peg as possible on which to hang their trash."

"It's not like sending a rock back. You'll be killing a human being."

"Not killing. There'll be no sensation. He'll simply be a Neanderthal boy in a Neanderthal world. He will no longer be a prisoner and alien. He will have a chance at a free life."

"What chance? He's only seven years old, used to being taken care of, fed, clothed, sheltered. He will be alone. His tribe may not be at the point where he left them now that four years have passed. And if they were, they would not recognize him. He will have to take care of himself. How will he know how?"

Hoskins shook his head in hopeless negative. "Lord, Miss

Fellowes, do you think we haven't thought of that? Do you think we would have brought in a child if it weren't that it was the first successful fix of a human or near-human we made and that we did not dare to take the chance of unfixing him and finding another fix as good? Why do you suppose we kept Timmie as long as we did, if it were not for our reluctance to send a child back into the past. It's just"—his voice took on a desperate urgency—"that we can wait no longer. Timmie stands in the way of expansion! Timmie is a source of possible bad publicity; we are on the threshold of great things, and I'm sorry, Miss Fellowes, but we can't let Timmie block us. We cannot. We cannot. I'm sorry, Miss Fellowes."

"Well, then," said Miss Fellowes sadly. "Let me say good-by. Give me five minutes to say good-by. Spare me that much."

Hoskins hesitated. "Go ahead."

Timmie ran to her. For the last time he ran to her and for the last time Miss Fellowes clasped him in her arms.

For a moment, she hugged him blindly. She caught at a chair with the toe of one foot, moved it against the wall, sat down.

"Don't be afraid, Timmie."

"I'm not afraid if you're here, Miss Fellowes. Is that man mad at me, the man out there?"

"No, he isn't. He just doesn't understand about us. Timmie, do you know what a mother is?"

"Like Jerry's mother?"

"Did he tell you about his mother?"

"Sometimes. I think maybe a mother is a lady who takes care of you and who's very nice to you and who does good things."

"That's right. Have you ever wanted a mother, Timmie?"

Timmie pulled his head away from her so that he could look into her face. Slowly, he put his hand to her cheek and hair and stroked her, as long, long ago she had stroked him. He said, "Aren't you my mother?"

"Oh, Timmie."

"Are you angry because I asked?"

"No. Of course not."

"Because I know your name is Miss Fellowes, but—but sometimes, I call you "Mother" inside. Is that all right?"

"Yes. Yes. It's all right. And I won't leave you any more and nothing will hurt you. I'll be with you to care for you always. Call me Mother, so I can hear you."

"Mother," said Timmie contentedly, leaning his cheek against hers.

She rose, and, still holding him, stepped up on the chair. The sudden beginning of a shout from outside went unheard and, with her free hand, she yanked with all her weight at the cord where it hung suspended between two eyelets.

And Stasis was punctured and the room was empty.

SIDEWISE IN TIME
by
Murray Leinster

First published in 1934 and rarely reprinted since then because of its length, "Sidewise in Time" is one of the great seminal stories of modern science fiction. This is the story in which the late Murray Leinster introduced the theme of parallel worlds and the mixing of past, present, and future that many s-f writers would work on in numerous variations. The passing years have simply confirmed the still-fresh excitement and overall excellence of this important story.

Looking back, it seems strange that only James Minott figured the thing out in advance. The indications were more than plain. In early December Professor Michaelson announced his finding that the speed of light was not an absolute—could not be considered invariable. That, of course, was one of the first indications of what was to happen. A second indication came on February 15th, when at 12:40 P.M. Greenwich mean time, the sun suddenly shone blue-white and the enormously increased rate of radiation raised the temperature of the earth's surface by twenty-two degrees Fahrenheit in five minutes. At the end of the five minutes, the sun went back to its normal rate of radiation without any other symptom of disturbance. A great many bids for scientific fame followed, of course, but no plausible explanation of the phenomenon accounted for a total lack of after-disturbances in the sun's photosphere.

For a third clear forerunner of the events of June, on March 10th, the male giraffe in the Bronx Zoological Park, in New York, ceased to eat. In the nine days following, it changed its form, absorbing all its extremities, even its neck and head, into an extraordinary, egg-shaped mass of still-living flesh and bone which on the tenth day began to divide spontaneously and on the twelfth was two slightly pulsating fleshy masses. A day later still, bumps appeared on the two masses. They grew, took form and design, and twenty days after the beginning of the phenomenon were legs, necks, and heads. Then two giraffes, both male, moved about the giraffe enclosure. Each was slightly less than half the weight of the original animal. They were identically marked. And they ate and moved and in every way seemed normal though immature animals. An exactly similar occurrence was reported from the Argentine Republic, in which a steer from the pampas was going through the same extraordinary method of reproduction under the critical eyes of Argentine scientists.

Nowadays it seems incredible that the scientists of the time should not have understood the meaning of these oddities. We now know something of the type of strain which produced them, though they no longer occur. But between January and June the news services of the nation were flooded with items of similar import. For two days the Ohio River flowed upstream. For six hours the trees in Euclid Park, in Cleveland, lashed their branches madly as if in a terrific storm, though not a breath of wind was stirring. And in New Orleans, near the last of May, fishes swam up out of the Mississippi River through the air, proceeded to "drown" in the air which in-

explicably upheld them, and then turned belly-up and floated
placidly at an imaginary water-level some fifteen feet above
the pavements of the city.

But it seems clear enough that Minott was the only man in
the world who guessed the meaning of these now clear-cut
indications of later events. He was then an instructor in mathematics on the faculty of Robinson College, in Fredericksburg,
Virginia. We know that he anticipated very nearly every one
of the happenings which we still only partly understand, though
they affected every human being in our world—and in other
worlds most of us had never dreamed could exist.

He made no attempt to share his knowledge with the rest
of us. At first glance it seems unbelievable, but actually the
attempt would have been useless. He was merely an instructor—not even a full professor—in what can only be called a
jerkwater college. He had no scientific reputation, and even
his fellow faculty members and all his former instructors at
Johns Hopkins University considered him brash, cocky, un-
reliable, and thoroughly in need of having his ears pinned
back. They would have taken great pleasure in putting him
in his place. Had he attempted to publicize his foreknowledge
he would surely have been firmly deprived of any chance at
a hearing. His mathematics, in any case, were undoubtedly
so far advanced that only a very limited number of people
would have been able to understand them—as was the case
with Einstein's relativity theory at the beginning—and there
could be no experimental proof except the universal experience which came later.

Even had he tried to use the preliminary signs—noted
above—as proofs of his explanation and mathematics, he would
have been considered insane.

And yet he knew. Whether his first clue was Michelson's report on the variable velocity of light, which proved the existence of strains of a sort never before reported—the speed of light has now ceased to be variable, by the way—or whether another of the eccentric variations in natural law suggested his calculations, we cannot even guess. But he knew what was going to happen before it did. He knew it so thoroughly that he had calculated our chances of survival at one in four. Which pessimistic estimate alone would have caused him to be shouted down instantly had he offered his knowledge ahead of time.

In any event, he made no effort to give warning. He bought revolvers and books. He had sandwiches prepared for the greatest danger that has ever existed, anywhere, and for the most exotic enterprise any man ever attempted. Maybe he succeeded. We shall never know.

The main features of his life are well enough established. He was the son of a small farmer in West Virginia, with no history of previous genius in his family. He attended a rural grammar and consolidated high school, and seems to have annoyed each and every teacher with whom he came in contact. He worked his way through Johns Hopkins University, in Baltimore, displaying the same talent for unpopularity. He had brains. We know that now! But he was aware of them too, and so pushingly ambitious to prove and use them that he aroused antagonism wherever he went. The story is now classic, of the term paper he submitted in his junior year, covering a problem in the calculus of probability. He solved the problem in wholly orthodox fashion, and added a scornful note:

"The above is what I was supposed to do to get a good grade. It happens to be idiotically wrong. The problem should be solved as below:"

And then he restated the problem in a fashion of which his instructor could not make head or tail, and got an answer normal mathematics would not justify. The term paper was preserved by accident, and after his genius had been proved it was closely studied. The result is that Minott's Equation is now regarded with reverence and has changed the whole mathematical treatment of some aspects of probability.

The world lost a great deal through the sheer unamiability of Minott's character. He was embittered by his own impatience, frustrated by his own intelligence, and undoubtedly cursed with an ambition not seemly in an instructor in mathematics at Robinson College, Fredericksburg. Perhaps if he had had normal emotional ties the world would have benefited. Perhaps he would have, also. But it is useless to guess. We do know that if we had the notes he burned on the night of June 4th our mathematics would be so greatly advanced as to be practically a new science bringing all knowledge into a new unity. The few unburned scraps found in the fireplace of his living room have given tantalizing glimpses of that science. They are invaluable. Some partly burned fragments have been infuriating in their incompleteness. But he must have taken his most valuable notes with him, into that unguessed-at place where he may still live and work.

He would be amused at the diligence with which his least-considered scribble is now discussed by men who would have ignored him before. Perhaps—it is quite possible—he may have invented a word for the scope of the catastrophe we escaped. We have no word for it as yet. There is no term which can indicate a disaster in which not only the earth but our whole solar system would have been destroyed. Not only our solar system but our galaxy. Not only our galaxy but every other island universe in all the space we know. And even more than that, the destruction of time itself, meaning not only the obliteration of present and future, but even the annihilation of the past so that it would never have been. And then, besides, all those other strange states of existence we now know of, those other universes, those other pasts and presents and futures—all to be shattered into nothingness. There is no word for such a catastrophe!

It would be interesting to know what Minott termed it to himself as he coolly prepared to take advantage of the one chance in four of survival if that should be the one to eventuate. But it is easier merely to wonder how he felt when the morning of June 5th dawned. We do not know, of course. We cannot know. All we can be certain of is how we felt—and what happened.

It was 7:30 A.M. of June 5th. The city of Joplin, Missouri, awaked from a comfortable, summer-night sleep. Dew glistened upon grass blades and leaves and the filmy webs of morning spiders glittered like diamond dust in the early sunshine. In the most easterly suburb a high school boy, yawning, came somnolently out of his house to mow the lawn before school time. A rather rickety family car roared a block away. It backfired, stopped, roared again, and throttled down to a steady, waiting hum. The voices of children sounded among the houses. A colored washerwoman appeared, striding beneath the trees which lined this strictly residential street. From an upper window a radio blatted: "—*one, two, three, four! Higher, now!—three, four! Put your weight into it!—two, three, four! . . .*" The radio suddenly squawked and began to emit an insistent, mechanical shriek which changed again to a squawk and then a terrific sound as of all the static of ten thousand thunderstorms on the air at once. Then it was silent.

The high school boy leaned mournfully on the push bar of the lawn mower. At the instant the static ended, the boy sat down suddenly on the dew-wet grass. The colored woman reeled and grabbed frantically at the nearest tree trunk. The basket of wash toppled and spilled in a snowstorm of starched, varicolored clothing. Howls of terror from children. Sharp shrieks from women. *"Earthquake! Earthquake!"* Figures appeared running, pouring out of houses. Someone fled out to a sleeping porch, slid down a supporting column, and in his pajamas tripped over a rose bush. In seconds, it seemed, the entire population of the street was out of doors.

And then there was a queer, blank silence. There was no earthquake. No house had fallen. No chimney had cracked. Not so much as a dish or windowpane had made a sound in smashing. The sensation every human being had felt was not an actual shaking of the ground. There had been movement, yes, and of the earth, but no such movement as any human being had ever dreamed of before. These people were to learn of that movement much later. Now they stared blankly at each other.

And in the sudden, dead silence broken only by the hum of an idling car and the wail of a frightened baby, a new sound became audible. It was the tramp of marching feet. With it came a curious clanking and clattering noise. And then a barked command, which was definitely not in the English language.

Down the street of a suburb of Joplin, Missouri, came a file of spear-armed, shield-bearing soldiers, in the short, skirt-like dress of ancient Rome. They wore helmets upon their heads. They peered about as if they were as blankly amazed as the citizens of Joplin who regarded them. A long column of marching men came into view, every man with shield and spear and the indefinable air of being used to just such weapons.

They halted at another barked order. A wizened short man with a short-sword snapped a question at the staring citizens. The high school boy jumped. The wizened man roared his question again. The high school boy stammered, and painfully formed syllables with his lips. The wizened man grunted in satisfaction. He talked, articulating clearly if impatiently. And the high school boy turned dazedly to the other Americans.

"He wants to know the name of this town," he said, disbelieving his own ears. "He's talking Latin, like I learn in school. He says this town isn't on the roadmaps, and he doesn't know where he is. But all the same he takes possession of it in the name of the Emperor Valerius Fabricius, emperor of Rome and the far corners of the earth." And then the schoolboy stuttered. "He—he says these are the first six cohorts of the Forty-Second Legion, on garrison duty in Messalia. That—that's supposed to be two days march up that way."

He pointed in the direction of St. Louis.

The idling motor car roared suddenly into life. Its gears whined and it came rolling out into the street. Its horn honked peremptorily for passage through the shield-clad soldiers. They gaped at it. It honked again and moved toward them.

A roared order, and they flung themselves upon it, spears thrusting, short-swords stabbing. Up to this instant there was not one single inhabitant of Joplin who did not believe the spear-armed soldiers motion-picture actors, or masqueraders, or something else equally insane but credible. But there was nothing make-believe about their attack on the car. They assaulted it as if it were a strange and probably deadly beast.

They flung themselves into battle with it in a grotesquely reckless valor.

And there was nothing at all make-believe in the thoroughness and completeness with which they speared Mr. Horace B. Davis, who had only intended to drive down to the cotton-brokerage office of which he was chief clerk. They thought he was driving this strange beast to slaughter them, and they slaughtered him instead. The high school boy saw them do it, growing whiter and whiter as he watched. When a swordsman approached the wizened man and displayed the severed head of Mr. Davis, with the spectacles dangling grotesquely from one ear, the high school boy fainted dead away.

It was sunrise of June 5th. Cyrus Harding gulped down his breakfast in the pale gray dawnlight. He had felt very dizzy and sick for just a moment, some little while since, but he was himself again now. The smell of frying filled the kitchen. His wife cooked. Cyrus Harding ate. He made noises as he emptied his plate. His hands were gnarled and work-worn, but his expression was of complacent satisfaction. He looked at a calendar hung on the wall, a Christmas sentiment from the Bryan Feed and Fertilizer Company, in Bryan, Ohio.

"Sheriff's goin' to sell out Amos today," he said comfortably. "I figger I'll get that north forty cheap."

His wife said tiredly:

"He's been offerin' to sell it to you for a year."

"Yep," agreed Cyrus Harding more complacently still. "Comin' down on the price, too. But nobuddy'll bid against me at the sale. They know I want it bad, an' I ain't a good neighbor to have when somebuddy takes somethin' from under my nose. Folks know it. I'll git it a lot cheaper'n Amos offered it to me for. He wanted to sell it t'meet his int'rest an' hol' on another year. I'll git it for half that."

He stood up and wiped his mouth. He strode to the door.

"That hired man shoulda got a good start with his harrowin'," he said expansively. "I'll take a look an' go over to the sale."

He went to the kitchen door and opened it. Then his mouth dropped open. The view from this doorway was normally that of a not-especially neat barnyard, with beyond it farmland flat as a floor, cultivated to the very fence rails, with a promising crop of corn as a border against the horizon.

Now the view was quite otherwise. All was normal as far as the barn. But beyond the barn was delirium. Huge, spreading tree-ferns soared upward a hundred feet. Lacy, foliated branches formed a roof of incredible density above sheer jungle such as no man on earth had ever seen before. The jungles of the Amazon basin were parklike by comparison with its thickness. It was a riotous tangle of living vegetation in which growth was battle, and battle was life, and life was deadly, merciless conflict. No man could have forced his way ten feet through such a wilderness. From it came a fetid exhalation which was part decay and part lush rank growing things, and part the overpowering perfumes of glaringly vivid flowers. It was jungle such as paleobotanists have described as existing in the Carboniferous period; as the source of our coal beds.

"It—it ain't so!" said Cyrus Harding weakly. "It—ain't so!"

His wife did not reply. She had not seen. Wearily, she began to clean up after her lord and master's meal.

He went down the kitchen steps, staring and shaken. He moved toward this impossible apparition which covered his crops. It did not disappear as he neared it. He went within twenty feet of it and stopped, still staring, still unbelieving, beginning to entertain the monstrous supposition that he had gone insane.

Then something moved in the jungle. A long, snaky neck, feet thick at its base and tapering to a mere sixteen inches behind a head the size of a barrel. The neck reached out the twenty feet to him. Cold eyes regarded him abstractedly. The mouth opened. Cyrus Harding screamed.

His wife raised her eyes. She looked through the open door and saw the jungle. She saw the jaws close upon her husband. She saw the colossal, abstracted eyes half close as Something gulped, and partly choked, and swallowed. She saw a lump in the monstrous neck move from the relatively slender portion just behind the head to the enormous mass of flesh where the neck joined its unseen body. She saw the head withdraw into the jungle and be instantly lost to sight.

Cyrus Harding's widow went very pale. She put on her hat and walked subduedly out of the front door. She began to walk steadily toward the house of the nearest neighbor. As she went, she said composedly to herself:

"It's come. I've gone crazy. They'll have to put me in an asylum. But I won't have to stand him any more. *I won't have to stand him any more!*"

And at 10:30 A.M. on the morning of June 5th, Instructor James Minott of Robinson College turned upon the party of students with a revolver in each hand. Gone was the appearance of the dour young instructor whose most destructive possibility was a below-passing mark in math. He had guns in his hands now, instead of chalk or pencil, and his eyes were glowing even as he smiled frostily. The four girls gasped. The

young men, accustomed to see him only in a classroom, realized that not only could he use the weapons in his hands,
but that he would. And suddenly they respected him as they
would respect—say—a burglar or a prominent gangster or a
well-known murderer. He was raised far above the level of a
mathematics instructor. He became instantly a leader, and by
virtue of his weapons, even a ruler.

"As you see," said Minott evenly, "I have anticipated the
situation in which we find ourselves. At any moment, to be
sure, we and all the human race may be wiped out with a
completeness of which you can form no idea. But we may
survive, and I am prepared equally to be wiped out or to make
the most of my chance of survival—if we live."

He looked steadily from one to another of the students who
had followed him to explore the extraordinary appearance of
a sequoia forest north of Fredericksburg.

"I know what has happened," said Minott coolly. "I also
know what is likely to happen. And I know what I intend to
do about it. Any of you who are prepared to follow me can
say so. Any of you who objects—well—I can't have mutinies!
I'll shoot him!"

"But Mr. Minott," said Blake nervously, "we ought to get
the girls home—"

"They will never go home," said Minott calmly. "Neither
will you nor any of the rest of us. As soon as you're quite
convinced that I'm ready to use these weapons, I'll tell you
what's happened and what it means. I've been preparing for
it for weeks."

It was noon of June 5th. The cell door opened and a very
grave, whiskered man in a curious gray uniform came in. He
tapped the prisoner gently on the shoulder.

"I'm Doctor Holloway," he said encouragingly. "Army Medical Corps. Suppose you tell me, suh, just what happened t'you? I'm right sure it can all be straightened out."

The prisoner sputtered:

"Why—why—dammit," he protested. "I drove down from Louisville this morning. I had a dizzy spell and—well—I must have missed my road, because suddenly I noticed that everything around me was unfamiliar. And then a man in a gray uniform yelled at me, and a minute later he began to shoot, and the first thing I knew they'd arrested me for having the American flag painted on my car! I'm a traveling salesman for the Uncle Sam Candy-Bar Company! Dammit, it's funny when a man can't fly his own country's flag—"

"In your own country, of co'se," assented the doctor, comfortingly. "But you must know, suh, that we don't allow any flag but ouah own to be displayed heah. You violated ouah laws, suh."

"Your laws!" The prisoner stared blankly. "What laws? Where in the United States is it illegal to fly the American flag?"

"Nowheah in the United States, suh." The doctor smiled. "You must have crossed ouah border unawares, suh. I will be frank, an' admit that it was suspected you were insane. I see now that it was just a mistake."

"Border—United—" The prisoner gasped. "I'm not in the United States? I'm not? Then where in hell am I?"

"Ten miles, suh, within the borders of the Confederacy," said the doctor, and laughed. "A queer mistake, suh, but theah was no intention of insult. You'll be released at once. Theah is enough tension between Washington an' Richmond without another border incident to upset ouah hotheads."

"Confederacy?" The prisoner choked. "You can't—you don't mean the Confederate States—"

"Of co'se, suh. The Confederate States of North America. Why not?"

The prisoner gulped.

"I—I've gone mad!" he stammered. "I must be mad! There was Gettysburg—there was—"

"Gettysburg? Oh, yes!" The doctor nodded indulgently. "We are very proud of ouah history, suh. You refer to the battle in the War of Separation, when the fate of the Confederacy rested on ten minutes' time. I have often wondered what would have been the result if Pickett's charge had been driven back. It was Pickett's charge that gained the day for us, suh. England recognized the Confederacy two days later, France in another week, an' with unlimited credit abroad we won out. But it was a tight squeeze, suh!"

The prisoner gasped again. He stared out of the window. And opposite the jail stood an unquestionable courthouse. Upon the courthouse stood a flagpole. And spread gloriously in the breeze above a government building—floated the Stars and Bars of the Confederacy!

It was night of June 5th. The postmaster of North Centerville, Massachusetts came out of his cubbyhole to listen to the narrative. The pot-bellied stove of the general store sent a comfortable, if unnecessary glow about. The eyewitness chuckled.

"Yeah. They come around the cape, thirty or forty of 'em in a boat all o' sixty feet long with a crazy square sail drawin'. Round things in the gun'le like—like shields. An' rowin' like hell. They stopped when they saw the town an' looked s'prised. Then they hailed us, talkin' some lingo that wa'n't American. Ole Peterson, he near dropped his line, with a fish on it too.

Then he tried t' talk back. They hadda lotta trouble understandin' him, or made out to. Then they turned around an' rowed back. Actors or somethin', tryin' to play a joke. It fell flat, though. Maybe some o' those rich folks up the coast pullin' it. Ho! Ho! Ole says they was talkin' a funny, old-fashioned Skowegian. They told him they was from Leifsholm, or some-thin' like that, just up the coast. That they couldn't make out how our town got here. They'd never seen it before! Can y' imagine that? Ole says they were Vikin's, an' they called this place Vinland, an' says—My Gawd! What's that?"

A sudden hubbub arose in the night. Screams. Cries. A shotgun boomed dully. The loafers in the general store crowded out on the porch. Flames rose from half a dozen places on the waterfront. In their light could be seen a full dozen serpent-ships, speeding for the shore, propelled by oars. Firelight glinted on swords, on shields. A woman screamed as a huge, yellow-maned man seized her. His brazen helmet and shield glittered. He was laughing. Then a figure in overalls hurtled toward the blond giant, an axe held threateningly—

The giant cut him down with an already dripping blade and roared. Men rushed to him and they plunged on to loot and burn. More of the armored figures leaped to the sand from another beached ship. Another house roared flames skyward. . . .

Tall trees rose around the party. Giant trees. Magnificient trees. They towered two hundred and fifty feet into the air, and their air of venerable calm was at once the most convincing evidence of their actuality, and the most improbable of all the things which had happened in the neighborhood of Fredericksburg, Virginia. The little group of people sat their horses affrightedly beneath the monsters of the forest. Minott re-

garded them estimatingly, these three young men and four
girls, all students of Robinson College.

Minott was now no longer the faculty member in charge of
a party of exploration, but a definitely ruthless leader.

At eight-thirty A.M. on June 5th the inhabitants of Fredericksburg had felt a curious, unanimous dizziness. It passed.
The sun shone brightly. There seemed to be no noticeable
change in any of the facts of everyday existence. But within
an hour, the sleepy little town was buzzing with excitement.
The road to Washington—Route One on all road-maps—
ceased abruptly some three miles north. A colossal, a gigantic
forest had appeared magically to block the way. Telegraphic
communication with Washington had ceased. Even the Washington broadcasting stations were no longer on the air. The
trees of the extraordinary forest were tall beyond the experience of any human being in town. They looked like the
photographs of the giant sequoias on the Pacific Coast, but—
well—the thing was simply impossible.

In an hour and a half, Instructor Minott had organized a
party of sightseers among the students. He seemed to pick
his party with a queer definiteness of decision. Three young
men and four girls. They would have piled into a rickety car
owned by one of the boys, but Minott negated the idea.

"The road ends at the forest," he said, smiling. "I'd rather
like to explore a magic forest. Suppose we ride horseback?
I'll arrange for horses."

In ten minutes the horses appeared. The girls had vanished
to get into riding breeches or knickers. They noted appreciatively on their return that besides the saddles, the horses had
saddle bags slung in place. Again Minott smiled.

"We're exploring," he said humorously. "We must dress the

part. Also, we'll probably want some lunch. And we can bring back specimens for the botanical lab to look over."

They rode forth; the girls thrilled, the young men pleased and excited, and all of them just a little bit disappointed at finding themselves passed by motor cars which whizzed by as all Fredericksburg went to look at the improbable forest ahead.

There were cars by hundreds where the road abruptly ended. A crowd stared at the forest. Giant trees, their roots fixed firmly in the ground. Undergrowth here and there. Over it all, an aspect of peace and utter serenity—and permanence. The watching crowd hummed and buzzed with speculation, with talk. The thing they saw was impossible. It could not have happened. This forest could not possibly be real. They were regarding some sort of mirage.

But as the party of riders arrived, half a dozen daring men came out of the forest. They had dared to enter it. Now they returned, still incredulous of their own experience, bearing leaves and branches and one of them certain small berries unknown on the Atlantic Coast.

A State Police officer held up his hand as Minott's party went toward the edge of the forest.

"Look here!" he said. "We been hearin' funny noises in there. I'm stoppin' anybody else from goin' in until we know what's what."

Minott nodded.

"We'll be careful. I'm a faculty member of Robinson College. We're going in after some botanical specimens. I have a revolver. We're all right."

He rode ahead. The State policeman, without definite orders for authority, shrugged his shoulders and bent his efforts to the prevention of other attempts to explore. In minutes, the eight horses and their riders were out of sight.

That was now three hours past. For three hours, Minott had led his charges a little south of northeast. In that time they saw no dangerous animals. They saw some—many— familiar plants. They saw rabbits in quantity, and once a slinking gray form which Tom Hunter, who was majoring in zoology, declared was a wolf. There are no wolves in the vicinity of Fredericksburg, but neither are there sequoias. And the party had seen no signs of human life, though Fredericksburg lies in farming country which is thickly settled. In three hours the horses must have covered between twelve and fifteen miles, even through the timber. It was just after sighting a shaggy beast which was unquestionably a woodland buffalo— extinct east of the Rockies as early as 1820—that young Blake protested uneasily against further travel.

"There's something awfully queer, sir," he said awkwardly. "I don't mind experimenting as much as you like, sir, but we've got the girls with us. If we don't start back pretty soon, we'll get in trouble with the dean!"

And then Minott drew his two revolvers and very calmly announced that none of them would ever go back. That he knew what had happened and what could be expected. And he added that he would explain as soon as they were convinced he would use his revolvers in case of a mutiny.

"Call us convinced now, sir," said young Blake. He was a bit pale about his lips, but he hadn't flinched. In fact, he'd moved to be between Maida Haynes and the gun muzzle. "We'd like very much to know how all these trees and plants, which ought to be three thousand miles away, happen to be growing in Virginia without any warning. Especially, sir, we'd like to know how it is that the topography underneath all this brand-new forest is the same. The hills trend the same way they used to, but everything that ever was on them has vanished, and something else is in its place."

Minott nodded approvingly.

"Splendid, Blake!" he said warmly. "Sound observation! I picked you because you're well spoken of in geology, even though there were—er—other reasons for leaving you behind. Let's go on over the next rise. Unless I'm mistaken, we should find the Potomac in view. Then I'll answer any questions you like. I'm afraid we've a good bit more riding to do today."

Reluctantly, the eight horses breasted the slope. They scrambled among underbrush. It was queer that in three hours they had seen not a trace of a road leading anywhere. But up at the top of the hill there was a road. It was a narrow, wandering cart track. Without a word, every one of the eight riders turned their horses to follow it. It meandered onward for perhaps a quarter of a mile. It dipped suddenly. And the Potomac lay before and below them.

Then seven of the eight riders exclaimed. There was a settlement upon the banks of the river. There were boats in harbor. There were other boats in view beyond; two beating down from the long reaches upstream, and three others coming painfully up from the direction of Chesapeake Bay. But neither the village nor the boats should have been upon the Potomac River. The village was small and mud-walled. Tiny, blue-clad figures moved about the fields outside. The buildings, the curving lines of the roofs, and more especially the unmistakable outline of a sort of temple near the center of the fortified hamlet—these were Chinese. The boats in sight were junks, save that their sails were cloth instead of slatted bamboo. The fields outside the squat mud walls were cultivated in a fashion altogether alien. Near the river, where marsh flats would be normal along the Potomac, rice fields intensely worked spread out instead.

Then a figure appeared nearby. Wide hat, wadded cotton-padded jacket, cotton trousers, and clogs, it was Chinese peasant incarnate, and all the more so when it turned a slant-eyed, terror-stricken face upon them and fled squawking. It left a monstrously heavy wooden yoke behind, from which dangled two buckets filled with berries it had gathered in the forest.

The riders stared. There was the Potomac. But a Chinese village nestled beside it, Chinese junks plied its waters....

"I—I think," said Maida Haynes unsteadily, "I—think I've—gone insane. Haven't I?"

Minott shrugged. He looked disappointed but queerly resolute.

"No," he said shortly. "You're not mad. It just happens that the Chinese happened to colonize America first. It's been known that Chinese junks touched the American shore—the Pacific Coast, of course—long before Columbus. Evidently they colonized it. They may have come all the way overland to the Atlantic, or maybe around the Panama. In any case, this is a Chinese continent now. This isn't what we want. We'll ride some more."

The fleeing, squawking figure had been seen from the village. A huge, discordant gong began to sound. Figures fled toward the walls from the fields round about. The popping of firecrackers began, with a chorus of most intimidating yells.

"Come on!" said Minott sharply. "We'd better move!"

He wheeled his horse about and started off at a canter. By

instinct, since he was the only one who seemed to have any definite idea what to do, the others flung after him.

And as they rode, suddenly the horses staggered. The humans atop them felt a queer, queazy vertigo. It lasted only for a second, but Minott paled a little.

"Now we'll see what's happened," he said composedly. "The odds are still fair, but I'd rather have had things stay as they were until we'd tried a few more places. . . ."

That same queasy vertigo affected the staring crowd at the end of the road leading north from Fredericksburg. For perhaps a second they felt an unearthly illness, which even blurred their vision. Then they saw clearly again. And in an instant they were babbling in panic, starting their motor cars in terror, some of them fleeing on foot.

The sequoia forest had vanished. In its place was a dreary waste of glittering white; stumpy trees buried under snow; rolling ground covered with a powdery, glittering stuff. . . .

In minutes dense fog shut off the view, as the warm air of a Virginia June morning was chilled by that frigid coating. But in minutes, too, the heavy snow began to melt. The cars fled away along the concrete road, and behind them an expanding belt of fog spread out—and the little streams and runlets filled with a sudden surplus of water, and ran more swiftly, and rose. . . .

There were only sparse trees and a tall, canelike grass. The ground was still rolling, but the air was misty. Clear vision was not possible for a very long distance. Still, the topography in terms of hills and valleys had not changed. But they saw a tapir—it looked like a pigmy elephant at first glance—and they had seen other things that looked human, but weren't. So two of the young men rode on ahead, watching lest there should be anything hidden in the breast-high grass, and Minott followed with the four girls, and another of the students followed twenty yards behind.

"I don't like this," said Minott coldly. "Not at all. But we'll keep going."

Lucy Blair rode beside him on one hand. He'd shown her how to use a revolver. Maida Haynes rode on the other.

"What were those—things we saw?" asked Lucy shakenly. "They—looked human. Were they, really?"

"Depends on what you mean by human," said Minott. "If you mean *Homo sapiens*—our species—probably not. The human family had a number of species, like the equine and feline families. There was Neanderthal man and Java man and so on. *Homo sapiens* wiped them out, in the world we came from. But in the history of this particular place the battle may have gone the other way."

Maida Haynes licked her lips. She was terribly tense.

"History," she said in a queer voice. "What has that to do with—what's happening to us? I—I still think I'm dreaming. I—I must be!"

"I think I'm dreaming too," said Lucy. "And I'm scared too, but so far it's rather wonderful. I—think I'll get over being scared, in time."

One of the two figures on ahead swerved to one side. He rode cautiously, and reined in, and then turned his horse and came racing back to Minott.

"Some of those—creatures lying in wait there," he said through chattering lips. "The—funny things that look like men. What'll we do?"

Minott considered coldly.

"If we planned to stay here," he said presently, without emotion, "we'd charge them and kill enough of them to teach a needed lesson. But we don't intend to stay here. It isn't worth the risk or trouble. We'd gain nothing. Swing wide of them. If they try to follow us we'll shoot one or two."

Harris sent his horse plunging back to join young Blake. They changed course. Beastly howlings arose from a spot they would now avoid. Loping, bouncing figures with long brown shaggy hair went leaping and bounding to intercept them. The figures carried clubs and spears.

Minott very calmly drew a revolver. He aimed and fired six times. A creature screamed up ahead. Its fellows fled away, howling. The wounded creature thrashed and shrieked. Then it suddenly made bubbling sounds and was still. Minott reloaded his revolver.

"You—killed it!" gasped Maida, horrified.

"To be sure," said Minott casually. "Killing one made the others run away. If they'd attacked us we'd have had to kill several, and it would have used up a good deal of ammunition.

"Intelligence isn't at a premium here," said Minott. "We can't make much out of this environment!"

He made no other comment. Far, far away, the misty air seemed to grow thicker. There was a white fog before them. It seemed to stretch out of sight on either hand. They rode toward it.

Lucy Blair said suddenly:

"Do you really think we'll come upon a civilization where we'll be welcomed, Mr. Minott?"

"Naturally!" His tone was dry. "I did not plan this expedition without some definite ideas!"

"And do you think we will—we will—"

"Rule it?" He said more dryly still: "I assure you that I will rule it. I need only to be received—to be accepted—in a community not too far advanced in culture, but a shade above savagery. Given that foothold, I can use my special knowledge to its full value. I need only a society still fluid, still malleable, not yet frozen in a pattern of conventional stability. I will end by ruling it. In our own culture, man is only afraid of losing what he has. I can do nothing with such people. But give me men who want what they have not, and I can give it to them! I can make them prosper as if by magic!"

"By mathematics?" asked Lucy dubiously.

He smiled faintly.

"You might call it that," he said ironically. "But by your definition mathematics is only a form of integration dealing with quantity. Logic is a form of integration which deals with ideas but not with quantity. There can be—there is!—a form of integration which deals with both and more besides. I discovered it. It is useless in our time, of course. It would upset too much that is solidly established. But it is as precise in its operation as either mathematics or logic. And I assure you that it will give me as much advantage in all dealings with men of a proper culture, as the ability to count gives in dealings with savages who cannot."

Lucy Blair looked at him oddly.

"That sounds like pure intellectuality. You act like something else entirely. Do you know, I've always thought you were lonely?"

"I always have been," said Minott bitterly. "I always will be. But I shall do things to make up for it now! Let me find just one community of men who are restless and desirous, and I will remake it, remold it, rule and guide it, and—"

But then he stopped. Lucy did not look shocked. She said interestedly:

"And how do we fit into that?"

"You will help me," he said calmly. "All of you. You have no choice, of course, but you will have such rewards as you cannot now imagine. I won't need to force any of you. You'll have no choice. But you will be glad, I think."

"But it's—preposterous—" protested Maida, shrilly, "not to—not to be able to go home again—"

"You will marry," said Minott practically. "Then you won't mind. Even that, though, will be of your own choice. Of course. You won't find semisavages interesting, any more than any of the rest of us would. You'll do all right."

The two girls stared at each other. There were four girls. Three students—and Minott.

"Yes," he said matter-of-factly. "I shall marry one of you. The most suitable for my plans. I shall want an intelligent empress."

But then he spurred ahead. The fog bank before them spread from one horizon to the other. As the horses went uneasily into it, the air turned icy cold.

The ferryboat from Berkeley, California plowed valorously through the fog. Its whistle howled mournfully at the proper intervals. Up in the pilothouse, the skipper said confidentially:

"I tell you, I had the funniest feelin' of my life, just now. I was dizzy an' sick all over, like seasick an' drunk together."

The mate said abstractedly:

"Me too, a little while ago. Somethin' we ate, prob'ly. Say, that's funny!"

"What?"

"Was a lot o' traffic in the harbor just now. Whistlin'. I ain't heard a whistle for minutes. Listen!"

Both men strained their ears. There was the rhythmic shudder of the vessel, itself a sound produced by the engines. There were fragmentary voice-noises from the passenger deck below. There was the wash of water by the ferryboat's bow. There was nothing else. Nothing at all.

"Funny!" said the skipper.

"Dam' funny!" agreed the mate.

The ferryboat went on. The fog cut down all visibility to a radius of perhaps two hundred feet.

"Funniest thing I ever saw!" said the skipper worriedly. He reached for the whistle cord and the mournful bellow of the horn resounded. "We're near our slip, though. I wish..."

With a little chugging, swishing sound a steam launch came out of the mist. It sheered off, the men in it staring blankly at the huge bulk of the ferry. It made a complete circuit of the big, clumsy craft. Then someone stood up and bellowed unintelligibly in the launch. He bellowed again. He was giving an order. He pointed to the flag at the stern of the launch—it was an unfamiliar flag—and roared furiously.

"What the hell's the matter with that guy?" wondered the mate.

A little breeze blew suddenly. The fog began to thin. The faintly brighter spot which was the sun overhead grew bright indeed. Faint sunshine struggled through the fog bank. The wind drove the fog back before it—and the bellowing man in the steam launch grew purple with rage as his orders went unheeded.

Then, quite abruptly, the last wisps of vapor blew away.

San Francisco stood revealed. But—San Francisco? This was not San Francisco! It was a wooden city. A small city. A dirty city with narrow streets and gas street-lamps and four monstrous, barracklike edifices fronting the harbor. Nob Hill stood, but it was barren of dwellings. And—

"My Gawd!" said the mate of the ferryboat.

He was staring at a colossal mass of masonry, four-square and huge, which rose to a gigantic spiral-fluted dome. A strange and alien flag fluttered in the breeze above certain buildings. Figures moved in the streets. There were motor cars, but they were clumsy and huge. The mate's eyes rested upon a horse-drawn carriage. It was drawn by three horses abreast, and they were either so trained or so check-reined that only the center one faced straight ahead. The necks of the other two were arched outward in the fashion of Tsarist Russia.

But that was natural enough, after all. When an interpreter could be found, the mate and skipper were savagely abused for entering the harbor of Novo Skevsky without obeying the ordinances in force by ukase of the Tsar Alexis of All the Russias. Those rules, they learned, were enforced with special rigor in all the Russian territory in America, from Alaska on south.

The eight riders were every one very pale. Even Minott seemed shaken but no less resolute when he drew rein.

"I imagine you will all be satisfied now," he said composedly. "Blake, you're the geologist of the party. Doesn't the shoreline there look familiar?"

Young Blake nodded. He was very white indeed. He pointed to the stream.

"Yes. The falls, too. This is the site of Fredericksburg,

sir, where we were this morning. There is where the main bridge was—or will be. The main highway to Richmond should run—" He licked his lips. "It should run where that very big oak tree is standing. The Princess Anne Hotel should be on the other side of that hill. I—I would say, sir, that somehow we've gone backwards in time or else forward into the future. It sounds insane, but I've been trying to figure it out..."

Minott nodded coolly.

"Very good. This is the site of Fredericksburg, to be sure. But we have not traveled backward or ahead in time. I hope that you noticed where we came out of the sequoia forest. There seems to be a sort of fault along that line, which it may be useful to remember." He paused. "We're not in the past or the future, Blake. We've traveled sidewise, in a sort of oscillation from one time-path to another. We happen to be in a—well—in a part of time where Fredericksburg has never been built, just as a little while since we were where the Chinese occupy the American continent. I think we'd better have lunch."

He dismounted. The four girls tended to huddle together. Maida Haynes' teeth chattered. Blake moved to the horses' heads.

"Don't get rattled," he said urgently. "We're here, wherever it is. Mr. Minott is going to explain things fully in a minute. Since he knows what's what, we're in no danger. Climb off your horses and let's eat. I'm hungry as a bear. Come on, Maida!"

Maida Haynes dismounted. She managed a rather shaky smile.

"I'm—afraid of—him," she said in a whisper. "More than—anything else—stay close to me, please!"

Blake frowned. Minott said dryly:

"Look in your saddlebags and you'll find sandwiches. Also you'll find firearms. You young men had better arm yourselves. Since there's now no conceivable hope of getting back to the world we know, I think you can be trusted with weapons."

Young Blake stared at him, then silently investigated his own saddlebags. He found two revolvers, with what seemed an abnormally large supply of cartridges. He found a mass of paper, which turned out to be books with their cardboard backs torn off. He glanced professionally at the revolvers and slipped them in his pockets. He put back the books.

"I appoint you second in command, Blake," said Minott, more dryly than before. "You understand nothing, but you want to understand. I made no mistake in choosing you, despite my reasons for leaving you behind. Sit down, and I'll tell you what happened!"

With a grunt and a puffing noise, a small black bear broke cover and fled across a place where only that morning a highly elaborate filing station had stood. The party started, then relaxed. The girls suddenly started to giggle foolishly, almost hysterically. Minott bit calmly into a sandwich and said pleasantly:

"I shall have to talk mathematics to you, but I'll try to make it more palatable than my classroom lectures have been. You see, everything that has happened can only be explained in terms of mathematics, and more especially certain concepts in mathematical physics. You young ladies and gentlemen being college men and women, I shall have to phrase things very simply, as for ten-year-old children. Hunter, you're staring. If you actually see something, such as an Indian, shoot at him and he'll run away. The probabilities are that he never heard the report of a firearm. We're not on the Chinese continent now."

Hunter gasped, and fumbled at his saddlebags. While he got out the revolvers in it, Minott went on imperturbably:

"There has been an upheaval of nature, which still continues. But instead of a shaking and jumbling of earth and rocks, there has been a shaking and jumbling of space and time. I go back to first principles. Time is a dimension. The past is one extension of it, the future is the other, just as east is one extension of a more familiar dimension and west is its opposite. But we ordinarily think of time as a line, a sort of tunnel, perhaps. We do not make that error in the dimensions about which we think daily. For example, we know that Annapolis, King George Court House, and—say—Norfolk are all to eastward of us. But we know that in order to reach any of them, as a destination, we would have to go not only east but north or south in addition. In imaginative travels into the future, however, we never think in such a common-sense fashion. We assume that the future is a line instead of a coordinate, a path instead of a direction. We assume that if we travel to futureward there is but one possible destination. And that is as absurd as it would be to ignore the possibility of traveling to eastward in any other line than due east, forgetting that there are northeast and southeast and a large number of intermediate points."

Young Blake said slowly:

"I follow you, sir, but it doesn't seem to bear—"

"On our problem? But it does!" Minott smiled, showing his teeth. He bit into his sandwich again. "Imagine that I come to a fork in a road. I flip a coin to determine which fork I shall

take. Whichever route I follow, I shall encounter certain landmarks, and certain adventures. But they will not be the same,
whether landmarks or adventures. In choosing between the
forks of the road I choose not only between two sets of landmarks I could encounter, but between two sets of events. I
choose between paths, not only on the surface of the earth,
but in time. And as those paths upon earth may lead to two
different cities, so those paths in the future may lead to two
entirely different futures. On one of them may lie opportu-
nities for riches. On the other may lie the most prosaic of hit-
and-run accidents which will leave me a mangled corpse, not
only upon one fork of a highway in the state of Virginia, but
upon one fork of a highway in time. In short, I am pointing
out that there is more than one future we can encounter, and
with more or less absence of deliberation we choose among
them. But the futures we fail to encounter, upon the roads
we do not take, are just as real as the landmarks upon those
roads. We never see them, but we freely admit their existence."

Again it was young Blake who protested:

"All this is interesting enough, sir, but still I don't see how
it applies to our present situation."

Minott said impatiently:

"Don't you see that if such a state of things exists in the
future, that it must also have existed in the past? We talk of
three dimensions and one present and one future. There is a
theoretic necessity—a mathematical necessity—to assume
more than one future. There are an indefinite number of
possible futures, any one of which we would encounter if we
took the proper 'forks' in time. There are any number of
destinations to eastward. There are any number to future-

ward. Start a hundred miles west and come eastward, choosing
your paths on earth at random, as you do in time. You may
arrive here. You may arrive to the north or south of this spot,
and still be east of your starting point. Now start a hundred
years back instead of a hundred miles west!"

Groping, young Blake said fumblingly:

"I think you're saying, sir, that—well, as there must be any
number of futures, there must have been any number of pasts
besides those written down in our histories. And—and it
would follow that there are any number of what you might
call 'presents.'"

Minott gulped down the last of his sandwich and nodded.

"Precisely! And today's convulsion of nature has jumbled
them, and still upsets them from time to time. The Northmen
once colonized America. In the sequence of events which
mark the pathway of our own ancestors through time, that
colony failed. But along another path through time that colony
throve and flourished. The Chinese reached the shores of
California. In the path our ancestors followed through time,
nothing developed from the fact. But this morning we touched
upon the pathway in which they have colonized and con-
quered the continent, though from the fear that one peasant
we saw displayed, they have not wiped out the Indians as our
ancestors did. Somewhere the Roman Empire still exists, and
may not improbably rule America as it once ruled Britain.
Somewhere, the conditions causing the glacial period still
obtain and Virginia is buried under a mass of snow. Somewhere even the Carboniferous period may exist. Or to come
more closely to the present we know, somewhere there is a
path through time in which Pickett's charge at Gettysburg
went desperately home, and the Confederate States of America is now an independent nation with a heavily fortified bor-

der and a chip-on-the-shoulder attitude toward the United States.

Blake alone had asked questions, but the entire party had been listening open-mouthed. Now Lucy Blair said:

"But—Mr. Minott, where are we now?"

"We are probably," said Minott, smiling, "in a path of time in which America has never been discovered by white men. That isn't a very satisfactory state of things. We're going to look for something better. We wouldn't be comfortable in wigwams, with skins for clothing. So we shall hunt for a more congenial environment. We will have some weeks in which to do our searching, I think. Unless, of course, all space and time is wiped out by the cause of our predicament."

Tom Hunter stirred uncomfortably.

"We haven't traveled backward or forward in time, then."

"No," repeated Minott. He got to his feet. "That odd nausea we felt seems to be caused by travel sidewise in time. It's the symptom of a time-oscillation. We'll ride on and see what other worlds await us. We're a rather well-qualified party for this sort of exploration. I chose you for your training. Hunter, zoology. Blake, engineering and geology. Harris—" He nodded to the rather undersized young man, who flushed at being noticed. "Harris is quite a competent chemist, I understand. Miss Ketterline is a capable botanist. Miss Blair—"

Maida Haynes rose slowly.

"You anticipated all this, Mr. Minott, and yet you brought us into it. You—you said we'll never get back home. Yet you deliberately arranged it. What—what was your motive? What did you do it for?"

Minott climbed into the saddle. He smiled, but there was bitterness in his smile.

"In the world we know," he told her, "I was an instructor

in mathematics in a small and unconsidered college. I had absolutely no chance of ever being more than a professor of mathematics in a small and unconsidered college. In this world I am, at least, the leader of a group of reasonably intelligent young people. In our saddlebags are arms and ammunition and—more important—books of reference for our future activities. We shall hunt for and find a civilization in which our technical knowledge is at a premium. We shall live in that world—if all time and space is not destroyed—and use our knowledge."

Maida Haynes said:

"But again—what for?"

"To conquer it!" said Minott in sudden fierceness. "To conquer it! We eight will rule a world as no world has been ruled since time began! I promise you that when we find the environment we seek, you will have wealth by millions, slaves by thousands, every luxury and all the power human beings could desire!"

Blake said evenly:

"And you, sir? What will you have?"

"Most power of all," said Minott steadily. "I shall be the emperor of the world!"

He turned his back to them and rode off to lead the way. Maida Haynes was deathly pale as she rode close to Blake. Her hand closed convulsively upon his arm.

"J-Jerry!" she whispered. "I'm—frightened!"

But Lucy Blair rode onward with an odd, excited smile on her face.

The boy ran shouting up to the village. *"Hey, Grampa! Hey, Grampa! Lookit the birds!"* He pointed as he ran. A man looked idly, and stood transfixed. A woman stopped, and stared. Lake Superior glowed bluely off to westward, and the little village most often turned its eyes in that direction. Now though, as the small boy ran shouting of what he had seen, men stared, and women marveled, and the children ran and shouted and whooped in the instinctive excitement of childhood at anything which entrances grown-ups.

Over the straggly pine forests birds were coming. They came in great dark masses. Not by dozens, or by hundreds, or even by thousands. They came in millions, in huge dark clouds which literally obscured the sky. There were two huge flights in sight at the boy's first shouting. There were six in view before he had reached his home and was panting a demand that his elders come and look. And there were others, incredible numbers of others, sweeping onward straight over the village.

Dusk fell abruptly as the first flock passed overhead. The whirring of wings was loud. It made people raise their voices as they asked each other what such birds could possibly be. Daylight again, and again darkness as the flocks poured on. The size of each flock was to be measured not in feet or yards, but in miles of front. Two—three miles of birds, flying steadily in a single enormous mass some four miles deep. Another such mass, and another, and another...

"What are they, Grampa? There must be millions of 'em!"

Somewhere, a shotgun went off. Small things dropped from the sky. Another gunshot, and another. A rain of birdshot went up from the village into the mass of whirring wings. And crazily careening small bodies fell down among the houses....

Grampa examined one of them, smoothing its rumpled plumage. He exclaimed. He gasped in excitement.

"It's a wild pigeon! What they used t' call passenger pigeons! Back in '78 there was these birds by billions. Folks said a billion was killed in Michigan that one year! But they' gone now. They' gone like the buffalo. There ain't any more."

The sky was dark with birds above him. A flock four miles wide and three miles long literally made lights necessary in the village. The air was filled with the sound of wings. Droppings fell like snow. The passenger pigeon had returned to a continent from which it had been absent for more than fifty years. Flocks of passenger pigeons flew overhead in thick masses equalling those seen by Audubon in 1813, when he computed the pigeons in flight above Kentucky at hundreds of billions in number. In flocks that were literally innumerable they flew to westward. The sun set, and still the air was filled with the sound of their flying. For hours after darkness fell, the whirring of wings continued without ceasing.

A great open fire licked at the rocks against which it had been built. The horses cropped uneasily at herbage nearby. The smell of fat meat cooking was undeniably savory, but one of the girls blubbered gustily on a bed of leaves. Harris tended the cookery. Tom Hunter brought wood. Blake stood guard a little beyond the firelight, revolvers ready, staring off into the blackness. Minott pored over a topographical map of Virginia. Lucy Blair tried to comfort the blubbering girl.

"Supper's ready," said Harris. He made even that announcement seem somehow shy and apologetic.

Minott put down his map. Tom Hunter began to cut great chunks of steaming meat from the haunch of venison. He put them on slabs of bark and began to pass them around. Minott reached out his hand and took one of them. He ate with obvious appetite. He seemed to have abandoned his preoccupation the instant he laid down his map. He was displaying the qualities of a capable leader.

"Hunter," he observed, "after you've eaten that stuff, you might relieve Blake. We'll arrange reliefs for the rest of the night. By the way, you men mustn't forget to wind your watches. We'll need to rate them, ultimately."

Hunter gulped down his food and moved out to Blake's hiding place. They exchanged low-toned words. Blake came back to the fire. He took the food Harris handed him and began to eat it. He looked at the blubbering girl on the bed of leaves.

"She's just scared," said Minott. "Barely slit the skin on her arm. But it is upsetting for a senior at Robinson College to be wounded by a flint arrowhead."

Blake nodded.

"I heard some noises off in the darkness," he said curtly. "I'm not sure, but my impression was that I was being stalked. And I thought I heard a human voice."

"We may be watched," admitted Minott. "But we're out of the path of time in which those Indians tried to ambush us. If any of them followed, they're too bewildered to be very dangerous."

"I hope so," said Blake.

His manner was devoid of cordiality, yet there was no exception to be taken to it. From his standpoint, Minott had deliberately gotten the party into a predicament from which there seemed to be no possibility of escape. He had organized it to get it into just that predicament. He was unquestionably the leader of the party, despite his action. Blake made no attempt to undermine his leadership. But Blake himself had some qualifications as a leader, young as he was. Perhaps the most promising of them was the fact that he made no attempt to exercise his talents until he knew as much as Minott of what was to be looked for; what was to be expected. He listened sharply, and then said:

"I think we've digested your lesson of this morning, sir. But—how long is this scrambling of space and time to continue? We left Fredericksburg and rode to the Potomac. It was Chinese territory. We rode back to Fredericksburg, and it wasn't there. Later we hit a highly primitive area with ape-men in it, and then a glacial area, and afterward we encountered Indians who let loose a flight of arrows at us and wounded Bertha Ketterline in the arm. We were nearly out of range at the time, though."

"They were scared," said Minott. "They'd never seen horses before. Our white skins probably upset them, too. And then our guns, and the fact that I killed one, should have chased them off."

"But—what happened to Fredericksburg? We rode away from it. Why couldn't we ride back?"

"The scrambling process has kept up," said Minott dryly. "You remember that queer vertigo? We've had it several times today, and every time, as I see it, there's been an oscillation of the earth we happened to be on. Hm . . . Look!"

He got up and secured the map over which he had been poring. He brought it back and pointed to a heavy penciled line.

"Here's a map of Virginia in our time. The Chinese continent appeared just about three miles north of Fredericksburg. The line of demarcation was, I consider, the line along which the giant sequoias appeared. While in the Chinese time we felt that giddiness and rode back toward Fredericksburg. We came out of the sequoia forest at the same spot as before. I made sure of it. But the continent of our time was no longer there. We rode east and before we reached the border of King George County there was another abrupt change in the vegetation. From a pine country to canelike grass and primitive trees and tapirs and ape-men, which are not exactly characteristic of this part of the world in our time. We saw no signs of any civilization. We turned south, and ran into that heavy fog and the snow beyond it. Evidently, there's a section of a time-path in which Virginia is still subject to a glacial climate."

Blake nodded. He listened again. Then he said:

"You've three sides of an—an island of time marked there."

"Just so," agreed Minott. "Exactly! In the scrambling process, the oscillating process, there seem to be natural 'faults' in the surface of the earth. Relatively large areas seem to shift back and forth as units from one time-path to another. In my own mind, I've likened them to elevators with many stories. We were on the Fredericksburg 'elevator,' or that section of our time-path, when it shifted. We rode off it onto the Chinese continent. While there, the section we started from shifted again, to another time altogether. When we rode back to where it had been—well—the town of Fredericksburg was in another time-path altogether."

Blake said sharply:

"Listen!"

A dull, dull mutter sounded far to the north. It lasted for an instant, and died away. There was a crashing of bushes nearby and a monstrous animal stepped alertly into the firelight. It was an elk, but such an elk! It was a giant, a colossal creature. One of the girls cried out affrightedly, and it turned and crashed away into the underbrush.

"There are no elk in Virginia," said Minott dryly.

Blake said sharply again:

"Listen!"

Again that dull muttering to the north. It grew louder now. It was an airplane motor. It increased in volume from a dull mutter to a growl, from a growl to a roar. Then the plane shot overhead, the navigation lights on its wings glowing brightly. It banked steeply and returned. It circled overhead, with a queer effect of helplessness. And then suddenly it dived down...

"An aviator from our time," said Blake, staring toward the sound. "He saw our fire. He's going to try to make a crash landing in the dark...."

The motor cut off. An instant in which there was only the crackling of the fire and the whistling of wind around gliding surfaces off there in the night. Then a terrific thrashing of branches. A crash...

Then a flare of flame. A roaring noise, and the lurid yellow of gasoline flames spouting skyward.

"Stay here!" snapped Blake. He was on his feet in an instant. "Harris, Minott! Somebody has to stay with the girls! I'll get Hunter and go help!"

He plunged off into the darkness, calling to Hunter. The two of them forced their way through the underbrush. Minott scowled and got out his revolvers. Still scowling, he slipped out of the firelight and took up the guard duty Hunter had abandoned.

A gasoline tank exploded, off there in the darkness. The glare of fire grew intolerably vivid. The sound of the two young men racing through undergrowth became fainter and died away.

A long time passed. A very long time. Then, very far away, the sound of thrashing bushes could be heard again. The gasoline flare dulled and dimmed. Figures came slowly back. They moved as if they were carrying something very heavy. They stopped beyond the glow of light from the campfire. Then Blake and Hunter reappeared, alone.

"He's dead," said Blake curtly. "Luckily, he was flung clear of the crash before the gas tanks caught. He came back to consciousness for a couple of minutes before he—died. Our fire was the only sign of human life he'd seen in hours. We brought him over here. We'll bury him in the morning."

There was silence. Minott's scowl was deep and savage as he came back to the firelight.

"What—what did he say?" asked Maida Haynes.

"He left Washington at five this afternoon," said Blake shortly. "From our time, or something like it. All of Virginia across the Potomac vanished at four-thirty, and virgin forest took its place. He went out to explore. At the end of an hour he came back, and Washington was gone. In its place was a fog bank, with snow underneath. He followed the Potomac down and saw palisaded homesteads with long, oared ships drawn up on shore."

"Vikings—Norsemen!" said Minott in satisfaction.

"He didn't land. He swept down, following the edge of the bay. He looked for Baltimore. Gone. Once, he's sure, he saw a city, but he was taken sick at about that time and when he recovered, it had vanished. He was heading north again and his gasoline was getting low when he saw our fire. He tried for a crash landing. He'd no flares with him. He crashed—and died."

"Poor fellow!" said Lucy shakenly.

"The point is," said young Blake, "that Washington was in

our present time at about four-thirty today. We've got a chance, though a slim one, of getting back! We've got to get to the edge of one of these blocks that go swinging through time, the edge of what Mr. Minott calls a 'time-fault,' and watch it! When the shifts come, we explore as quickly as we can. We've no great likelihood, perhaps, of getting back exactly to our own period, but we can get nearer to it than we are now! Mr. Minott said that somewhere the Confederacy exists. Even that, among people of our own race and speaking our own language, would be better than to be marooned forever among Indians, or among Chinese or Norsemen."

Minott said harshly:

"Blake, we'd better have this out right now! I give the orders in this party! You jumped quickly when the plane crashed, and you gave orders to Harris and to me; I let you get away with it, but we can have but one leader. I am that leader! See you remember it!"

Blake swung about. Minott had a revolver bearing on his body.

"And you are making plans for a return to our time," he went on savagely. "I won't have it! The odds are still that we'll all be killed. But if I do live, I mean to take advantage of it! And my plans do not include a return to an instructorship in mathematics at Robinson College!"

"Well?" said Blake coolly. "What of it, sir?"

"Just this! I'm going to take your revolvers. I'm going to make the plans and give the orders hereafter. We are going to look for the time-path in which a Viking civilization thrives in America. We'll find it, too, because these disturbances will last for weeks yet. And once we find it, we will settle down among those Norsemen and when space and time are stable again I shall begin the formation of my empire! And you will obey orders or you'll be left afoot while the rest of us go on."

Blake said very quietly indeed:

"Perhaps, sir, we'd all prefer to be left to our own destinies rather than be merely the tools by which you attain to yours."

Minott stared at him an instant. His lips tensed.

"It is a pity," he said coldly. "I could have used your brains, Blake. But I can't have mutiny. I shall have to shoot you."

His revolver came up remorselessly.

The British Academy of Sciences was in extraordinary session to determine the cause of various untoward events. Its members were weary, bleary-eyed, but still conscious of their dignity and the importance of their task. A venerable, whiskered physicist spoke with fitting definiteness and solemnity.

"... And so, gentlemen, I see nothing more that remains to be said. The extraordinary events of the past hours seem to follow from certain facts about our own closed space. The gravitational fields of point 10^{79} particles of matter will close space about such an aggregation. No cosmos can be larger. No cosmos can be smaller. And if we envision the creation of such a cosmos we will observe its galaxies vanish at the instant the 10^{79}th particle adds its own mass to those which were present before it. However, the fact that space has closed about such a cosmos does not imply its annihilation. It means merely its separation from its original space, the isolation of itself in space and time because of the curvature of space due to its gravitational field. And if we assume the existence of more than one area of closed space, we assume in some sense the existence of a hyperspace separating the closed spaces; hyperspatial coordinates which mark their relative hyperspatial positions; hyper—"

A gentleman with even longer and whiter whiskers than

the speaker said in a loud and decided voice:

"Fiddlesticks! Stuff and nonsense!"

The speaker paused. He glared.

"Sir! Do you refer—"

"I do!" said the gentleman with the longer and whiter whiskers. "It is stuff and nonsense! Next you'd be saying that in this hyperspace of yours the closed spaces would be subject to hyperlaws, revolve about each other in hyperorbits regulated by hypergravitation, and undoubtedly at times there would be hyperearthtides or hypercollisions, producing decidedly hypercatastrophes!"

"Such, sir," said the whiskered gentleman on the rostrum, quivering with indignation, "such is the fact, sir!"

"Then the fact," rejoined the scientist with the longer and whiter whiskers, "the fact, sir, makes me sick!"

And as if to prove it, he reeled. But he was not alone in reeling. The entire venerable assembly shuddered in abrupt, nauseating vertigo. And then the British Academy of Sciences adjourned without formality and in a panic. It ran away. Because abruptly there was no longer a rostrum nor any end to its assembly hall. Where their speaker had been was open air. In the open air was a fire. About the fire were certain brutish figures incredibly resembling the whiskered scientists who fled from them. They roared at the fleeing, venerable men. Snarling, wielding crude clubs, they plunged into the hall of the British Academy of Sciences. It is known that they caught one person—a biologist of highly eccentric views. It is believed that they ate him.

But it has long been surmised that some, at least, of the extinct species of humanity such as the Piltdown and Neanderthal men were cannibals. If in some pathway of time they happened to exterminate their more intelligent rivals—if somewhere *Pithecanthropus erectus* survives and *Homo sapiens* does not—well, in that pathway of time cannibalism is the custom of society.

With a gasp, Maida Haynes flung herself before Blake. But Harris was even quicker. Apologetic and shy, he had just finished cutting a smoking piece of meat from the venison haunch. He threw it, swiftly, and the searing mass of stuff flung Minott's hand aside at the same instant that it burned it painfully.

Blake was on his feet, his gun out.

"If you pick up that gun, sir," he said rather breathlessly but with unquestionable sincerity, "I'll put a bullet through your arm!"

Minott swore. He retrieved the weapon with his left hand and thrust it in his pocket.

"You young fool!" he snapped. "I'd no intention of shooting you. I did intend to scare you thoroughly! Harris, you're an ass! Maida—I shall discuss your action later! The worst punishment I could give the lot of you would be to leave you to yourselves!"

He stalked out of the firelight and off into the darkness. Something like consternation came upon the group. The glow of fire where the plane had crashed flickered fitfully. The base of the dull-red light seemed to widen a little.

"That's the devil!" said Hunter uneasily. "He does know more about this stuff than we do. If he leaves us, we're messed up!"

"We are," agreed Blake grimly. "And perhaps if he doesn't."

Lucy Blair said:

"I—I'll go and talk to him. He—used to be nice to me in class. And—and his hand must hurt terribly. It's burnt."

She moved away from the fire, a long and angular shadow going on before her. Minott's voice came sharply.

"Go back! There's something moving out here!"

Instantly after, his revolver flashed. A howl arose, and the weapon flashed again and again. Then there were many crashings. Figures fled. Minott came back to the firelight, scornfully.

"Your leadership is at fault, Blake," he commented sardonically. "You forgot about a guard. And you were the man who thought he heard voices! They've run away now, though. Indians, of course."

Lucy Blair said hesitantly:

"Could I—could I do something for your hand? It's burnt..."

"What can you do?" he asked angrily.

"There's some fat," she told him. "Indians used to dress wounds with bear fat. I suppose deer fat would do as well."

He permitted her to dress the burn, though it was far from a serious one. She begged handkerchiefs from the others to complete the job. There was distinct uneasiness all about the campfire. This was no party of adventurers, prepared for anything. It had started out as an outing of undergraduates. Minott scowled as Lucy Blair worked on his hand. Harris looked as apologetic as possible, because he had made the injury. Bertha Ketterline blubbered—less noisily, now, because nobody paid her any attention. Young Blake frowned meditatively at the fire.

The horses moved uneasily. Bertha Ketterline, between her blubberings, sneezed. Lucy felt her eyes smarting. She was the first one to see the spread of the blaze started by the gas tanks of the aeroplane. Her cry of alarm roused the others.

The plane had crashed a good mile from the campfire. The blazing of its tanks had been fierce but brief. The burning of the wings and chassis-fabric had been short, as well. The fire had died down to seeming dull embers. But there were more than embers ablaze out there now.

The fire had died down, to be sure, but only that it might spread among thick and tangled underbrush. It had spread widely on the ground before some climbing vine, blazing, carried flames up to resinous pine branches overhead. A small but steady wind was blowing. And as Lucy looked off to see the source of smoke which stung her eyes, one tall tree was blazing, a long line of angry red flame crept along the ground, and then at two more, three more, a dozen points bright fire roared upward toward the sky.

The horses snorted and reared. Minott snapped:

"Harris! Get the horses! Hunter, see that the girls get mounted, and quickly!"

He pointedly gave Blake no orders. He pored intently over his map as more trees and still more caught fire and blazed upward. He stuffed it in his pocket. Blake calmly rescued the haunch of venison, and when Minott sprang into the saddle among the snorting, scared horses, Blake was already by Maida Haynes' side, ready to go.

"We ride in pairs," said Minott curtly. "A man and a girl. You men, look after them. I've a flashlight. I'll go ahead. We'll hit the Rappahannock River sooner or later, if we don't get around the fire first—and if we can keep ahead of it."

They topped a little hillock and saw more of the extent of their danger. In a half-mile of spreading, the fire had gained three times as much breadth. And to their right, the fire even then roared in among the trees of a forest so thick as to be jungle. The blaze fairly raced through it as if the fire made its own wind, which in fact it did. To their left it crackled fiercely in underbrush which, as they fled, blazed higher.

And then, as if to add mockery to their very real danger, a genuinely brisk breeze sprang up suddenly. Sparks and blazing bits of leaves, fragments of ash and small, unsubstantial coals began to fall among them. Bertha Ketterline yelped suddenly as a tiny live coal touched the flesh of her cheek. Harris's horse squealed and kicked as something singed it. The eight of them galloped madly ahead. Trees rose about them. The white beam of Minott's flashlight seemed almost ludicrous in the fierce red glare from behind, but at least it showed the way.

Something large and dark and clumsy lumbered cumbersomely into the space between Grady's statue and the post office building. The arc lights showed it clearly, and it was not anything which should be wandering in the streets of Atlanta, Georgia, at any hour of the day or night. A taxicab chauffeur saw it, and nearly tore off a wheel in turning around to get away. A policeman saw it, and turned very pale as he grabbed at his beat-telephone to report it. But there had been too many queer things happening this day for him to suspect his own sanity, and the *Journal* had printed too much news from elsewhere for him to disbelieve his own eyes.

The Thing was monstrous, reptilian, loathsome. It was eighty feet long, of which at least fifty was head and tail and the rest flabby-fleshed body. It may have weighed twenty-five or thirty tons, but its head was not much larger than that of a rather large horse. That tiny head swung about stupidly. The Thing was bewildered. It put down a colossal foot—and water gushed up from a broken water main beneath the pavement. The Thing did not notice. It moved vaguely, exhaling a dank and musty odor.

The clang of police emergency cars and the scream of fire-engine sirens filled the air. An ambulance flashed into view—and was struck by a balancing sweep of the mighty tail. The ambulance careened and crashed.

The Thing uttered a plaintive cry, ignoring the damage its tail had caused. The sound was like that of a bleat, a thousand times multiplied. It peered ceaselessly around, seeming to feel trapped by the tall buildings about it, but it was too stupid to retrace its steps for escape.

Somebody screamed in the distance as police cars and fire engines reached the spot where the first Thing swayed and peered and moved in quest of escape. Two other Things, smaller than the first, came lumbering after it. Like it, they had monstrous bodies and disproportionately tiny heads. One of them blundered stupidly into a hook-and-ladder truck. Truck and beast went down, and the beast bleated like the first.

Then some fool began to shoot. Other fools joined in. Steel-jacketed bullets poured into the mountains of reptilian flesh. Police submachine guns raked the monsters. Those guns were held by men of great daring, who could not help noting the utter stupidity of the Things out of the great swamp which had appeared where Inman Park used to be.

The bullets stung. They hurt. The three beasts bleated and tried bewilderedly and very clumsily indeed to escape. The largest tried to climb a five-story building, and brought it down in sheer wreckage.

Before the last of them was dead—or rather, before it ceased to move its great limbs, because the tail moved jerkily for a long time and its heart was still beating spasmodically when loaded on a city dump cart next day—before the last of them was dead they had made sheer chaos of three blocks of business buildings in the heart of Atlanta, and killed seventeen men—and the best testimony is that they made not one attempt to fight. Their whole and only thought was to escape. The destruction they wrought and the deaths they caused were due to their clumsiness and stupidity.

The leading horses floundered horribly. They sank to their fetlocks in something soft and spongy. Bertha Ketterline squawked in terror as her mount's motion changed. Blake said crisply in the blackness:

"It feels like plowed ground. Better use the light again, Mr. Minott!"

The sky behind them glowed redly. The forest fire still trailed them. For miles of front, now, it shot up sparks and flame and a harsh red glare which illumined the clouds of its own smoke.

The flashlight stabbed at the earth. The ground was plowed. It was softened by the hands of men. Minott kept the light on as little gasps of thankfulness arose. Then he said sardonically:

"Do you know what this crop is? It's lentils. Are lentils grown in Virginia? Perhaps! We'll see what sort of men these may happen to be!"

He swung to follow the line of the furrows. Tom Hunter said miserably:

"If that's plowed ground, it's a dam' shallow furrow. A one-horse plow'd throw up more dirt than that!"

A light glowed palely in the distance. Every person in the party saw it at the same instant. As if by instinct, the head of every horse swerved for it.

"We'll want to be careful," said Blake quietly. "These may be Chinese, too."

The light was all of a mile distant. They moved over the plowed ground cautiously. . . .

Suddenly the hoofs of Lucy Blair's horse rang on stone. The noise was startingly loud. Other horses, following hers, clattered thunderously. Minott flashed down the light again. Dressed stone. Cut stone. A roadway built of dressed stone blocks, some six- or eight-feet wide. Then one of the horses shivered and snorted. It pranced agitatedly, edging away from something on the road. Minott swept the flashlight beam along the narrow way.

"The only race," he said dryly, "that ever built roads like these was the Romans. They made their military roads like this. But they didn't discover America that we know of."

The beam touched something dark. It came back and steadied. One of the girls uttered a stiffled exclamation. The beam showed dead men. One was a man with shield and sword and a helmet such as the soldiers of ancient Rome are pictured as having worn. He was dead. Half his head had been blown off. Lying atop him was a man in a curious gray uniform. He had died of a sword wound.

The beam searched around. More bodies. Many Roman-accoutred figures. Four or five men in what looked remarkably like the uniform that might be worn by soldiers of the Confederate Army—if a Confederate Army could be supposed to exist.

"There's been fighting," said Blake, composedly. "I guess somebody from the Confederacy—that time-path, say— started to explore what must have seemed a damned strange happening. And these Romans—if they're Romans—jumped them."

Something came shambling through the darkness. Minott threw the flash-beam upon it. It was human, yes. But it was three parts naked, and it was chained, and it had been beaten horribly, and there were great sores upon its body from other beatings. It was bony and emaciated. The insensate ferocity of sheer despair marked it. It was brutalized by its sufferings until it was just human, barely human, and nothing more.

It squinted at the light, too dull of comprehension to be afraid.

Then Minott spoke, and at his words it automatically groveled in the dirt. Minott spoke harshly, in half-forgotten Latin, and the groveling figure mumbled words which had been barbarous Latin to begin with, and through its bruised lips were still further mutilated.

"It's a slave," said Minott coldly. "Strange men—Confederates, I suppose—came from the north today. They fought and killed some of the guards at this estate. This slave denies it, but I imagine he was heading north in hopes of escaping to them. When you think of it, I suppose we're not the only explorers to be caught out of our own time-path by some shift or another."

He growled at the slave and rode on, still headed for the distant light.

"What—what are you going to do?" asked Maida faintly.

"Go on to the villa yonder and ask questions," said Minott dryly. "If Confederates hold it, we'll be well received. If they don't, we'll still manage to earn a welcome. I intend to camp along a time-fault and cross over whenever a time-shift brings a Norse settlement in sight. Consequently, I want exact news of places where they've been seen, if such news is to be had."

Maida Haynes pressed close to Blake. He put a reassuring hand on her arm as the horses trudged on over the soft ground. The firelight behind them grew brighter. Occasional resinous, coniferous trees flared upward and threw fugitive red glows upon the riding figures. But gradually the glare grew steadier and stronger. The white walls of a rambling stucco house became visible. Outbuildings. Barns. A monstrous structure which looked startlingly like a barracks.

It was a farm, an estate, a Roman villa transplanted to the very edge of a wilderness. It was—Blake remembered vaguely—like a picture he had once seen of a Roman villa in England, restored to look as it had looked before Rome withdrew her legions from Britain and left the island to savagery and darkness. There were small mounds of curing hay about them, through which the horses picked their way. Blake suddenly wrinkled his nostrils suspiciously. He sniffed. . . .

Maida pressed close to him. Her lips formed words. Lucy Blair rode close to Minott, glancing up at him from time to time. Harris rode apologetically beside Bertha Ketterline, and Bertha sat her horse as if she were saddle sore. Tom Hunter clung close to Minott as if for protection, leaving Janet Thompson to look out for herself.

"J-Jerry," said Maida. "What—what do you think?"

"I don't like it," admitted Blake in a low tone. "But we've got to tag along. I think I smell—"

Then a sudden swarm of figures leaped at the horses. Wild figures, naked figures, sweaty and reeking and almost maniacal figures, some of whom clanked chains as they leaped. A voice bellowed orders at them from a distance, and a whip cracked ominously.

Before the struggle ended, there were just two shots fired. Minott fired them both and wheeled about. . . . Then a horse streaked away, and Bertha Ketterline was bawling plaintively, and Tom Hunter babbled hysterically, and Harris swore with a complete lack of his customary air of apology.

Blake seemed to be buried under a mass of foul bodies like the rest, but he rasped at his captors in an authoritative tone. They fell away from him, cringing as if by instinct. And then torches appeared suddenly and slaves appeared in their light, slaves of every possible degree of filth and degradation, of every possible racial mixture, but unanimous in a desperate abjectness before their master amid the torchbearers.

He was a short, fat man in an only slightly modified toga. He drew it close about his body as the torchbearers held their flares close to the captives. The torchlight showed the captives, to be sure, but also it showed the puffy, self-indulgent and invincibly cruel features of the man who owned these slaves and the villa. By his pose and the orders he gave in a curiously corrupt Latin, he showed that he considered he owned the captives too.

The deputy from Aisne-le-Sur decided that it had been very wise indeed for him to walk in the fresh air. Paris at night is stimulating. That curious attack of vertigo had come of too much champagne. The fresh air had dispelled the fumes. But it was odd that he did not know exactly where he was, though he knew his Paris well. These streets were strange. The houses were unlike any that he remembered ever having seen before.

In the light of the street lamps—and they were unusual, too!—there was a certain unfamiliar quality about their architecture. He puzzled over it, trying to identify the peculiar *flair* these houses showed.

He became impatient. After all, it was necessary for him to return home some time, even though his wife... The deputy from Aisne-le-Sur shrugged. Then he saw bright lights ahead. He hastened his steps. A magnificent mansion, brilliantly illuminated.

The clattering of many hoofs. A cavalry escort, forming up before the house. A pale young man emerged, escorted by a tall, fat man who kissed his hand as if in an ecstasy of admiration. Dismounted cavalrymen formed a lane from the gateway to the car. Two young officers followed the pale young man. They were ablaze with decorations. The deputy from Aisne-le-Sur noted subconsciously that he did not recognize their uniforms. The car door was open and waiting. There was some oddity about the car, but the deputy could not see clearly just what it was.

There was much clicking of heels. Steel blades at salute. The pale young man patiently allowed the fat man to kiss his hand again. He entered the car. The two bemedaled young officers climbed in after him. The car rolled away. Instantly, the cavalry escort clattered with it, before it, behind it, all around it....

The fat man stood on the sidewalk, beaming and rubbing his hands together. The dismounted cavalrymen swung to their saddles and trotted briskly after the others.

The deputy from Aisne-le-Sur stared blankly. He saw another pedestrian, halted like himself to regard the spectacle. He was disturbed by the fact that this pedestrian was clothed in a fashion as perturbingly unfamiliar as these houses, and the spectacle he had witnessed.

"Pardon, *m'sieur*," said the deputy from Aisne-le-Sur. "I do not recognize my surroundings. Would you tell me—"

"The house," said the other, caustically, "is the hotel of M. le Duc de Montigny. It is possible that one does not know of M. le Duc? Or more especially of Madame la Duchesse, and what she is and where she lives?"

The deputy from Aisne-le-Sur blinked.

"Montigny?—Montigny? No," he confessed. "And the young man of the car, whose hand was kissed by—"

"Kissed by M. le Duc?" The stranger stared frankly. "*Mon dieu!* Where have you come from that you do not recognize Louis the Twentieth? He has but departed from a visit to Madame his mistress."

"Louis—Louis the Twentieth!" stammered the deputy from Aisne-le-Sur. "I—I do not understand!"

"Fool!" said the stranger impatiently, "that was the King of France, who succeeded his father as a child of ten and has been free of the regency for but six months—and already ruins France!"

The long-distance operator plugged in with a shaking hand, "*Number please ... I am sorry, sir, but we are unable to connect you with Camden.... The lines are down.... I am sorry, sir, but we are unable to connect you with Jenkinstown. The lines are down.... Very sorry, sir.*"

Another call buzzed and lighted up.

"*Hello ... I am sorry, sir. We are unable to connect you with Dover. The lines are down....*" Her hands worked automatically. "*Hello ... I am sorry, but we are unable to connect you*

*with New York. The lines are down....No, sir. We cannot
route it by Atlantic City. The lines are down....Yes, sir, I
know the telegraph companies cannot guarantee delivery....
No, sir, we cannot reach Pittsburgh, either, to get a message
through....*" Her voice quivered. "*No, sir, the lines are down
to Scranton....And Harrisburg too. Yes, sir....I am sorry,
but we cannot get a message of any sort out of Philadelphia
in any direction....We have tried to arrange communication
by radio, but no calls are answered....*"

She covered her face with her hands for an instant. Then
she plugged in and made a call herself.

"*Minnie! Haven't they heard anything? ...Not anything?
...What? They phoned for more police? ...The—the operator out there says there's fighting? ...She hears a lot of
shooting? ...What is it, Minnie? Don't they even know? ...
They—they're using the armored cars from the banks to fight
with, too? ...But what are they fighting? What? ...My folks
are out there, Minnie! My folks are out there!*"

The doorway of the slave barracks closed and great bars
slammed against its outer side. Reeking, foul, unbreathable
air closed about them like a wave. Then a babbling of voices
all about. The clanking of chains. The rustling of straw, as if
animals moved. Someone screeched; howled above the others. He began to gain the ascendancy. There was almost some
attention paid to him, though a minor babbling continued all
about.

Maida said in a strained voice:

"I—I can catch a word here and there. He's—telling these
other slaves how we were captured. It's—Latin—of sorts."

Bertha Ketterline squalled suddenly, in the absolute dark.

"Somebody touched me!" she bawled. "A man!"

A voice spoke humorously, somewhere near. There was laughter. It was the howled laughter of animals. Slaves were animals, according to the Roman notion. A rustling noise, as in the noisome freedom of their barracks the utterly brutalized slaves drew nearer to the newcomers. There could be sport with new-captured folk, not yet degraded to their final status.

Lucy Blair cried out in a stifled fashion. There was a sharp, incisive "*crack.*" Somebody fell. More laughter.

"I knocked him out!" snapped Blake. "Harris! Hunter! Feel around for something we can use as clubs! These slaves intend to haze us, and in their own den there's no attempt to control them! Even if they kill us they'll only be whipped for it. And the girls—"

Something, snarling, leaped for him in the darkness. The authoritative tone of Blake's voice was hateful. A yapping sound arose. Other figures closed in. Reduced to the status of animals, the slaves of the Romans behaved as beasts when locked in their monster kennel. The newcomers were hateful if only because they had been freemen, not slaves. The women were clean and they were frightened—and they were prey. Chains clanked ominously. Foul breaths tainted the air. The reek of utter depravity, of human beings brought lower than beasts— who at least do not foul their own dens—filled the air. It was utterly dark.

Bertha Ketterline began to blubber noisily. There was the sudden savage sound of a blow meeting flesh. Then pandemonium, and battle, and the sudden terrified screams of Lucy Blair. . . . The panting of men who fought. The sound of blows. A man howled. Another shrieked curses. A woman screamed shrilly. . . .

"Bang! Bang! Bang-bang!" Shots outside, a veritable fusillade of them. Running feet. Shouts. The bars at the doorway fell. The great doors opened, and men stood in the opening with whips and torches, bellowing for the slaves to come out and attack something yet unknown. They were being called from their kennel like dogs. Four of the whip men came inside, flogging the slaves out, while the sound of shots continued. The slaves shrank away, or bounded howling for the open air. But there were three of them who would never shrink or cringe again.

Blake and Harris stood embattled in a corner of the slave shed. Blake held a heavy beam in a desperate readiness for further battle. Harris, likewise, held a clumsy club. With torchlight upon him, his air of savage defiance turned to one of quaint apology for the dead slave at his feet. And Hunter and two of the girls competed in stark panic for a position behind him. Lucy Blair, dead-white, stood backed against a wall, a jagged fragment of gnawed bone held daggerwise.

The whips lashed out at them. Voices snarled at them. The whips again . . . Blake struck out furiously, a huge welt across his face. . . .

And revolvers cracked at the great door. Minott stood there, a revolver in each hand, his eyes blazing. A torch-bearer dropped, and the torches flared smokily in the foul mud of the flooring.

"All right," said Minott fiercely. "Come on out!"

Hunter was the first to reach him, babbling and gasping. There was sheer uproar all about. A huge grain shed roared upward in flames. Figures rushed crazily all about it. From the flames came another explosion, then two, then three more.

"Horses over here by the stables," said Minott, his face dead-white and very deadly indeed. "They haven't unsaddled

them. The stable slaves haven't figured out the cinches yet.
I put some revolver bullets in the straw when I set fire to
that grain shed. They're going off from time to time."

A figure with whip and dagger raced around an outbuilding
and confronted them. Minott shot him down. Blake said
hoarsely:

"Give me a revolver, Minott! I want to—"

"Horses first!" snapped Minott.

They raced into a courtyard. Two shots. The slaves fled,
howling. Out of the courtyard, bent low in the saddle. They
swept close to the villa itself. On a little raised terrace before
it raged a stout man in an only-slightly-modified toga. A slave
groveled before him. He kicked the abject figure and strode
out, shouting commands in a voice that cracked with fury.
The horses loomed up and he shook his fists at the riders,
purple with wrath, incapable of fear because of his beastly
rage.

Minott shot him dead, swung off his horse, and stripped
the toga from him. He flung it to Lucy.

"Take this!" he said savagely. "By God, I could kill..."

There was now no question of his leadership. He led the
retreat from the villa. The eight horses headed north again,
straight for the luridly flaming forest.

They stopped once more. Behind them, another building
at the estate had caught from the first. Sheer confusion ruled.
The slaughter of the master disrupted all organization. The
roof of the slave barracks caught. Screams and howls of pure
panic reached even the fugitives. Then there were racing,
maddened figures rushing here and there in the glare of the
fires.... Suddenly there was fighting. A howling ululation
arose....

Minott worked savagely, stripping clothing from the bodies slain in that incredible, unrecorded conflict of Confederate soldiers and Roman troops, in some unguessable pathway of space and time. Blake watched behind, but Minott curtly commanded the salvaging of rifles and ammunition from the dead Confederates—if they were Confederates.

And as Hunter, still gasping hysterically, took the load of yet unfamiliar weapons upon his horse, the eight felt a certain incredible, intolerable vertigo and nausea. The burning forest ahead vanished from their sight. Instead, there was darkness. A noisome smell came down wind; dampness and strange, overpowering perfumes of monstrous colored flowers. . . . Something huge and deadly bellowed, in the space before them which smelled like a monstrous swamp.

The liner *City of Baltimore* plowed through the open sea in the first pale light of dawn. The skipper, up on the bridge, wore a worried frown. The radio operator came up. He carried a sheaf of radiogram forms. His eyes were blurry with loss of sleep.

"Maybe it was me, sir," he reported heavily. "I felt awful funny for a while last night, an' then all night long I couldn't raise a station. I checked everything an' couldn't find anything wrong. But just now I felt awful sick an' funny for a minute, an' when I come out of it the air was full o' code. Here's some of it. I don't understand how I coulda been sick so I couldn't hear code, sir, but—"

The skipper said abruptly:

"I had that sick feeling too. Dizzy. So did the man at the wheel. So did everybody. Give me the messages."

His eyes ran swiftly over the yellow forms.

"...News flash. Half of London disappeared at 2:00 A.M. this morning..." "...S.S. Manzanillo reporting. Sea serpent which attacked this ship during the night and seized four sailors returned and was rammed five minutes ago. It seems to be dying. Our bow badly smashed. Two forward compartments flooded...." "...Warning to all mariners. Pack ice seen floating fifty miles off New York harbor...." "...news flash. Madrid, Spain, has undergone inexplicable change. All buildings formerly known now unrecognizable from the air. Airfields have vanished. Mosques seem to have taken the place of churches and cathedrals. A flag bearing the crescent floats...." "...European population of Calcutta seems to have been massacred. S.S. Carib reports harbor empty, all signs of European domination vanished, and hostile mobs lining shore...."

The skipper of the *City of Baltimore* passed his hand over his forehead. He looked uneasily at the radio operator.

"Sparks," he said gently, "you'd better go see the ship's doctor. Here! I'll detail a man to go with you."

"I know," said Sparks bitterly. "I guess I'm nuts, all right! But that's what came through!"

He marched away with his head hanging, escorted by a sailor. A little speck of smoke appeared dead ahead. It became swiftly larger. With the combined speed of the two vessels, in a quarter of an hour the other ship was visible. In half an hour it could be made out clearly. It was long, and low, and painted black, but the first incredible thing was that it was a paddle steamer, with two sets of paddles instead of one, and the after set revolving more swiftly than the forward.

The skipper of the *City of Baltimore* looked more closely through his glasses, and nearly dropped them in stark amazement. The flag flying on the other ship was black and white only. A beam wind blew it out swiftly. A white death's-head, with two crossed bones below it. The traditional flag of piracy!

Signal flags fluttered up in the rigging of the other ship. The skipper of the *City of Baltimore* gazed at them, stunned.

"Gibberish!" he muttered. "It don't make sense! They aren't International Code. Not the same flags at all!"

Then a gun spoke. A monstrous puff of black-powder smoke billowed over the other ship's bow. A heavy shot crashed into the forepart of the *City of Baltimore*. An instant later it exploded.

"I'm crazy too!" said the skipper dazedly.

A second shot. A third and fourth. The black steamer sheered off and started to pound the *City of Baltimore* in a businesslike fashion. Half the bridge went overside. The forward cargo hatch blew up with a cloud of smoke from an explosion underneath.

Then the skipper came to. He roared orders. The big ship heeled as it came around. It plunged forward at vastly more than its normal cruising speed. The guns on the other ship doubled and redoubled their rate of fire. Then the black ship tried to dodge. But it had not time.

The *City of Baltimore* rammed it. At the very last minute the skipper felt certain of his own insanity. But it was too late to save the other ship then. The *City of Baltimore* cut it in two.

The pale gray light of dawn filtered down through an incredible thickness of foliage. It was a subdued, a tiny feeble twilight when it reached the earth where a tiny campfire burned. That fire gave off thick smoke from water-soaked wood. Hunter tended it, clad in ill-assorted remnants of a gray uniform. Harris worked patiently at a rifle, trying to understand exactly how it worked. It was unlike any rifle with which he was familiar. The bolt-action was not really a bolt-action at all, and he'd noticed that there was no rifling in the barrel. He was trying to understand how the long bullet was made to revolve. Harris, too, had substituted Confederate gray for the loincloth flung him for sole covering when with the others he was thrust into the slave pen of the Roman villa. Minott sat with his head in his hands, staring at the opposite side of the stream. On his face was all bitterness.

Lucy Blair darted furtive, somehow wistful glances at him. Presently she moved to sit beside him. She asked him an anxious question. The other three girls sat by the fire. Bertha Ketterline was slouched back against a tree-fern trunk. Her head had fallen back. She snored. With the exception of Blake, all of them were barefoot. Those who had been enslaved had, of course, been plundered of all their possessions.

Blake came back to the fire. He nodded across the little stream.

"We seem to have come to the edge of a time-fault, sir," he observed hopefully. "This side of the stream is definitely carboniferous-period vegetation. The other side isn't as primitive, but it isn't of our time, anyhow. Mr. Minott!"

Minott lifted his head.

"Well?" he demanded.

"We've been here for hours, sir," said Blake. "And there's been no further change in time-paths that we've noticed. Is it likely that the scrambling of time and space is ended, sir? If it has, and the time-paths stay jumbled, we'll never find our world intact, of course, but as you said, we can hunt for colonies or even cities of our own kind of people."

Minott shrugged.

"I expect," he said deliberately, "that the oscillations of time-paths will keep up for at least two weeks—if we aren't all annihilated."

Lucy Blair said something in a low tone. She regarded him worshipfully.

"No," he snapped. "I find that I am a fool—or I was!—I thought that young men, at least, even of Robinson College, would want things they did not have! But they're already frozen into the pattern of law-abiding citizens. They'd be useless. That business at the villa was proof enough! Attacked, what did they do? They used their fists! Beautiful, civilized, tame-animal thinking! They'd be no good to me! I was the only one who fired a pistol! They didn't have time to think—so they fought like little boys!"

Lucy murmured again. Minott glowered.

"I am a faculty member of Robinson College," he said in exquisite sarcasm. "You students are in my care. I'd make kings of the men—I'd make them lords of men and nations! —but they want to go back and be insurance salesmen. So back they go!"

"Really, sir," said Blake defensively.

"Hush!" said Lucy. "He's going to explain to you so you can tell everybody what's happened. Listen!"

Blake had already unconsciously reassumed some of his former respectful manner. His capture and scornful dismissal to the status of slave had shaken all his self-confidence. Before, he had felt himself not only a member of a superior race, but as a college student a superior member of that race. In being enslaved he had been both degraded and scorned. His vanity was still gnawed at by that memory, and his self-confidence shattered by the fact that he had been able to kill two utterly brutalized slaves in the slave barracks, without in the least contributing to his own freedom. Now he winced at the scorn in Minott's voice.

"We—we know that gravity warps space," said Minott harshly. "From observation we have been able to discover the amount of warping produced by a given mass. We can calculate the mass necessary to warp space so that it will close in completely, making a closed universe which is unreachable and undetectable in any of the dimensions we know. We know, for example, that if two gigantic star masses of a certain combined mass were to rush together, at the instant of their collision there would not be a great cataclysm. They would simply vanish. But they would not cease to exist. They would merely cease to exist in our space and time. They would have created a space and time of their own."

Harris said apologetically:

"Like crawling in a hole and pulling the hole in after you. I read something like that in a Sunday supplement, once, sir."

Minott nodded. He went on scornfully:

"Now, imagine that two such universes have been formed. They are both invisible from the space and time in which they originated. Each exists in its own space and time, just as our universe does. But each must also exist in a certain—well— hyperspace, because if closed spaces are separated, there must be some sort of something in between them, else they would be together."

"Really," said Blake, "you're talking about something we can infer, but ordinarily can't possibly learn anything about by observation."

"I did!" said Minott. "From published observations! If our space is closed, we must assume that there are other closed spaces. And don't forget that other closed spaces would be as real—are as real—as our closed space is."

"But what does it mean?" asked Blake.

"If there are other closed spaces like ours, and they exist in a common medium—the hyperspace from which they and we alike are sealed off—they might be likened to—say—stars and planets in our space, which are separated by space and yet affect each other through space. Since these various closed spaces are separated by a logically necessary hyperspace, it is at least probable that they should affect each other through that hyperspace."

Blake said slowly:

"Then these shiftings of time-paths—well—they're the result of something on the order of tidal strains? If another star got close to the sun, our planets would crack up from tidal strains alone. You're suggesting that another closed space has gotten close to our closed space in hyperspace. . . . It's awfully confused, sir."

"I have calculated it," said Minott harshly. "The odds are three to one that space and time and universe, every star and every galaxy in the skies, will be obliterated in one monstrous destruction when even the past will never have been! But there is one chance in four, and I planned to take full advantage of it. I planned—I planned—"

Then he stood up suddenly. His figure straightened. He struck his hands together savagely.

"By God, it can still be done if you're more than worms! We have arms! We have books, technical knowledge, formulas—the cream of the technical knowledge of earth packed in our saddlebags! Listen to me! We cross this stream now! When the next change comes, we strike across whatever time-path takes the place of this. We make for the Potomac, where that aviator saw Norse ships drawn up! I have Anglo-Saxon and early Norse vocabularies in the saddlebags! We'll make friends with them! We'll teach them! We'll lead them! We'll make ourselves masters of the world—"

Harris said apologetically:

"I'm sorry, sir, but I promised Bertha I'd take her home, if it was humanly possible. I have to do it. I can't join you in becoming an emperor, even if the breaks are right."

Minott scowled at him.

"Hunter?"

"I—I'll do as the others do," said Hunter uneasily. "I—I'd rather go home...."

"Fool!" snarled Minott.

Lucy Blair said loyally:

"I—I'd like to be an empress, Mr. Minott."

Maida Haynes stared at her. She opened her mouth to speak. Blake absently pulled a revolver from his pocket and looked at it meditatively as Minott clenched and unclenched his hands. The veins stood out on his forehead. He began to breathe heavily.

"Fools!" he roared. "Fools! You'll never be more than shoe clerks or professors! Yet you throw away—"

Swift, sharp, agonizing vertigo smote them all. The revolver fell from Blake's hands. He looked up. Familiar pine and fields. More—houses. Familiar ones. A dead silence fell. They hardly dared to breathe. Then Blake said shakily:

"That—" He swallowed. "That is King George Court House, in King George County, in Virginia, in our time I think— Hell! Let's get across that stream!"

He feverishly seized Maida. He carried her toward the stream in his arms. Minott said desperately:

"Wait!"

He looked at them in a sort of bitter hope.

"I offer you, for the last time—I offer riches, power—lordships—everything that any man could long for—"

Blake waded across and put Maida safely down upon the shore. Hunter was splashing frantically through the shallow water. Harris was shaking Bertha Ketterline to wake her. Blake splashed back. He rounded up the horses, in trembling haste. He loaded the salvaged weapons over a saddle. He shepherded the three remaining girls across. Hunter was out of sight. He had fled toward the painted buildings of the village. Blake drove the horses across. Minott watched. His eyes blazed with scorn.

"Better come along," said Blake, generously.

"And be an instructor in mathematics?" Minott laughed. "No! I stay here!"

Blake considered. Minott was a strange, an unprepossessing figure. Standing against the background of a carboniferous jungle, he was even pitiable—to Blake. But he was utterly contemptuous of the younger men.

"Wait sir," said Blake in conscious nobility.

He stripped the saddlebags from six of the horses. He heaped them on the remaining two. he led them back across the stream. Minott regarded him with implacable scorn.

"You'll graduate," he said, biting off each word separately. "You'll get a job. You'll spend your life paying bills, when you could have sailed a longship! You'll be a pedestrian—when you could have been a king. But I won't! I may die, but if I don't—"

Blake shrugged. He went back across the stream and re-

mounted. Lucy Blair looked doubtfully at the lonely figure of
Minott, whom probably nobody else in all the world had ever
admired.

A faint, almost imperceptible dizziness affected all of them.
It passed. By instinct they looked back at the tall jungle. It
stood unchanged. Minott laughed at them. Bitterly.

"I—I've got something to say to him!" panted Lucy Blair
suddenly. "D-don't wait for me!"

She rode for the stream. Again that faint, nearly imperceptible dizziness. Lucy slapped her horse's flank frantically. Maida
cried:

"Come back, Lucy! It's going to shift—"

"That's what I want," cried Lucy joyfully, over her shoulder.
"I mean to stay—"

She was half way across the stream. More than half way.
Then the vertigo struck all of them.

Everyone knows the rest of the story. For two weeks longer
there were still occasional shiftings of the time-paths. But
gradually, it became noticeable that the number of "time-
faults"—in Minott's phrase—were decreasing in number. At
the most drastic period, it has been estimated that no less
than twenty-five percent of the whole earth's surface was at
a given moment at some other time-path than its own. We do
not know of any portion of the earth which did not vary from
its own time-path at some period of the disturbance.

That means, of course, that practically one hundred percent
of the earth's population encountered the conditions caused
by the earth's extraordinary oscillations sidewise in time. Our
scientists are no longer quite as dogmatic as they used to be.
The dialectics of philosophy have received a serious jolt. Basic

ideas in botany, zoology, and even philology have been altered by the new facts made available by our unintended travels.

Because of course it was the fourth chance which happened, and the earth survived. In our time-path, at any rate. The six survivors of Minott's exploring party reached King George Court House barely a quarter of an hour after the time-shift which carried Minott and Lucy Blair out of our space and time forever. Blake and Harris searched for a means of transmitting the information they possessed to the world at large. Through a lonely radio amateur a mile from the village, they sent out Minott's theory on short waves. Shorn of Minott's pessimistic analysis of the probabilities of survival, it went swiftly to every part of the world then in its proper relative position. It was valuable, in that it checked explorations in force which in some places had been planned. It prevented, for example, a punitive military expedition from going beyond a time-fault in Georgia, past which a scalping party of Indians from an uncivilized America had retreated. It prevented the dispatch of a squadron of destroyers to find and seize Leifsholm, from which a Viking foray had been made upon North Centerville, Massachusetts. A squadron of mapping planes was recalled from reconnaissance work above a carboniferous swamp in West Virginia, just before the time-shift which would have isolated them forever.

Some things, though, no knowledge could prevent. It has been estimated that no less than five thousand daring persons in the United States are missing from their own space and time through having adventured into the strange landscapes which appeared so suddenly. Many must have perished. Some, we feel sure, have come in contact with one or another of the distinct civilizations we now know to exist. Conversely, we have gained inhabitants from other time-paths. Two cohorts of the Twenty-Second Roman Legion were left upon our soil near Ithaca, New York. Four families of Chinese peasants essayed to pick berries in what they considered a miraculous strawberry patch in Virginia, and remained there when that section of ground returned to its proper *milieu*. A Russian village remains in Colorado. A French trading settlement in the—in their time undeveloped—Middle West. A part of the northern herd of buffalo has returned to us, two hundred thousand strong, together with a village of Cheyenne Indians who had never seen either horses or firearms. The passenger pigeon, to the number of a billion and a half birds, has returned to North America.

But our losses are heavy. Besides those daring individuals who were carried away upon the strange territories they were exploring, there are the overwhelming disasters affecting Detroit, and Tokyo, and Rio de Janeiro. The last two we understand. When the causes of oscillation sidewise in time were removed, most of the earth sections returned to their proper positions in their own time-paths. But not all. There is a section of Post-Cambrian jungle left in eastern Tennessee. The Russian village in Colorado has been mentioned, and the French trading post in the Middle West. In some cases sections of the oscillating time-paths remained in new positions, remote from their points of origin.

That is the cause of the utter disappearance of Rio and Tokyo. Where Rio stood an untouched jungle remains. It is of our own geological period, but it is simply from a path in time in which Rio de Janeiro never happened to be built. On the site of Tokyo stands a forest of extraordinarily primitive type, about which botanists and paleontologists still debate. Somewhere, in some space and time, Tokyo and Rio yet exist and their people still live on. But Detroit....

We still do not understand what happened to Detroit. It was upon an oscillating segment of earth. It vanished from our time, and it returned to our time. But its inhabitants did not come back with it. The city was empty; deserted as if the hundreds of thousands of human beings who lived in it had simply evaporated into the air. There have been some few signs of struggle seen, but they may have been the result of panic. The city of Detroit returned to its own space and time untouched, unharmed, unlooted, and undisturbed. But no living thing, not even a domestic animal or a caged bird, was in it when it came back. We do not understand that at all.

Perhaps if Minott had returned to us, he could have guessed at the answer to the riddle. What fragmentary papers of his that have been shown to refer to the time-upheaval have been of inestimable value. Our whole theory of what happened depends upon the papers Minott left behind as too unimportant to bother with—plus, of course, Blake's and Harris's account of his explanations to them. Tom Hunter can remember little that is useful. Maida Haynes has given some worthwhile data, but it covers ground we have other observers for. Bertha Ketterline also reports very little.

The answers to a myriad problems yet elude us, but in the saddlebags given to Minott by Blake as preparation for his desperate journey through space and time, the solutions to many must remain. Our scientists labor diligently to understand and to elaborate the figures Minott thought of trivial significance. And throughout the world many, many minds turn longingly to certain saddlebags, loaded on a led horse, following Minott and Lucy Blair through unguessable landscapes, to unimaginable adventures, with revolvers and textbooks as their armament for the conquest of a world.

CONSIDER HER WAYS
by
John Wyndham

The late John Wyndham is perhaps most familiar to casual readers of science fiction as the author of two good novels that became films—The Day of the Triffids and Village of the Damned (from his book The Midwich Cuckoos). He excelled at the kind of rich, descriptive prose associated with the British school of "disaster writers," but he also had considerable skill with social commentary, as evidenced by this excellent story of a woman thrust into a future society that is entirely female.

There was nothing but myself.

I hung in a timeless, spaceless, forceless void that was neither light nor dark. I had entity, but no form; awareness, but no senses; mind, but no memory. I wondered, is this—this nothingness—my soul? And it seemed that I had wondered that always, and should go on wondering it forever. . . .

But, somehow, timelessness ceased. I became aware that there *was* a force: that I was being moved, and that spacelessness had, therefore, ceased, too. There was nothing to show that I moved; I knew simply that I was being drawn. I felt happy because I knew there was something or someone to whom I wanted to be drawn. I had no other wish than to turn like a compass needle and then fall through the void.

But I was disappointed. No smooth, swift fall followed.

Instead, other forces fastened on me. I was pulled this way, and then that. I did not know how I knew it; there was no outside reference, no fixed point, no direction even; yet I could feel that I was tugged hither and thither, as though against the resistance of some inner gyroscope. It was as if one force were in command of me for a time, only to weaken and lose me to a new force. Then I would seem to slide towards some unknown point, until I was arrested, and diverted upon another course. I wafted this way and that, with the sense of awareness continually growing firmer; and I wondered whether rival forces were fighting for me, good and evil, perhaps, or life and death.

The sense of pulling back and forth became more definite until I was almost jerked from one course to another. Then, abruptly, the feeling of struggle finished. I had a sense of travelling faster and faster still, plunging like a wandering meteorite that had been trapped at last.

"All right," said a voice. "Resuscitation was a little retarded, for some reason. Better make a note of that on her card. What's the number? Oh, only her fourth time. Yes, certainly make a note. It's all right. Here she comes!"

It was a woman's voice speaking, with a slightly unfamiliar accent. The surface I was lying on shook under me. I opened my eyes, saw the ceiling moving along above me, and let them close. Presently, another voice, again with an unfamiliar intonation, spoke to me:

"Drink this," she said.

A hand lifted my head, and a cup was pressed against my lips. After I had drunk the stuff I lay back with my eyes closed again. I dozed for a little while, and came out of it feeling stronger. For some minutes I lay looking up at the ceiling and wondering vaguely where I was. I could not recall any ceiling that was painted just this pinkish shade of cream. Then, suddenly, while I was still gazing up at the ceiling, I was shocked, just as if something had hit my mind a sharp blow. I was frighteningly aware that it was not just the pinkish ceiling that was *unfamiliar*—everything was unfamiliar. Where there should have been memories there was just a great gap. I had no idea who I was, or where I was; I could recall nothing of how or why I came to be here. . . . In a rush of panic I tried to sit up, but a hand pressed me back, and presently held the cup to my lips again.

"You're quite all right. Just relax," the same voice told me, reassuringly.

I wanted to ask questions, but somehow I felt immensely weary, and everything was too much trouble. The first rush of panic subsided, leaving me lethargic. I wondered what had happened to me—had I been in an accident, perhaps? Was this the kind of thing that happened when one was badly shocked? I did not know, and now for the moment I did not care: I was being looked after. I felt so drowsy that the questions could wait.

I suppose I dozed, and it may have been for a few minutes, or for an hour. I know only that when I opened my eyes again I felt calmer—more puzzled than alarmed—and I lay for a time without moving. I had recovered enough grasp now to console myself with the thought that if there had been an accident, at least there was no pain.

Presently I gained a little more energy, and, with it, curiosity to know where I was. I rolled my head on the pillow to see more of the surroundings.

A few feet away I saw a contrivance on wheels, something between a bed and a trolley. On it, asleep with her mouth open, was the most enormous woman I had ever seen. I stared, wondering whether it was some kind of cage over her to take the weight of the covers that gave her the mountainous look, but the movement of her breathing soon showed me that it was not. Then I looked beyond her and saw two more trolleys, both supporting equally enormous women.

I studied the nearest one more closely, and discovered to my surprise that she was quite young—not more than twenty-two, or twenty-three, I guessed. Her face was a little plump, perhaps, but by no means over fat; indeed, with her fresh, healthy young coloring and her short-cropped gold curls, she was quite pretty. I fell to wondering what curious disorder of the glands could cause such a degree of anomaly at her age.

Ten minutes or so passed, and there was a sound of brisk, businesslike footsteps approaching. A voice inquired:

"How are you feeling now?"

I rolled my head to the other side, and found myself looking into a face almost level with my own. For a moment I thought its owner must be a child, then I saw that the features under the white cap were certainly not less than thirty years old. Without waiting for a reply she reached under the bedclothes and took my pulse. Its rate appeared to satisfy her, for she nodded confidently.

"You'll be all right now, Mother," she told me.

I stared at her, blankly.

"The car's only just outside the door there. Do you think you can walk it?" she went on.

Bemusedly, I asked:

"What car?"

"Why, to take you home, of course," she said, with professional patience. "Come along now." And she pulled away the bedclothes.

I started to move, and looked down. What I saw there held me fixed. I lifted my arm. It was like nothing so much as a plump, white bolster with a ridiculous little hand attached at the end. I stared at it in horror. Then I heard a far-off scream as I fainted. . . .

When I opened my eyes again there was a woman—a normal-sized woman—in a white overall with a stethoscope round her neck, frowning at me in perplexity. The white-capped woman I had taken for a child stood beside her, reaching only a little above her elbow.

"—I don't know, Doctor," she was saying. "She just suddenly screamed and fainted."

"What is it? What's happened to me? I know I'm not like this—I'm not, I'm not," I said, and I could hear my own voice wailing the words.

The doctor went on looking puzzled.

"What does she mean?" she asked.

"I've no idea, Doctor," said the small one. "It was quite sudden, as if she'd had some kind of shock—but I don't know why."

"Well, she's been passed and signed off, and, anyway, she can't stay here. We need the room," said the doctor. "I'd better give her a sedative."

"But what's happened? Who am I? There's something terribly wrong. I know I'm not like this. P-please t-tell me—" I implored her, and then somehow lost myself in a stammer and a muddle.

The doctor's manner became soothing. She laid a hand gently on my shoulder.

"That's all right, Mother. There's nothing to worry about. Just take things quietly. We'll soon have you back home."

Another white-capped assistant, no taller than the first,

hurried up with a syringe, and handed it to the doctor.

"No!" I protested. "I want to know where I am. Who am I? Who are you? What's happened to me?" I tried to slap the syringe out of her hand, but both the small assistants flung themselves on my arm, and held on to it while she pressed in the needle.

It was a sedative, all right. It did not put me out, but it detached me. An odd feeling: I seemed to be floating a few feet outside myself and considering me with an unnatural calmness. I was able, or felt that I was able, to evaluate matters with intelligent clarity. Evidently I was suffering from amnesia. A shock of some kind had caused me to "lose my memory," as it is often put. Obviously it was only a very small part of my memory that had gone—just the personal part—who I was, what I was, where I lived—all the mechanism for day-to-day getting along seemed to be intact: I'd not forgotten how to talk, or how to think, and I seemed to have quite a well-stored mind to think with.

On the other hand there was a nagging conviction that everything about me was somehow *wrong*. I *knew*, somehow, that I'd never before seen the place I was in; I *knew*, too, that there was something queer about the presence of the two small nurses; above all, I *knew*, with absolute certainty, that this massive form lying here was not mine. I could not recall what face I ought to see in a mirror, not even whether it would be dark or fair, or old or young, but there was no shadow of doubt in my mind that, whatever it was like, it had never topped such a shape as I had now.

And there were the other enormous young women, too. Obviously, it could not be a matter of glandular disorder in all of us, or there'd not be this talk of sending me "home," wherever that might be. . . .

I was still arguing the situation with myself in, thanks no doubt to the sedative, a most reasonable-seeming manner, though without making any progress at all, when the ceiling above my head began to move again, and I realized I was being wheeled along. Doors opened at the end of the room, and the trolley tilted a little beneath me as we went down a gentle ramp beyond.

At the foot of the ramp, an ambulancelike car, with pink coachwork polished until it gleamed, was waiting with the rear doors open. I observed interestedly that I was playing a part in a routine procedure. A team of eight diminutive attendants carried out the task of transferring me from the trolley to a sprung couch in the ambulance as if it were a kind of drill. Two of them lingered after the rest to tuck in my coverings and place another pillow behind my head. Then they got out, closing the doors behind them, and in a minute or two we started off.

It was at this point—and possibly the sedative helped in this, too—that I began to have an increasing sense of balance and a feeling that I was perceiving the situation. Probably there *had* been an accident, as I had suspected, but obviously my error, and the chief cause of my alarm, proceeded from my assumption that I was a stage further on than I actually was. I had assumed that after an interval I had recovered consciousness in these baffling circumstances, whereas the true state of affairs must clearly be that I had *not* recovered consciousness. I must be still in a suspended state, very likely with concussion, and this was a dream, or hallucination. Presently, I should wake up in conditions that would at least be sensible, if not necessarily familiar.

I wondered now that this consoling and stabilizing thought had not occurred to me before, and decided that it was the alarming sense of detailed reality that had thrown me into panic. It had been astonishingly stupid of me to be taken in to the extent of imagining that I really was a kind of Gulliver among rather oversize Lilliputians. It was quite characteristic of most dreams, too, that I should lack a clear knowledge of my identity, so we did not need to be surprised at that. The thing to do was to take an intelligent interest in all I observed: the whole thing must be chockful of symbolic content which it would be most interesting to work out later.

The discovery quite altered my attitude and I looked about me with a new attention. It struck me as odd right away that there was so much circumstantial detail, and all of it in focus— there was none of that sense of foreground in sharp relief against a muzzy, or even nonexistent, background that one usually meets in a dream. Everything was presented with a most convincing, three-dimensional solidity. My own sensations, too, seemed perfectly valid. The injection, in particular, had been quite acutely authentic. The illusion of reality fascinated me into taking mental notes with some care.

The interior of the van, or ambulance, or whatever it was, was finished in the same shell pink as the outside—except for the roof, which was powder blue with a scatter of small silver stars. Against the front partition were mounted several cupboards, with plated handles. My couch, or stretcher, lay along the left side: on the other were two fixed seats, rather small, and upholstered in a semiglazed material to match the color of the rest. Two long windows on each side left little solid wall. Each of them was provided with curtains of a fine net, gathered back now in pink braid loops, and had a roller blind furled above it. Simply by turning my head on the pillow I was able to observe the passing scenery—though somewhat jerkily, for either the springing of the vehicle scarcely matched its appointments, or the road surface was bad: whichever the cause, I was glad my own couch was independently and quite comfortably sprung.

The external view did not offer a great deal of variety save in its hues. Our way was lined by buildings standing back behind some twenty yards of tidy lawn. Each block was three stories high, about fifty yards long, and had a tiled roof of somewhat low pitch, suggesting a vaguely Italian influence. Structurally the blocks appeared identical, but each was differently colored, with contrasting window frames and doors, and carefully considered, uniform curtains. I could see no one behind the windows; indeed there appeared to be no one about at all except here and there a woman in overalls mowing a lawn, or tending one of the inset flowerbeds.

Further back from the road, perhaps two hundred yards away, stood larger, taller, more utilitarian-looking blocks, some of them with high, factory-type chimneys. I thought they might actually be factories of some kind, but at the distance, and because I had no more than fugitive views of them between the foreground blocks, I could not be sure.

The road itself seldom ran straight for more than a hundred yards at a stretch, and its windings made one wonder whether the builders had not been more concerned to follow a contour line than a direction. There was little other traffic, and what there was consisted of lorries, large or small, mostly large. They were painted in one primary color or other, with only a fivefold combination of letters and figures on their sides for further identification. In design they might have been any lorries anywhere.

We continued this uneventful progress at a modest pace for some twenty minutes, until we came to a stretch where the road was under repair. The car slowed, and the workers moved

to one side, out of our way. As we crawled forward over the
broken surface I was able to get a good look at them.
They were all women or girls dressed in denimlike trousers,
sleeveless singlets and working boots. All had their hair cut
quite short, and a few wore hats. They were tall and broad-
shouldered, bronzed and healthy-looking. The biceps of their
arms were like a man's, and the hafts of their picks and shovels
rested in the hard, strong hands of manual toilers.

They watched with concern as the car edged its way on to
the rough patch, but when it drew level with them they trans-
ferred their attention, and jostled and craned to look inside
at me.

They smiled widely, showing strong white teeth in their
browned faces. All of them raised their right hands, making
some sign to me, still smiling. Their goodwill was so evident
that I smiled back. They walked along, keeping pace with the
crawling car, looking at me expectantly while their smiles
faded into puzzlement. They were saying something but I
could not hear the words. Some of them insistently repeated
the sign. Their disappointed look made it clear that I was
expected to respond with more than a smile. The only way
that occurred to me was to raise my own right hand in imitation
of their gesture. It was at least a qualified success; their faces
brightened though a rather puzzled look remained. Then the
car lurched on to the made-up road again and their still somewhat troubled faces slid back as we speeded up to our former
sedate pace. More dream symbols, of course—but certainly
not one of the stock symbols from the book. What on earth,
I wondered, could a party of friendly Amazons, equipped with
navvying implements instead of bows, stand for in my sub-
concious? Something frustrated, I imagined. A suppressed
desire to dominate? I did not seem to be getting much further

along that line when we passed the last of the variegated but nevertheless monotonous blocks, and ran into open country.

The flower beds had shown me already that it was spring, and now I was able to look on healthy pastures, and neat arable fields already touched with green; there was a hazelike green smoke along the trim hedges, and some of the trees in the tidily placed spinneys were in young leaf. The sun was shining with a bright benignity upon the most precise countryside I had ever seen; only the cattle dotted about the fields introduced a slight disorder into the careful dispositions. The farmhouses themselves were part of the pattern; hollow squares of neat buildings with an acre or so of vegetable garden on one side, an orchard on another, and a rickyard on a third. There was a suggestion of a doll's landscape about it—Grandma Moses, but tidied up and rationalized. I could see no random cottages, casually sited sheds, or unplanned outgrowths from the farm buildings. And what, I asked myself, should we conclude from this rather pathological exhibition of tidiness? That I was a more uncertain person than I had supposed, one who was subconsciously yearning for simplicity and security? Well, well. . . .

An open lorry which must have been traveling ahead of us turned off down a lane bordered by beautifully laid hedges, towards one of the farms. There were half a dozen young women in it, holding implements of some kind; Amazons, again. One of them, looking back, drew the attention of the rest to us. They raised their hands in the same sign that the others had made, and then waved cheerfully. I waved back.

Rather bewildering, I thought: Amazons for domination *and* this landscape for passive security: the two did not seem to tie up very well.

We trundled on, at our unambitious pace of twenty miles

an hour or so, for what I guessed to be three-quarters of an hour, with the prospect changing very little. The country undulated gently and appeared to continue like that to the foot of a line of low, blue hills many miles away. The tidy farmhouses went by with almost the regularity of milestones, though with something like twice the frequency. Occasionally there were working parties in the fields; more rarely, one saw individuals busy about the farms, and others hoeing with tractors, but they were all too far off for me to make out any details. Presently, however, came a change.

Off to the left of the road, stretching back at right angles to it for more than a mile, appeared a row of trees. At first I thought it just a wood, but then I noticed that the trunks were evenly spaced, and the trees themselves topped and pruned until they gave more the impression of a high fence.

The end of it came to within twenty feet of the road, where it turned, and we ran along beside it for almost half a mile until the car slowed, turned to the left and stopped in front of a pair of tall gates. There were a couple of toots on the horn.

The gates were ornamental, and possibly of wrought iron under their pink paint. The archway that they barred was stucco-covered, and painted the same color.

Why, I inquired of myself, this prevalence of pink, which I regard as a namby-pamby color, anyway? Flesh-color? Symbolic of an ardency for the flesh which I had insufficiently gratified? I scarcely thought so. Not pink. Surely a burning red. . . . I don't think I know anyone who can be really ardent in a pink way.

While we waited, a feeling that there was something wrong with the gatehouse grew upon me. The structure was a single-story building, standing against the left, inner side of the archway, and colored to match it. The woodwork was pale blue, and there were white net curtains at the windows. The door opened, and a middle-aged woman in a white blouse-and-trouser suit came out. She was bareheaded, with a few gray locks in her short, dark hair. Seeing me, she raised her hand in the same sign the Amazons had used, though perfunctorily, and walked over to open the gates. It was only as she pushed them back to admit us that I suddenly saw how small she was—certainly not over four feet tall. And that explained what was wrong with the gatehouse: it was built entirely to her scale.

I went on staring at her and her little house as we passed. Well, what about that? Mythology is rich in gnomes and "little people," and they are fairly pervasive of dreams, too. Somebody, I was sure, must have decided that they are a standard symbol of something, but for the moment I did not recall what it was. Would it be repressed philoprogenitiveness, or was that too unsubtle? I stowed that away, too, for later contemplation and brought my attention back to the surroundings.

We were on our way, unhurriedly, along something more like a drive than a road, with surroundings that suggested a compromise between a public garden and a municipal housing estate. There were wide lawns of an unblemished velvet green, set here and there with flower beds, delicate groups of silver birch, and occasional larger, single trees. Among them stood pink, three-story blocks, dotted about, seemingly to no particular plan.

A couple of the Amazon-types in singlets and trousers of a faded rust red were engaged in planting out a bed close beside the drive, and we had to pause while they dragged their handcart full of tulips onto the grass to let us pass. They gave me the usual salute and amiable grin as we went by.

158   CONSIDER HER WAYS

A moment later I had a feeling that something had gone wrong with my sight, but as we passed one block we came in sight of another. It was white instead of pink, but otherwise exactly similar to the rest—except that it was scaled down by at least one-third.

I blinked at it and stared hard, but it continued to seem just the same size.

A little farther on, a grotesquely huge woman in pink draperies was walking slowly and heavily across a lawn. She was accompanied by three of the small, white-suited women looking, in contrast, like children, or very animated dolls: one was involuntarily reminded of tugs fussing round a liner.

I began to feel swamped: the proliferation and combination of symbols was getting well out of my class.

The car forked to the right, and presently we drew up before a flight of steps leading to one of the pink buildings—a normal-sized building, but still not free from oddity, for the steps were divided by a central balustrade; those to the left of it were normal, those to the right smaller and more numerous.

Three toots on the horn announced our arrival. In about ten seconds half a dozen small women appeared in the doorway and came running down the right-hand side of the steps. A door slammed as the driver got out and went to meet them. When she came into my range of view I saw that she was one of the little ones, too, but not in white as the rest were; she wore a shining pink suit like a livery that exactly matched the car.

They had a word together before they came round to open the door behind me, then a voice said brightly:

"Welcome, Mother Orchis. Welcome home."

The couch or stretcher slid back on runners, and between them they lowered it to the ground. One young woman whose blouse was badged with a pink St. Andrew's cross on the left breast leaned over me. She inquired considerately:

"Do you think you can walk, Mother?"

It did not seem the moment to inquire into the form of address. I was obviously the only possible target for the question.

"Walk?" I repeated. "Of course I can walk." And I sat up, with about eight hands assisting me.

"Of course" had been an overstatement. I realized that by the time I had been heaved to my feet. Even with all the help that was going on around me it was an exertion which brought on heavy breathing. I looked down at the monstrous form that billowed under my pink draperies, with a sick revulsion and a feeling that, whatever this particular mass of symbolism disguised, it was likely to prove a distasteful revelation later on. I tried a step. "Walk" was scarcely the word for my progress. It felt like, and must have looked like, a slow series of forward surges. The women, at little more than my elbow height, fluttered about me like a flock of anxious hens. Once started, I was determined to go on, and I progressed with a kind of wave motion, first across a few yards of gravel, and then, with ponderous deliberation, up the left-hand side of the steps.

There was a perceptible sense of relief and triumph all round as I reached the summit. We paused there a few moments for me to regain my breath, then we moved on into the building. A corridor led straight ahead, with three or four closed doors on each side; at the end it branched right and left. We took the left arm, and, at the end of it, I came face to face, for the first time since the hallucination had set in, with a mirror.

It took every volt of my resolution not to panic again at

what I saw in it. The first few seconds of my stare were spent in fighting down a leaping hysteria.

In front of me stood an outrageous travesty, an elephantine female form, looking the more huge for its pink swathings. Mercifully, they covered everything but the head and hands, but these exposures were themselves another kind of shock, for the hands, though soft and dimpled and looking utterly out of proportion, were not uncomely, and the head and face were those of a girl.

She was pretty, too. She could not have been more than twenty-one, if that. Her curling fair hair was touched with auburn lights, and cut in a kind of bob. The complexion of her face was pink and cream, her mouth was gentle, and red without any artifice. She looked back at me, and at the little women anxiously clustering round me, from a pair of blue-green eyes beneath lightly arched brows. And this delicate face, this little Fragonard, was set upon that monstrous body: no less outrageously might a blossom of freesia sprout from a turnip.

When I moved my lips, hers moved; when I bent my arm, hers bent; and yet, once I got the better of that threatening panic, she ceased to be a reflection. She was nothing like me, so she must be a stranger whom I was observing, though in a most bewildering way. My panic and revulsion gave way to sadness, an aching pity for her. I could weep for the shame of it. I did. I watched the tears brim on her lower lids; mistily, I saw them overflow.

One of the little women beside me caught hold of my hand.

"Mother Orchis, dear, what's the matter?" she asked, full of concern.

I could not tell her: I had no clear idea myself. The image

in the mirror shook her head, with tears running down her cheeks. Small hands patted me here and there; small, soothing voices encouraged me onward. The next door was opened for me and, amid concerned fussing, I was led into the room beyond.

We entered a place that struck me as a cross between a boudoir and a ward. The boudoir impression was sustained by a great deal of pink—in the carpet, coverlets, cushions, lampshades, and filmy window curtains; the ward motif, by an array of six divans, or couches, one of which was unoccupied.

It was a large enough room for three couches, separated by a chest, a chair and table for each, to be arranged on each side without an effect of crowding, and the open space in the middle was still big enough to contain several expansive easy chairs and a central table bearing an intricate flower arrangement. A not displeasing scent faintly pervaded the place, and from somewhere came the subdued sound of a string quartette in a sentimental mood. Five of the bed-couches were already mountainously occupied. Two of my attendant party detached themselves and hurried ahead to turn back the pink satin cover on the sixth.

Faces from all the five other beds were turned towards me. Three of them smiling in welcome, the other two less committal.

"Hello, Orchis," one of them greeted me in a friendly tone. Then, with a touch of concern, she added: "What's the matter, dear? Did you have a bad time?"

I looked at her. She had a kindly, plumply pretty face, framed by light brown hair as she lay back against a cushion. The face looked about twenty-three or twenty-four years old.

The rest of her was a huge mound of pink satin. I couldn't make any reply, but I did my best to return her smile as we passed.

Our convoy hove to by the empty bed. After some preparation and positioning I was helped into it by all hands, and a cushion was arranged behind my head.

The exertion of my journey from the car had been considerable, and I was thankful to relax. While two of the little women pulled up the coverlet and arranged it over me, another produced a handkerchief and dabbed gently at my cheeks. She encouraged me:

"There you are, dear. Safely home again now. You'll be quite all right when you've rested a bit. Just try to sleep for a little."

"What's the matter with her?" inquired a forthright voice from one of the other beds. "Did she make a mess of it?"

The little woman with the handkerchief—she was the one who wore the St. Andrew's cross and appeared to be in charge of the operation—turned her head sharply.

"There's no need for that tone, Mother Hazel. Of course Mother Orchis had four beautiful babies—didn't you, dear?" she added to me. "She's just a bit tired after the journey, that's all."

"H'mph," said the girl addressed, in an unaccommodating tone, but she made no further comment.

A degree of fussing continued. Presently the small woman handed me a glass of something that looked like water, but had unsuspected strength. I spluttered a little at the first taste, but quickly felt the better for it. After a little more tidying and ordering my retinue departed, leaving me propped against my cushion, with the eyes of the five other monstrous women dwelling upon me speculatively.

An awkward silence was broken by the girl who had greeted me as I came in.

"Where did they send you for your holiday, Orchis?"

"Holiday?" I asked blankly.

She and the rest stared at me in astonishment.

"I don't know what you're talking about," I told them.

They went on staring, stupidly, stolidly.

"It can't have been much of a holiday," observed one, obviously puzzled. "I'll not forget my last one. They sent me to the sea, and gave me a little car so that I could get about everywhere. Everybody was lovely to us, and there were only six Mothers there, including me. Did you go by the sea, or in the mountains?"

They were determined to be inquisitive, and one would have to make some answer sooner or later. I chose what seemed the simplest way out for the moment.

"I can't remember," I said. "I can't remember a thing. I seem to have lost my memory altogether."

That was not very sympathetically received, either.

"Oh," said the one who had been addressed as Hazel, with a degree of satisfaction. "I thought there was something. And I suppose you can't even remember for certain whether your babies were Grade One this time, Orchis?"

"Don't be stupid, Hazel," one of the others told her. "Of course they were Grade One. If they'd not been, Orchis wouldn't be back here now—she'd have been re-rated as a Class Two Mother, and sent to Whitewich." In a more kindly tone she asked me: "When did it happen, Orchis?"

"I—I don't know," I said. "I can't remember anything before this morning at the hospital. It's all gone entirely."

"Hospital!" repeated Hazel, scornfully.

"She must mean the Center," said the other. "But do you mean to say you can't even remember *us*, Orchis?"

"No," I admitted, shaking my head. "I'm sorry, but everything before I came round in the Hosp—in the Center, is all blank."

"That's queer," Hazel said, in an unsympathetic tone. "Do they know?"

One of the others took my part.

"Of course they're bound to know. I expect they don't think that remembering or not has anything to do with having Grade One babies. And why should it, anyway? But look, Orchis..."

"Why not let her rest for a bit," another cut in. "I don't suppose she's feeling too good after the Center, and the journey, and getting in here. I never do myself. Don't take any notice of them, Orchis, dear. You just go to sleep for a bit. You'll probably find it's all quite all right when you wake up."

I accepted her suggestion gratefully. The whole thing was far too bewildering to cope with at the moment; moreover, I did feel exhausted. I thanked her for her advice, and lay back on my pillow. Insofar as the closing of one's eyes can be made ostentatious, I made it so. What was more surprising was that, if one can be said to sleep within an hallucination or a dream, I slept. . . .

In the moment of waking, before opening my eyes, I had a flash of hope that I should find the illusion had spent itself. Unfortunately, it had not. A hand was shaking my shoulder gently, and the first thing that I saw was the face of the little women's leader, close to mine.

In the way of nurses she said:

"There, Mother Orchis, dear. You'll be feeling a lot better after that nice sleep, won't you?"

Beyond her, two more of the small women were carrying

a short-legged bed tray towards me. They set it down so that
it bridged me and was convenient to reach. I stared at the
load on it. It was, with no exception, the most enormous and
nourishing meal I had ever seen put before one person. The
first sight of it revolted me—but then I became aware of a
schism within, for it did not revolt the physical form that I
occupied: that, in fact, had a watering mouth, and was eager
to begin. An inner part of me marveled in a kind of semi-
detachment while the rest consumed two or three fish, a whole
chicken, some slices of meat, a pile of vegetables, fruit hidden
under mounds of stiff cream, and more than a quart of milk,
without any sense of surfeit. Occasional glances showed me
that the other "Mothers" were dealing just as thoroughly with
the contents of their similar trays.

I caught one or two curious looks from them, but they were
too seriously occupied to take up their inquisition again at the
moment. I wondered how to fend them off later, and it occurred to me that if only I had a book or a magazine I might
be able to bury myself effectively, if not very politely, in it.

When the attendants returned, I asked the badged one if
she could let me have something to read. The effect of such
a simple request was astonishing: the two who were removing
my tray all but dropped it. The one beside me gaped for an
amazed moment before she collected her wits. She looked at
me, first with suspicion and then with concern.

"Not feeling quite yourself yet, dear?" she suggested.

"But I am," I protested. "I'm quite all right now."

The look of concern persisted, however.

"If I were you I'd try to sleep again," she advised.

"But I don't want to. I'd just like to read quietly," I objected.

She patted my shoulder, a little uncertainly.

"I'm afraid you've had an exhausting time, Mother. Never

mind, I'm sure it'll pass quite soon."

I felt impatient. "What's wrong with wanting to read?" I demanded.

She smiled a smug, professional-nurse smile.

"There, there, dear. Just you try to rest a little more. Why, bless me, what on earth would a Mother want with knowing how to read?"

With that she tidied my coverlet, and bustled away, leaving me to the wide-eyed stares of my five companions. Hazel gave a kind of contemptuous snigger; otherwise there was no audible comment for several minutes.

I had reached a stage where the persistence of the hallucination was beginning to wear away my detachment. I could feel that under a little more pressure I should be losing my confidence and starting to doubt its unreality. I did not at all care for its calm continuity: inconsequent exaggerations and jumps, foolish perspectives, indeed, any of the usual dream characteristics would have been reassuring; but, instead, it continued to present obvious nonsense, with an alarming air of conviction and consequence. Effects, for instance, were unmistakably following causes. I began to have an uncomfortable feeling that were one to dig deep enough one might begin to find logical causes for the absurdities, too. The integration was far too good for mental comfort—even the fact that I had enjoyed my meal as if we were fully awake, and was consciously feeling the better for it, encouraged the disturbing quality of reality.

"Read!" Hazel said suddenly, with a scornful laugh. "And write, too, I suppose?"

"Well, why not?" I retorted.

They all gazed at me more attentively than ever, and then exchanged meaning glances among themselves. Two of them smiled at one another. I demanded irritably: "What on earth's wrong with that? Am I supposed not to be able to read or write, or something?"

One said kindly, soothingly:

"Orchis, dear. Don't you think it would be better if you were to ask to see the doctor? Just for a check-up?"

"No," I told her flatly. "There's nothing wrong with me. I'm just trying to understand. I simply ask for a book, and you all look at me as if I were mad. Why?"

After an awkward pause the same one said humoringly, and almost in the words of the little attendant:

"Orchis, dear, do try to pull yourself together. What sort of good would reading and writing be to a Mother? How could they help her to have better babies?"

"There are other things in life besides having babies," I said, shortly.

If they had been surprised before, they were thunderstruck now. Even Hazel seemed bereft of suitable comment. Their idiotic astonishment exasperated me and made me suddenly sick of the whole nonsensical business. Temporarily, I *did* forget to be the detached observer of a dream.

"Damn it," I broke out. "What *is* all this rubbish? Orchis! Mother Orchis!—for God's sake! Where am I? Is this some kind of lunatic asylum?"

I stared at them, angrily, loathing the sight of them, wondering if they were all in some spiteful complicity against me. Somehow I was quite convinced in my own mind that whoever, or whatever, I was, I was not a mother. I said so, forcibly, and then, to my annoyance, burst into tears.

For lack of anything else to use, I dabbed at my eyes with

my sleeve. When I could see clearly again I found that four
of them were looking at me with kindly concern. Hazel, however, was not.

"I said there was something queer about her," she told the
others, triumphantly. "She's mad, that's what it is."

The one who had been most kindly disposed before, tried
again:

"But, Orchis, *of course* you are a Mother. You're a Class
One Mother—with three births registered. Twelve fine Grade
One babies, dear. You *can't* have forgotten that!"

For some reason I wept again. I had a feeling that something
was trying to break through the blankness in my mind; but I
did not know what it was, only that it made me feel intensely
miserable.

"Oh, this is cruel, cruel! Why can't I stop it? Why won't it
go away and leave me?" I pleaded. "There's a horrible cruel
mockery here—but I don't understand it. What's wrong with
me? I'm not obsessional—I'm not—I—oh, can't somebody
help me . . . ?"

I kept my eyes tight shut for a time, willing with all my
mind that the whole hallucination should fade and disappear.

But it did not. When I looked again they were still there,
their silly, pretty faces gaping stupidly at me across the revolting mounds of pink satin.

"I'm going to get out of this," I said.

It was a tremendous effort to raise myself to a sitting position. I was aware of the rest watching me, wide-eyed, while
I made it. I struggled to get my feet round and over the side
of the bed, but they were all tangled in the satin coverlet and
I could not reach to free them. It was the true, desperate
frustration of a dream. I heard my voice pleading: "Help me!
Oh, Donald, darling, please help me. . . ."

And suddenly, as if the word "Donald" had released a spring, something seemed to click in my head. The shutter in my mind opened, not entirely, but enough to let me know who I was. I understood, suddenly, where the cruelty had lain.

I looked at the others again. They were still staring half-bewildered, half-alarmed. I gave up the attempt to move, and lay back on my pillows again.

"You can't fool me any more," I told them. "I know who I am, now."

"But, Mother Orchis—" one began.

"Stop that," I snapped at her. I seemed to have swung suddenly out of self-pity into a kind of masochistic callousness. "I am *not* a mother," I said harshly. "I am just a woman who, for a short time, had a husband, and who hoped—but only hoped—that she would have babies by him."

A pause followed that; a rather odd pause, where there should have been at least a murmur. What I had said did not seem to have registered. The faces showed no understanding; they were as uncomprehending as dolls.

Presently, the most friendly one seemed to feel an obligation to break up the silence. With a little vertical crease between her brows: "What," she inquired tentatively, "what is a husband?"

I looked hard from one face to another. There was no trace of guile in any of them; nothing but puzzled speculation such as one sometimes sees in a child's eyes. I felt close to hysteria for a moment, then I took a grip on myself. Very well, then, since the hallucination would not leave me alone, I would play it at its own game, and see what came of that. I began to explain with a kind of dead-pan, simple-word seriousness:

"A husband is a man whom a woman takes..."

Evidently, from their expressions I was not very enlightening. However, they let me go on for three or four sentences without interruption. Then, when I paused for breath, the kindly one chipped in with a point which she evidently felt needed clearing up:

"But what," she asked, in evident perplexity, "what is a man?"

A cool silence hung over the room after my exposition. I had an impression I had been sent to Coventry, or semi-Coventry, by them, but I did not bother to test it. I was too much occupied trying to force the door of my memory farther open, and finding that beyond a certain point it would not budge.

I knew now that I was Jane. I had been Jane Summers, and had become Jane Waterleigh when I had married Donald.

I was—had been—twenty-four when we were married; just twenty-five when Donald was killed, six months later. And there it stopped. It seemed like yesterday, but I couldn't tell. . . .

Before that, everything was perfectly clear. My parents and friends, my home, my schools, my training, my job as Dr. Summers at the Wraychester Hospital. I could remember my first sight of Donald when they brought him in one evening with a broken leg—and all that followed. . . .

I could remember now the face that I ought to see in a looking-glass—and it was certainly nothing like that I had seen in the corridor outside. It should be more oval, with a complexion looking faintly suntanned; with a smaller, neater mouth; surrounded by chestnut hair that curled naturally; with brown eyes rather wide apart and perhaps a little grave as a rule.

I knew, too, how the rest of me should look—slender, long-legged, with small, firm breasts—a nice body but one that I had simply taken for granted until Donald gave me pride in it by loving it.

I looked down at the repulsive mound of pink satin, and shuddered. A sense of outrage came welling up. I longed for Donald to comfort and pet me and love me and tell me it would be all right; that I wasn't as I was seeing myself at all, and that it *really was* a dream. At the same time I was stricken with horror at the thought that he should ever see me gross and obese like this. And then I remembered that Donald would never see me again at all—never any more—and I was wretched and miserable, and the tears trickled down my cheeks again.

The five others just went on looking at me, wide-eyed and wondering. Half an hour passed, still in silence, then the door opened to admit a whole troop of the little women, all in white suits. I saw Hazel look at me, and then at the leader. She seemed about to speak, and then to change her mind. The little women split up, two to a couch. Standing one on each side, they stripped away the coverlet, rolled up their sleeves, and set to work at massage.

At first it was not unpleasant, and quite soothing. I lay back and relaxed. Presently, however, I liked it less: soon I found it offensive.

"Stop that!" I told the one on the right, sharply.

She paused, smiled at me amiably, though a trifle uncertainly, and then continued.

"I said stop it," I told her, pushing her away.

Her eyes met mine. They were troubled and hurt, although a professional smile still curved her mouth.

"I mean it," I added, curtly.

She continued to hesitate, and glanced across at her partner on the further side of the bed.

"You, too," I told the other. "That'll do."

She did not even pause in her rhythm. The one on the right plucked a decision and returned. She restarted just what I had stopped. I reached out and pushed her, harder this time. There must have been a lot more muscle in that bolster of an arm than one would have supposed. The shove carried her half across the room, and she tripped and fell.

All movement in the room suddenly ceased. Everybody stared, first at her, and then at me. The pause was brief. They all set to work again. I pushed away the girl on the left, too, though more gently. The other one picked herself up. She was crying and she looked frightened, but she set her jaw doggedly and started to come back.

"You keep away from me, you little horrors," I told them threateningly.

That checked them. They stood off, and looked miserably at one another. The one with the badge of seniority fussed up. "What's the trouble, Mother Orchis?" she inquired.

I told her. She looked puzzled.

"But that's quite right," she expostulated.

"Not for me. I don't like it, and I won't have it," I replied. She stood awkwardly, at a loss.

Hazel's voice came from the other side of the room:

"Orchis is off her head. She's been telling us the most disgusting things. She's quite mad."

The little woman turned to regard her, and then looked inquiringly at one of the others. When the girl confirmed with a nod and an expression of distaste she turned back to me, giving me a searching inspection.

"You two go and report," she told my discomfited masseuses.

They were both crying now, and they went wretchedly down the room together. The one in charge gave me another long, thoughtful look, and then followed them.

A few minutes later all the rest had packed up and gone. The six of us were alone again. It was Hazel who broke the ensuing silence.

"That was a bitchy piece of work. The poor little devils were only doing their job," she observed.

"If that's their job, I don't like it," I told her.

"So you just get them a beating, poor things. But I suppose that's the lost memory again. You wouldn't remember that a Servitor who upsets a Mother is beaten, would you?" she added sarcastically.

"Beaten?" I repeated, uneasily.

"Yes, beaten," she mimicked. "But you don't care what becomes of them, do you? I don't know what happened to you while you were away, but whatever it was it seems to have produced a thoroughly nasty result. I never did care for you, Orchis, though the others thought I was wrong. Well, now we all know."

None of the rest offered any comment. The feeling that they shared her opinion was strong, but luckily I was spared confirmation by the opening of the door.

The senior attendant reentered with half a dozen small myrmidons, but this time the group was dominated by a handsome woman of about thirty. Her appearance gave me immense relief. She was neither little nor Amazonian, nor was she huge. Her present company made her look a little overtall, perhaps, but I judged her at about five feet ten; a normal, pleasant-featured young woman with brown hair, cut somewhat short, and a pleated black shirt showing beneath a white overall. The senior attendant was almost trotting to keep up with her longer steps, and was saying something about delusions and "only back from the Center to-day, Doctor."

The woman stopped beside my couch while the smaller women huddled together, looking at me with some misgiving. She thrust a thermometer into my mouth and held my wrist. Satisfied on both these counts, she inquired:

"Headache? Any other aches or pains?"

"No," I told her.

She regarded me carefully. I looked back at her.

"What—?" she began.

"She's mad," Hazel put in from the other side of the room. "She says she's lost her memory and doesn't know us."

"She's been talking about horrid, disgusting things," added one of the others.

"She's got delusions. She thinks she can read and write," Hazel supplemented.

The doctor smiled at that.

"Do you?" she asked me.

"I don't see why not—but it should be easy enough to prove," I replied, brusquely.

She looked startled, a little taken aback, then she recovered her tolerant half smile.

"All right," she said, humoring me.

She pulled a small note pad out of her pocket and offered it to me, with a pencil. The pencil felt a little odd in my hand; the fingers did not fall into place readily on it, nevertheless I wrote:

"I'm only too well aware that I have delusions—and that you are part of them."

Hazel tittered as I handed the pad back.

The doctor's jaw did not actually drop, but her smile came right off. She looked at me very hard indeed. The rest of the room, seeing her expression, went quiet, as though I had performed some startling feat of magic. The doctor turned towards Hazel.

"What sort of things has she been telling you?" she inquired.

Hazel hesitated, then she blurted out:

"Horrible things. She's been talking about two human sexes—just as if we were like the animals. It was disgusting!"

The doctor considered a moment, then she told the senior attendant:

"Better get her along to the sick bay. I'll examine her there."

As she walked off there was a rush of little women to fetch a low trolley from the corner to the side of my couch. A dozen hands assisted me on to it, and then wheeled me briskly away.

"Now," said the doctor grimly, "let's get down to it. Who told you all this stuff about two human sexes? I want her name."

We were alone in a small room with a gold-dotted pink wallpaper. The attendants, after transferring me from the trolley to a couch again, had taken themselves off. The doctor was sitting with a pad on her knee and a pencil at the ready. Her manner was that of an unbluffable inquisitor.

I was not feeling tactful. I told her not to be a fool.

She looked staggered, flushed with anger for a moment, and then took a hold on herself. She went on:

"After you left the Clinic you had your holiday, of course. Now, where did they send you?"

"I don't know," I replied. "All I can tell you is what I told the others—that this hallucination, or delusion, or whatever it is, started in that hospital place you call the Center."

With resolute patience she said:

"Look here, Orchis. You were perfectly normal when you left here six weeks ago. You went to the Clinic and had your babies in the ordinary way. *But* between then and now somebody has been filling your head with all this rubbish—and teaching you to read and write, as well. Now you are going to tell me who that somebody was. I warn you you won't get away with this loss of memory nonsense with me. If you are able to remember this nauseating stuff you told the others, then you're able to remember where you got it from."

"Oh, for heaven's sake, talk sense," I told her. She flushed again.

"I can find out from the Clinic where they sent you, and I can find out from the Rest Home who were your chief associates while you were there, but I don't want to waste time following up all your contacts, so I'm asking you to save trouble by telling me now. You might just as well. We don't want to have to *make* you talk," she concluded, ominously.

I shook my head.

"You're on the wrong track. As far as I am concerned this whole hallucination, including my connection with this Orchis, began somehow at the Center—how it happened I can't tell you, and what happened to her before that just isn't there to be remembered."

She frowned, obviously disturbed.

"What hallucination?" she inquired, carefully.

"Why this fantastic setup—and you, too." I waved my hand to include it all. "This revolting great body, all those little women, everything. Obviously it is all some projection of the subconscious—and the state of my subconscious is worrying me, for it's certainly no wish-fulfillment."

She went on staring at me, more worried now.

"Who on earth has been telling you about the subconscious and wish-fulfillments?" she asked, uncertainly.

"I don't see why, even in an hallucination, I am expected to be an illiterate moron," I replied.

"But a Mother doesn't know anything about such things. She doesn't need to."

"Listen," I said. "I've told you, as I've told those poor grotesques in the other room, that I am *not* a Mother. What I am is just an unfortunate M.B. who is having some kind of nightmare."

"M.B.?" she inquired, vaguely.

"Bachelor of Medicine. I practice medicine," I told her.

She went on looking at me curiously. Her eyes wandered over my mountainous form, uncertainly.

"You are claiming to be a doctor?" she said, in an odd voice.

"Colloquially—yes," I agreed.

There was indignation mixed with bewilderment as she protested:

"But this is sheer nonsense! You were brought up and developed to be a Mother. You *are* a Mother. Just look at you!"

"Yes," I said, bitterly. "Just look at me!"

There was a pause.

"It seems to me," I suggested at last, "that, hallucination or not, we shan't get much further simply by going on accusing one another of talking nonsense. Suppose you explain to me what this place is, and who you think I am. It might jog my memory."

She countered that. "Suppose," she said, "that first you tell me what you *can* remember. It would give me more idea of what is puzzling you."

"Very well," I agreed, and launched upon a potted history of myself as far as I could recollect it—up to the time, that is to say, when Donald's aircraft crashed.

It was foolish of me to fall for that one. Of course, she had no intention of telling me anything. When she had listened to all I had to say, she went away, leaving me impotently furious.

I waited until the place quieted down. The music had been switched off. An attendant had looked in to inquire, with an air of polishing off the day's duties, whether there was anything I wanted, and presently there was nothing to be heard. I let a margin of half an hour elapse, and then struggled to get up—taking it by very easy stages this time. The greatest part of the effort was to get onto my feet from a sitting position, but I managed it at the cost of heavy breathing. Presently I crossed to the door, and found it unfastened. I held it a little open, listening. There was no sound of movement in the corridor, so I pulled it wide open, and set out to discover what I could about the place for myself. All the doors of the rooms were shut. Putting my ear close to them I could hear regular, heavy breathing behind some, but there were no other sounds in the stillness. I kept on, turning several corners, until I recognized the front door ahead of me. I tried the latch, and found that it was neither barred nor bolted. I paused again, listening for some moments, and then pulled it open and stepped outside.

The parklike garden stretched out before me, sharp-shadowed in the moonlight. Through the trees to the right was a glint of water, to the left was a house similar to the one behind me, with not a light showing in any of its windows.

I wondered what to do. Trapped in this huge carcass, all

but helpless in it, there was very little I could do, but I decided to go on and at least find out what I could while I had the chance. I went forward to the edge of the steps that I had earlier climbed from the ambulance, and started down them cautiously, holding on to the balustrade.

"Mother," said a sharp, incisive voice behind me. "What are you doing?"

I turned and saw one of the little women, her white suit gleaming in the moonlight. She was alone. I made no reply, but took another step down. I could have wept at the outrage of the heavy, ungainly body, and the caution it imposed on me.

"Come back. Come back at once," she told me.

I took no notice. She came pattering down after me and laid hold of my draperies.

"Mother," she said again, "you must come back. You'll catch cold out here."

I started to take another step, and she pulled at the draperies to hold me back. I leant forward against the pull. There was a sharp tearing sound as the material gave. I swung round and lost my balance. The last thing I saw was the rest of the flight of steps coming up to meet me. . . .

As I opened my eyes a voice said:

"That's better, but it was very naughty of you, Mother Orchis. And lucky it wasn't a lot worse. Such a silly thing to do. I'm ashamed of you—really, I am."

My head was aching, and I was exasperated to find that the whole stupid business was still going on; altogether I was in no mood for reproachful drip. I told her to go to hell. Her small face goggled at me for a moment, and then became icily prim. She applied a piece of lint and plaster to the left side of my forehead, in silence, and then departed, stiffly.

Reluctantly, I had to admit to myself that she was perfectly right. What on earth had I been expecting to do—what on earth *could* I do, encumbered by this horrible mass of flesh? A great surge of loathing for it and a feeling of helpless frustration brought me to the verge of tears again. I longed for my own nice, slim body that pleased me and did what I asked of it. I remembered how Donald had once pointed to a young tree swaying in the wind, and introduced it to me as my twin sister. And only a day or two ago...

Then, suddenly, I made a discovery which brought me struggling to sit up. The blank part of my mind had filled up. I could remember everything. . . . The effort made my head throb, so I relaxed and lay back once more, recalling it all, right up to the point where the needle was withdrawn and someone swabbed my arm. . . .

But what had happened after that? Dreams and hallucinations I had expected . . . but not the sharp-focused, detailed sense of reality . . . not this state which was like a nightmare made solid. . . .

What, what in heaven's name, had they done to me . . . ?

I must have fallen asleep again soon, for when I opened my eyes there was daylight outside, and a covey of little women had arrived to attend to my toilet.

They spread their sheets dexterously and rolled me this way and that with expert technique as they cleaned me up. I suffered their industry patiently, feeling the fresher for it, and glad to discover that the headache had all but gone.

When we were almost at the end of our ablutions there came a peremptory knock, and without invitation two figures, dressed in black uniforms with silver buttons, entered. They were the Amazon type, tall, broad, well setup, and handsome. The little women dropped everything and fled with squeaks of dismay into the far corner of the room where they cowered in a huddle.

The two gave me the familiar salute. With an odd mixture of decision and deference one of them inquired:

"You are Orchis—Mother Orchis?"

"That's what they're calling me," I admitted.

The girl hesitated, then in a tone rather more pleading than ordering she said:

"I have orders for your arrest, Mother. You will please come with us."

An excited, incredulous twittering broke out among the little women in the corner. The uniformed girl quelled them with a look.

"Get the Mother dressed and make her ready," she commanded.

The little women came out of their corner hesitantly, directing nervous, propitiatory smiles towards the pair. The second one told them briskly, though not altogether unkindly:

"Come along now. Jump to it."

They jumped.

I was almost swathed in my pink draperies again when the doctor strode in. She frowned at the two in uniform.

"What's all this? What are you doing here?" she demanded.

The leader of the two explained.

"Arrest!" exclaimed the doctor. "Arrest a Mother! I never heard such nonsense. What's the charge?"

The uniformed girl said, a little sheepishly:

"She is accused of Reactionism."

The doctor simply stared at her.

"A reactionist Mother! What'll you people think of next? Go on, get out, both of you."

The young woman protested:

"We have our orders, Doctor."

"Rubbish. There's no authority. Have you ever heard of a Mother being arrested?"

"No, Doctor,"

"Well, you aren't going to make a precedent now. Go on." The uniformed girl hesitated unhappily, then an idea occurred to her.

"If you would let me have a signed refusal to surrender the Mother...?" she suggested helpfully.

When the two had departed, quite satisfied with their piece of paper, the doctor looked at the little women gloomily.

"You can't help tattling, you Servitors, can you? Anything you happen to hear goes through the lot of you like a fire in a cornfield, and makes trouble all round. Well, if I hear any more of this I shall know where it comes from." She turned to me. "And you, Mother Orchis, will in future please restrict yourself to yes-and-no in the hearing of these nattering little pests. I'll see you again shortly. We want to ask you some questions," she added, as she went out, leaving a subdued, industrious silence behind her.

She returned just as the tray which had held my gargantuan breakfast was being removed, and not alone. The four women who accompanied her and looked as normal as herself were followed by a number of little women lugging in chairs which they arranged beside my couch. When they had departed, the five women, all in white overalls, sat down and regarded me as if I were an exhibit. One appeared to be much the same age as the first doctor, two nearer fifty, and one sixty, or more.

"Now, Mother Orchis," said the doctor, with an air of opening the proceedings, "it is quite clear that something highly unusual has taken place. Naturally we are interested to understand just what and, if possible, why. You don't need to worry about those police this morning—it was quite improper of them to come here at all. This is simply an inquiry—a scientific inquiry—to establish what has happened."

"You can't want to understand more than I do," I replied. I looked at them, at the room about me, and finally at my massive prone figure. "I am aware that all this must be an hallucination, but what is troubling me most is that I have always supposed that any hallucination must be deficient in at least one dimension—must lack reality to some of the senses. But this does not. I have all my senses, and can use them. Nothing is insubstantial: I am trapped in flesh that is very palpably too, too solid. The only striking deficiency, so far as I can see, is reason—even symbolic reason."

The four other women stared at me in astonishment. The doctor gave them a sort of now-perhaps-you'll-believe-me glance, and then turned to me again.

"We'll start with a few questions," she said.

"Before you begin," I put in, "I have something to add to what I told you last night. It has come back to me."

"Perhaps the knock when you fell," she suggested, looking at my piece of plaster. "What were you trying to do?"

I ignored that. "I think I'd better tell you the missing part—it might help—a bit, anyway."

"Very well," she agreed. "You told me you were—er—married, and that your—er—husband was killed soon afterwards." She glanced at the others; their blankness of expression was somehow studious. "It was the part after that that was missing," she added.

"Yes," I said. "He was a test pilot." I explained to them. "It happened six months after we were married—only one month before his contract was due to expire.

"After that, an aunt took me away for some weeks. I don't suppose I'll ever remember that part very well—I—I wasn't noticing anything very much. . . .

"But then I remember waking up one morning and suddenly seeing things differently, and telling myself that I couldn't go on like that. I knew I must have some work, something that would keep me busy.

"Dr. Hellyer, who is in charge of the Wraychester Hospital, where I was working before I married, told me he would be glad to have me with them again. I went back, and worked very hard, so that I did not have much time to think. That would be about eight months ago, now.

"Then one day Dr. Hellyer spoke about a drug that a friend of his had succeeded in synthesizing. I don't think he was really asking for volunteers, but I offered to try it out. From what he said it sounded as if the drug might have some quite important properties. It struck me as a chance to do something useful. Sooner or later, someone would try it, and as I didn't have any ties and didn't care very much what happened anyway, I thought I might as well be the one to try it."

The spokesman doctor interrupted to ask:

"What was this drug?"

"It's called chuinjuatin," I told her. "Do you know it?"

She shook her head. One of the others put in:

"I've heard the name. What is it?"

"It's a narcotic," I told her. "The original form is in the leaves of a tree that grows chiefly in the south of Venezuela. The tribe of Indians who live there discovered it somehow, like others did quinine, and mescalin. And in much the same way they use it for orgies. Some of them sit and chew the leaves—they have to chew about six ounces of them—and gradually they go into a zombielike, trance state. It lasts three or four days during which they are quite helpless and incapable of doing the simplest thing for themselves, so that other members of the tribe are appointed to look after them as if they were children, and to guard them.

"It's necessary to guard them because the Indian belief is that chuinjuatin liberates the spirit from the body, setting it free to wander anywhere in space and time, and the guardian's most important job is to see that no other wandering spirit shall slip into the body while the true owner is away. When the subjects recover they claim to have had wonderful mystical experiences. There seem to be no physical ill effects, and no craving results from it. The mystical experiences, though, are said to be intense, and clearly remembered.

"Dr. Hellyer's friend had tested his synthesized chuinjuatin on a number of laboratory animals and worked out the dosage, and tolerances, and that kind of thing, but what he could not tell, of course, was what validity, if any, the reports of the mystical experiences had. Presumably they were the product of the drug's influence on the nervous system—but whether that effect produced a sensation of pleasure, ecstasy, awe, fear, horror, or any of a dozen more, it was impossible to tell without a human guinea pig. So that was what I volunteered for."

I stopped. I looked at their serious, puzzled faces, at the billow of pink satin in front of me. . . .

"In fact," I added, "it appears to have produced a combination of the absurd, the incomprehensible, and the grotesque."

They were earnest women, these, not to be sidetracked. They were there to disprove an anomaly—if they could.

"I see," said the spokeswoman with an air of preserving reasonableness, rather than meaning anything. She glanced down at a paper on which she had made a note from time to time.

"Now, can you give us the time and date at which this experiment took place?"

I could, and did, and after that the questions went on and on and on.

The least satisfactory part of it from my point of view was that even though my answers caused them to grow more uncertain of themselves as we went on, they did at least get them; whereas when I put a question it was usually evaded, or answered perfunctorily, as an unimportant digression.

They went on steadily, and only broke off when my next meal arrived. Then they went away, leaving me thankfully in peace—but little the wiser. I half expected them to return, but when they did not I fell into a doze from which I was awakened by the incursion of a cluster of the little women once more. They brought a trolley with them, and in a short time were wheeling me out of the building on it—but not by the way I had arrived. This time we went down a ramp where another, or the same, pink ambulance waited at the bottom. When they had me safely loaded aboard three of them climbed in, too, to keep me company. They were chattering as they did so, and they kept it up inconsequently, and almost incomprehensibly, for the whole hour and a half of the journey that ensued.

The countryside differed little from that I had already seen. Once we were outside the gates there were the same tidy fields and standardized farms. The occasional built-up areas were not extensive and consisted of the same types of blocks close by, and we ran on the same, not very good, road surfaces. There were groups of the Amazon types, and, more rarely, individuals, to be seen at work in the fields; the sparse traffic was lorries, large or small, and occasional buses, but with never a private car to be seen. My illusion, I reflected, was remarkably consistent in its details. Not a single group of Amazons, for instance, failed to raise its right hands in friendly, respectful greeting to the pink car.

Once, we crossed a cutting. Looking down from the bridge I thought at first that we were over the dried bed of a canal, but then I noticed a post leaning at a crazy angle among the grass and weeds: most of its attachments had fallen off, but there were enough left to identify it as a railway signal.

We passed through one concentration of identical blocks which was in size, though in no other way, quite a town, and then, two or three miles farther on, ran through an ornamental gateway into a kind of park.

In one way it was not unlike the estate we had left, for everything was meticulously tended; the lawns like velvet, the flower beds vivid with spring blossoms, but it differed essentially in that the buildings were not blocks. They were houses, quite small for the most part, and varied in style, often no larger than roomy cottages. The place had a subduing effect on my small companions; for the first time they left off chattering, and gazed about them with obvious awe.

The driver stopped once to inquire the way of an overalled Amazon who was striding along with a hood on her shoulder. She directed us, and gave me a cheerful, respectful grin through the window, and presently we drew up again in front of a neat little two-story Regency-styled house.

This time there was no trolley. The little women, assisted by the driver, fussed over helping me out, and then half supported me into the house, a kind of buttressing formation.

Inside, I was maneuvered with some difficulty through a door on the left, and found myself in a beautiful room, elegantly decorated and furnished in the period style of the house. A white-haired woman in a purple silk dress was sitting in a wing chair beside a wood fire. Both her face and her hands told of considerable age, but she looked at me from keen, lively eyes.

"Welcome, my dear," she said, in a voice which had no trace of the quaver I half expected.

Her glance went to a chair. Then she looked at me again, and thought better of it.

"I expect you'd be more comfortable on the couch," she suggested.

I regarded the couch—a genuine Georgian piece, I thought—doubtfully.

"Will it stand it?" I wondered.

"Oh, I think so," she said, but not too certainly.

The retinue deposited me there carefully, and stood by, with anxious expressions. When it was clear that, though it creaked, it was probably going to hold, the old lady shooed them away, and rang a little silver bell. A diminutive figure, a perfect parlormaid three-foot-ten in height, entered.

"The brown sherry, please, Mildred," instructed the old lady. "You'll take sherry, my dear?" she added to me.

"Y-yes—yes, thank you," I said, faintly. After a pause I added: "You will excuse me, Mrs.—er—Miss—?"

"Oh, I should have introduced myself. My name is Laura—

not Miss, or Mrs., just Laura. You, I know, are Orchis—Mother Orchis."

"So they tell me," I owned, distastefully.

We studied one another. For the first time since the hallucination had set in I saw sympathy, even pity, in someone else's eyes. I looked round the room again, noticing the perfection of details.

"This is—I'm not mad, am I?" I asked.

She shook her head slowly, but before she could reply the miniature parlormaid returned, bearing a cut-glass decanter and glasses on a silver tray. As she poured out a glass for each of us I saw the old lady glance from her to me and back again, as though comparing us. There was a curious, uninterpretable expression on her face. I made an effort.

"Shouldn't it be madeira?" I suggested.

She looked surprised, and then smiled, and nodded appreciatively.

"I think you have accomplished the purpose of this visit in one sentence," she said.

The parlormaid left, and we raised our glasses. The old lady sipped at hers and then placed it on an occasional table beside her.

"Nevertheless," she went on, "we had better go into it a little more. Did they tell you why they have sent you to me, my dear?"

"No." I shook my head.

"It is because I am a historian," she informed me. "Access to history is a privilege. It is not granted to many of us nowadays—and then somewhat reluctantly. Fortunately, a feeling that no branches of knowledge should be allowed to perish entirely still exists—though some of them are pursued at the cost of a certain political suspicion." She smiled deprecatingly, and then went on. "So when confirmation is required it is necessary to appeal to a specialist. Did they give you any report on their diagnosis?"

I shook my head again.

"I thought not. So like the profession, isn't it? Well, I'll tell you what they told me on the telephone from the Mothers' Home, and we shall have a better idea of what we are about. I was informed that you have been interviewed by several doctors whom you have interested, puzzled—and, I suspect, distressed—very much, poor things. None of them has more than a minimum smattering of history, you see. Well, briefly, two of them are of the opinion that you are suffering from delusions of a schizophrenic nature, and three are inclined to think you are a genuine case of projected perception. It is an extremely rare condition. There are not more than three reliably documented cases, and one that is more debatable, they tell me; but of those confirmed two are associated with the drug chuinjuatin, and the third with a drug of very similar properties.

"Now, the majority of three found your answers coherent for the most part, and felt that they were authentically circumstantial. That is to say that nothing you told them conflicted directly with what they know, but, since they know so little outside their professional field, they found a great deal of the rest both hard to believe and impossible to check. Therefore, I, with my better means of checking, have been asked for my opinion."

She paused, and looked me over thoughtfully.

"I rather think," she added, "that this is going to be one of the most curiously interesting things that has happened to me in my quite long life—Your glass is empty, my dear."

"Projected perception," I repeated wonderingly, as I held

out my glass. "Now, if *that* were possible—"

"Oh, there's no doubt about the *possibility*. Those three cases I mentioned are fully authenticated."

"It might be that—almost," I admitted. "At least, in some ways it might be—but not in others. There *is* this nightmare quality. *You* seem perfectly normal to me, but look at me, myself—and at your little maid! There's certainly an element of delusion. I *seem* to be here, like this, and talking to you, but it can't really be so, so where am I?"

"I can understand, better than most, I think, how unreal this must seem to you. In fact, I have spent so much of my time in books that it sometimes seems unreal to me—as if I did not quite belong anywhere. Now, tell me, my dear, when were you born?"

I told her. She thought for a moment.

"H'm," she said. "George the Sixth—but you'd not remember the second big war?"

"No," I agreed.

"But you might remember the coronation of the next monarch? Whose was that?"

"Elizabeth—Elizabeth the Second. My mother took me to see the procession," I told her.

"Do you remember anything about it?"

"Not a lot really—except that it rained, nearly all day," I admitted.

We went on like that for a little while, then she smiled, reassuringly.

"Well, I don't think we need any more to establish our point. I've heard about that coronation before—at secondhand. It must have been a wonderful scene in the Abbey." She mused a moment, and gave a little sigh. "You've been very patient with me, my dear. It is only fair that you should have your turn—but I'm afraid you must prepare yourself for some shocks."

"I think I must be inured after my last thirty-six hours—or what has appeared to be thirty-six hours," I told her.

"I doubt it," she said, looking at me seriously.

"Tell me," I asked her. "Please, explain it all—if you can."

"Your glass, my dear. Then I'll get the crux of it over." She poured for each of us, then she asked:

"What strikes you as the oddest feature of your experience, so far?"

I considered. "There's so much..."

"Might it not be that you have not seen a single man?" she suggested.

I thought back. I remembered the wondering tone of one of the Mothers asking: "What is a man?"

"That's certainly one of them," I agreed. "Where are they?"

She shook her head, watching me steadily.

"There aren't any, my dear. Not any more. None at all."

I simply went on staring at her. Her expression was perfectly serious and sympathetic. There was no trace of guile there or deception while I struggled with the idea. At last I managed:

"But—but that's impossible! There must be some somewhere.... You couldn't—I mean, how—? I mean..." My expostulation trailed off in confusion.

She shook her head.

"I know it must seem impossible to you, Jane—may I call you Jane? But it is so. I am an old woman now, nearly eighty, and in all my long life I have never seen a man—save in old pictures and photographs. Drink your sherry, my dear. It will do you good." She paused. "I'm afraid this upsets you."

I obeyed, too bewildered for further comment at the moment, protesting inwardly, yet not altogether disbelieving, for certainly I had not seen one man, nor sign of any. She went on quietly, giving me time to collect my wits:

"I can understand a little how you must feel. I haven't had to learn all my history entirely from books, you see. When I was a girl, sixteen or seventeen, I used to listen a lot to my grandmother. She was as old then as I am now, but her memory of her youth was still very good. I was able almost to see the places she talked about—but they were part of such a different world that it was difficult for me to understand how she felt. When she spoke about the young man she had been engaged to, tears would roll down her cheeks, even then— not just for him, of course, but for the whole world that she had known as a girl. I was sorry for her, although I could not really understand how she felt—how should I? But now that I am old, too, and have read so much, I am perhaps a little nearer to understanding her feelings, I think." She looked at me curiously. "And you, my dear. Perhaps you, too, were engaged to be married?"

"I was married—for a little time," I told her.

She contemplated that for some seconds, then:

"It must be a very strange experience to be owned," she remarked, reflectively.

"Owned?" I exclaimed in astonishment.

"Ruled by a husband," she explained, sympathetically.

I stared at her.

"But it—it wasn't like that—it wasn't like that at all," I protested. "It was..." But there I broke off, with tears too close. To steer her away I asked:

"But what happened? What on earth happened to the men?"

"They all died," she told me. "They fell sick. Nobody could do anything for them, so they died. In a little more than a year they were all gone—all but a very few."

"But surely—surely everything would collapse?"

"Oh, yes. Very largely it did. It was very bad. There was a dreadful lot of starvation. The industrial parts were the worst hit, of course. In the more backward countries and in rural areas women were able to turn to the land and till it to keep themselves and their children alive, but almost all the large organizations broke down entirely. Transport ceased very soon: petrol ran out, and no coal was being mined. It was quite a dreadful state of affairs because, although there were a great many women, and they had outnumbered the men, in fact, they had only really been important as consumers and spenders of money. So when they crisis came it turned out that scarcely any of them knew how to do any of the important things because they had nearly all been owned by men, and had to lead their lives as pets and parasites."

I started to protest, but her frail hand waved me aside.

"It wasn't their *fault*—not entirely," she explained. "They were caught up in a process, and everything conspired against their escape. It was a long process, going right back to the eleventh century, in Southern France. The Romantic conception started there as an elegant and amusing fashion for the leisured classes. Gradually, as time went on, it permeated through most levels of society, but it was not until the latter part of the nineteenth century that its commercial possibilities were intelligently perceived, and not until the twentieth that it was really exploited.

"At the beginning of the twentieth century women were starting to have their chance to lead useful, creative, interesting lives. But that did not suit commerce: it needed them much more as mass consumers than as producers—except on the most routine levels. So Romance was adopted and developed as a weapon against their further progress and to promote consumption, and it was used intensively.

"Women must never for a moment be allowed to forget their sex, and compete as equals. Everything had to have a 'feminine angle' which must be different from the masculine angle, and be dinned in without ceasing. It would have been unpopular for manufacturers actually to issue an order 'back to the kitchen,' but there were other ways. A profession without a difference, called 'housewife,' could be invented. The kitchen could be glorified and made more expensive; it could be made to seem desirable, and it could be shown that the way to realize this heart's desire was through marriage. So the presses turned out, by the hundred thousand a week, journals which concentrated the attention of women ceaselessly and relentlessly upon selling themselves to some man in order that they might achieve some small, uneconomic unit of a home upon which money could be spent.

"Whole trades adopted the romantic approach and the glamour was spread thicker and thicker in the articles, the write-ups, and most of all in the advertisements. Romance found a place in everything that women might buy, from underclothes to motorcycles, from health foods to kitchen stoves, from deodorants to foreign travel, until soon they were too bemused to be amused any more.

"The air was filled with frustrated moanings. Women maundered in front of microphones yearning only to 'surrender,' and 'give themselves,' to adore and to be adored. The cinema most of all maintained the propaganda, persuading the main and important part of their audience, which was female, that nothing in life was worth achieving but dewy-eyed passivity in the strong arms of Romance. The pressure became such that the majority of young women spent all their leisure time dreaming of Romance, and the means of securing it. They were brought to a state of honestly believing that to be owned by some man and set down in a little brick box to buy all the things that the manufacturers wanted them to buy would be the highest form of bliss that life could offer."

"But..." I began to protest again. The old lady was now well launched, however, and swept on without a check.

"All this could not help distorting society, of course. The divorce rate went up. Real life simply could not come near to providing the degree of romantic glamour which was being represented as every girl's proper inheritance. There was probably, in the aggregate, more disappointment, disillusion, and dissatisfaction among women than there had ever been before. Yet, with this ridiculous and ornamented ideal grained in by unceasing propaganda, what could a conscientious idealist do but take steps to break up the short-weight marriage she had made, and seek elsewhere for the ideal which was hers, she understood, by right?

"It was a wretched state of affairs brought about by deliberately promoted dissatisfactions; a kind of rat race with, somewhere safely out of reach, the glamorized romantic ideal always luring. Perhaps an exceptional few almost attained it, but, for all except those very few, it was a cruel, tantalizing sham on which they spent themselves, and of course their money, in vain."

This time I did get in my protest.

"But it wasn't like that. Some of what they say may be true—but that's all the superficial part. It didn't feel a bit like the way you put it. I was in it. I *know*."

She shook her head reprovingly.

"There is such a thing as being too close to make a proper evaluation. At a distance we are able to see more clearly. We can perceive it for what it was—a gross and heartless exploitation of the weaker-willed majority. Some women of education and resolution were able to withstand it, of course, but at a cost. There must always be a painful price for resisting majority pressure—even they could not always altogether escape the feeling that they might be wrong, and that the rat racers were having the better time of it.

"You see, the great hopes for the emancipation of women with which the century had started had been outflanked. Purchasing power had passed into the hands of the ill-educated and highly suggestible. The desire for Romance is essentially a selfish wish, and when it is encouraged to dominate every other it breaks down all corporate loyalties. The individual woman thus separated from, and yet at the same time thrust into competition with, all other women was almost defenseless; she became the prey of organized suggestion. When it was represented to her that the lack of certain goods or amenities would be fatal to Romance she became alarmed and, thus, eminently exploitable. She could only believe what she was told, and spent a great deal of time worrying about whether she was doing all the right things to encourage Romance. Thus, she became, in a new, a subtler way, more exploited, more dependent, and less creative than she had ever been before."

"Well," I said, "this is the most curiously unrecognizable account of my world that I have ever heard—it's like something copied, but with all the proportions wrong. And as for 'less creative'—well, perhaps families were smaller, but women still went on having babies. The population was still increasing."

The old lady's eyes dwelt on me a moment.

"You are undoubtedly a thought-child of your time, in some

ways," she observed. "What makes you think there is anything creative about having babies? Would you call a plant-pot creative because seeds grow in it? It is a mechanical operation— and, like most mechanical operations, is most easily performed by the least intelligent. Now, bringing up a child, educating, helping her to become a *person*, that *is* creative. But unfortunately, in the time we are speaking of, women had, in the main, been successfully conditioned into bringing up their daughters to be unintelligent consumers, like themselves."

"But," I said helplessly, "I *know* the time. It's my time. This is all distorted."

"The perspective of history must be truer," she told me again, unimpressed, and went on: "But if what happened *had* to happen, then it chose a fortunate time to happen. A hundred years earlier, even fifty years earlier, it would very likely have meant extinction. Fifty years later might easily have been too late—it might have come upon a world in which all women were profitably restricted to domesticity and consumership. Luckily, however, in the middle of the century women were still entering the professions, and by far the greatest number of professional women was to be found in medicine—which is to say that they were only really numerous in, and skilled in, the very profession which immediately became of vital importance if we were to survive at all.

"I have no medical knowledge, so I cannot give you any details of the steps they took. All I can tell you is that there was intensive research on lines which will probably be more obvious to you than they are to me.

"A species, even our species, has great will to survive, and the doctors saw to it that the will had the means of expression. Through all the hunger, and the chaos, and the other privations, babies somehow continued to be born. That had to be.

Reconstruction could wait: the priority was the new genera-
tion that would help in the reconstruction, and then inherit
it. So babies were born: the girl babies lived, and the boy
babies died. That was distressing, and wasteful, too, and so,
presently, only girl babies were born—again, the means by
which that could be achieved will be easier for you to understand than for me.

"It is, they tell me, not nearly so remarkable as it would
appear at first sight. The locust, it seems, will continue to
produce female locusts without male or any other kind of
assistance; the aphis, too, is able to go on breeding alone and
in seclusion, certainly for eight generations, perhaps more.
So it would be a poor thing if we, with all our knowledge and
powers of research to assist us, should find ourselves inferior
to the locust and the aphis in this respect, would it not?"

She paused, looking at me somewhat quizzically for my response. Perhaps she expected amazed—or possibly shocked—
disbelief. If so, I disappointed her: technical achievements have
ceased to arouse simple wonder since atomic physics showed
how barriers fall before the pressure of a good brains team. One
can take it that most things are possible—whether they are desirable, or worth doing, is a different matter—and one that
seemed to me particularly pertinent to her question. I asked
her:

"And what is it that you have achieved?"

"Survival," she said, simply.

"Materially," I agreed, "I suppose you have. But when it
has cost all the rest, when love, art, poetry, excitement, and
physical joy have all been sacrificed to mere continued existence, what is left but a soulless waste? What reason is there
any longer for survival?"

"As to the reason, I don't know—except that survival is a

desire common to all species. I am quite sure that the *reason* for that desire was no clearer in the twentieth century than it is now. But, for the rest, why should you assume that they are gone? Did not Sappho write poetry? And your assumption that the possession of a soul depends upon a duality of sexes surprises me: it has so often been held that the two are in some sort of conflict, has it not?"

"As a historian who must have studied men, women, and motives you should have taken my meaning better," I told her.

She shook her head with reproof. "You are so much the conditioned product of your age, my dear. They told you, on all levels, from the words of Freud to that of the most nugatory magazines for women, that it was sex, civilized into romantic love, that made the world go round—and you believed them. But the world continues to go round for others, too—for the insects, the fish, the birds, the animals—and how much do you suppose they know of romantic love, even in their brief mating seasons? They hoodwinked you, my dear. Between them they channeled your interests and ambitions along courses that were socially convenient, economically profitable, and almost harmless."

I shook my head.

"I just don't believe it. Oh, yes, you know something of my world—from the outside. But you don't understand it, or feel it."

"That's your conditioning, my dear," she told me, calmly.

Her repeated assumption irritated me. I asked:

"Suppose I were to believe what you say, what is it, then, that *does* make the world go round?"

"That's simple, my dear. It is the will to power. We have that as babies; we have it still in old age. It occurs in men and women alike. It is more fundamental, and more desirable, than sex; I tell you, you were misled—exploited, sublimated for economic convenience.

"After the disease had struck, women ceased, for the first time in history, to be an exploited class. Without male rulers to confuse and divert them they began to perceive that all true power resides in the female principle. The male had served only one brief useful purpose; for the rest of his life he was a painful and costly parasite.

"As they became aware of power, the doctors grasped it. In twenty years they were in full control. With them were the few women engineers, architects, lawyers, administrators, some teachers, and so on, but it was the doctors who held the keys of life and death. The future was in their hands and, as things began gradually to revive, they, together with the other professions, remained the dominant class and became known as the Doctorate. It assumed authority; it made the laws, it enforced them.

"There was opposition, of course. Neither the memory of the old days, nor the effect of twenty years of lawlessness, could be wiped out at once, but the doctors had the whip hand—any woman who wanted a child had to come to them, and they saw to it that she was satisfactorily settled in a community. The roving gangs dwindled away, and gradually order was restored.

"Later on, they faced better organized opposition. There was a party which contended that the disease which had struck down the men had run its course, and the balance could, and should, be restored—they were known as Reactionists, and they became an embarrassment.

"Most of the Council of the Doctorate still had clear memories of a system which used every weakness of women, and had been no more than a more civilized culmination of their exploitation through the ages. They remembered how they themselves had only grudgingly been allowed to qualify for their careers. They were now in command: they felt no obligation to surrender their power and authority, and eventually, no doubt, their freedom, to a creature whom they had proved to be biologically, and in all other ways, expendable. They refused unanimously to take a step that would lead to corporate suicide, and the Reactionists were proscribed as a subversive criminal organization.

"That, however, was just a palliative. It quickly became clear that they were attacking a symptom and neglecting the cause. The Council was driven to realize that it had an unbalanced society at its hands—a society that was capable of continuity, but was in structure, you might say, little more than the residue of a vanished form. It could not continue in that truncated shape and, as long as it tried to, disaffection would increase. Therefore, if power were to become stable, a new form suitable to the circumstances must be found.

"In deciding the shape it shoud take, the natural tendencies of the little-educated and uneducated woman were carefully considered—such qualities as her feeling for hierarchical principles and her disposition to respect artificial distinctions. You will no doubt recollect that in your own time any fool of a woman whose husband was ennobled or honored at once acquired increased respect and envy from other women though she remained the same fool; and also, that any gathering or society of unoccupied women would soon become obsessionally enmeshed in the creation and preservation of social distinctions. Allied to this is the high value they usually place upon a feeling of security. Important, too, is the capacity for devoted self-sacrifice, and slavery to conscience within the canons of any local convention. We are naturally very biddable creatures. Most of us are happiest when we are being ortho-dox, however odd our customs may appear to an outsider; the difficulty in handling us lies chiefly in establishing the re-quired standards of orthodoxy.

"Obviously, the broad outline of a system which was going to stand any chance of success would have to provide scope for these and other characteristic traits. It must be a scheme where the interplay of forces would preserve equilibrium and respect for authority. The details of such an organization, how-ever, were less easy to determine.

"An extensive study of social forms and orders was under-taken, but for several years every plan put forward was re-jected as in some way unsuitable. The architecture of that finally chosen was said, though I do not know with how much truth, to have been inspired by the Bible—a book at that time still unprohibited, and the source of much unrest. I am told that it ran something like: 'Go to the ant, thou sluggard; consider her ways.'

"The Council appears to have felt that this advice, suitably modified, could be expected to lead to a state of affairs which would provide most of the requisite characteristics.

"A four-class system was chosen as the basis, and strong differentiations were gradually introduced. These, now that they have become well established, greatly help to ensure stability: there is scope for ambition within one's class, but none for passing from one class to another. Thus, we have the Doctorate—the educated ruling classes, fifty percent of whom are actually of the medical profession. The Mothers, whose title is self-explanatory. The Servitors, who are numerous and, for psychological reasons, small. The Workers, who are phys-ically and muscularly strong, to do the heavier work. All the three lower classes respect the authority of the Doctorate. Both the employed classes revere the Mothers. The Servitors consider themselves more favored in their tasks than the Workers; and the Workers tend to regard the puniness of the Servitors with semiaffectionate contempt.

"So you see a balance has been struck, and though it works somewhat crudely as yet, no doubt it will improve. It seems likely, for instance, that it would be advantageous to introduce subdvisions into the Servitor class before long, and the police are thought by some to be put at a disadvantage by having no more than a little education to distinguish them from the ordinary Worker. . . ."

She went on explaining with increasing detail while the enormity of the whole process gradually grew upon me.

"Ants!" I broke in, suddenly. "The ant nest! You've taken *that* for your model?"

She looked surprised, either at my tone, or the fact that what she was saying had taken so long to register.

"And why not?" she asked. "Surely it is one of the most enduring social patterns that nature has evolved—though of course some adaptation—"

"You're—are you telling me that only the Mothers have children?" I demanded.

"Oh, members of the Doctorate do, too, when they wish," she assured me.

"But . . . but . . ."

"The Council decides the ratios," she went on to explain. "The doctors at the clinic examine the babies and allocate them suitably to the different classes. After that, of course, it is just a matter of seeing to their specialized feeding, glandular control, and proper training."

"But," I objected wildly, "what's it *for?* Where's the sense in it? What's the good of being alive, like that?"

"Well, what *is* the sense in being alive? You tell me," she suggested.

"But we're *meant* to love and be loved, to have babies we love by people we love."

"There's your conditioning again; glorifying and romanticizing primitive animalism. Surely you consider that we are superior to the animals?"

"Of course I do, but—"

"Love, you say, but what can you know of the love there can be between mother and daughter when there are no men to introduce jealousy? Do you know of any purer sentiment than the love of a girl for her little sisters?"

"But you don't understand," I protested again. "How should you understand a love that colors the whole world? How it centers in your heart and reaches out from there to pervade your whole being, how it can affect everything you are, everything you touch, everything you hear. . . . It can hurt dreadfully, I know, oh, I know, but it can run like sunlight in your veins. . . . It can make you a garden out of a slum; brocade out of rags; music out of a speaking voice. It can show you a whole universe in someone else's eyes. Oh, you don't understand . . . you don't know . . . you can't. . . . Oh, Donald, darling, how can I show her what she's never even guessed at . . . ?"

There was an uncertain pause, but presently she said:

"Naturally, in your form of society it was necessary for you to be given such a conditioned reaction, but you can scarcely expect us to surrender our freedom, to connive at our own resubjection by calling our oppressors into existence again."

"Oh, you *won't* understand. It was only the more stupid

men and women who were continually at war with one another. Lots of us were complementary. We were pairs who formed units."

She smiled. "My dear, either you are surprisingly ill-informed on your own period, or else the stupidity you speak of was astonishingly dominant. Neither as myself, nor as a historian, can I consider that we should be justified in resurrecting such a state of affairs. A primitive stage of our development has now given way to a civilized era. Woman, who is the vessel of life, had the misfortune to find man necessary for a time, but now she does so no longer. Are you suggesting that such a useless and dangerous encumbrance ought to be preserved, out of sheer sentimentality? I will admit that we have lost some minor conveniences—you will have noticed, I expect, that we are less inventive mechanically, and tend to copy the patterns we have inherited; but that troubles us very little; our interests lie not in the inorganic, but in the organic and the sentient. Perhaps men could show us how to travel twice as fast, or how to fly to the moon, or how to kill more people more quickly; but it does not seem to us that such kinds of knowledge would be good payment for reenslaving ourselves. No, our kind of world suits us better—all of us except a few Reactionists. You have seen our Servitors. They are a little timid in manner, perhaps, but are they oppressed, or sad? Don't they chatter among themselves as brightly and perkily as sparrows? And the Workers—those you called the Amazons—don't they look strong, healthy, and cheerful?"

"But you're robbing them all—robbing them of their birthright."

"You mustn't give me cant, my dear. Did not your social system conspire to rob a woman of her 'birthright' unless she married? You not only let her know it, but socially you rubbed it in. Here, our Servitors and Workers do not know it, and they are not worried by a sense of inadequacy. Motherhood is the function of the Mothers, and understood as such."

I shook my head. "Nevertheless, they *are* being robbed. A woman has a right to love..."

For once she was a little impatient as she cut me short.

"You keep repeating to me the propaganda of your age. The love you talk about, my dear, existed in your little sheltered part of the world by polite and profitable convention. You were scarcely ever allowed to see its other face, unglamourized by Romance, *You* were never openly bought and sold, like livestock; *you* never had to sell yourself to the first comer in order to live; *you* did not happen to be one of the women who through the centuries screamed in agony and suffered and died under invaders in a sacked city—nor were you ever flung into a pit of fire to be saved from them; *you* were never compelled to suttee upon your dead husband's pyre; *you* did not have to spend your whole life imprisoned in a harem; *you* were never part of the cargo of a slave ship; *you* never retained your own life only at the pleasure of your lord and master....

"That is the other side—the age-long side. There is going to be no more of such things. They are finished at last. Dare you suggest that we should call them back, to suffer them all again?"

"But most of these things had already gone," I protested. "The world was getting better."

"Was it?" she said. "I wonder if the women of Berlin thought so when it fell? Was it, indeed? Or was it on the edge of a new barbarism?"

"But if you can only get rid of evil by throwing out the good, too, what is there left?"

"There is a great deal. Man was only a means to an end.

We needed him in order to have babies. The rest of his vitality accounted for all the misery in the world. We are a great deal better off without him."

"So you really consider that you've improved on nature?"

"Tcha!" she said, impatient with my tone. "Civilization *is* improvement on nature. Would you want to live in a cave and have most of your babies die in infancy?"

"There are some things, some fundamental things..." I began, but she checked me, holding up her hand for silence.

Outside, the long shadows had crept across the lawns. In the evening quiet I could hear a choir of women's voices singing some little distance away. We listened for some minutes until the song was finished.

"Beautiful!" said the old lady. "Could angels themselves sing more sweetly? They sound happy enough, don't they? Our own lovely children—two of my granddaughters are there among them. They are happy, and they've reason to be happy: they're not growing up into a world where they must gamble on the goodwill of some man to keep them; they'll never need to be servile before a lord and master; they'll never stand in danger of rape and butchery, either. Listen to them!"

Another song had started and came lilting lightly to us out of the dusk.

"Why are you crying?" the old lady asked me as it ended.

"I know it's stupid—I don't really believe any of this is what it seems to be—so I suppose I'm crying for all you would have lost if it were true," I told her. "There should be lovers out there under the trees; they should be listening hand in hand to that song while they watch the moon rise. But there are no lovers now, there won't be any more..." I looked back at her.

"Did you ever read the lines: 'Full many a flower is born to blush unseen, and waste its sweetness on the desert air'? Can't you feel the forlornness of this world you've made? Do you *really* not understand?" I asked.

"I know you've only seen a little of us, but do *you* not begin to understand what it can be like when women are no longer forced to fight one another for the favors of men?" she countered.

We talked on while the dusk gave way to darkness and the lights of other houses started to twinkle through the trees. Her reading had been wide. It had given her even an affection for some periods of the past, but her approval of her own era was unshaken. She felt no aridity in it. Always it was my "conditioning" which prevented me from seeing that the golden age of woman had begun at last.

"You cling to too many myths," she told me. "You speak of a full life, and your instance is some unfortunate woman hugging her chains in a suburban villa. Full life, fiddlesticks! But it was convenient for the traders that she could be made to think so. A truly full life would be an exceedingly short one, in any form of society."

And so on....

At length, the little parlormaid reappeared to say that my attendants were ready to leave when it should be convenient. But there was one thing I very much wanted to know before I left. I put the question to the old lady.

"Please tell me. How did it—how could it—happen?"

"Simply by accident, my dear—though it was the kind of accident that was entirely the product of its time. A piece of research which showed unexpected, secondary results, that's all."

"But how?"

"Rather curiously—almost irrelevantly, you might say. Did you ever hear of a man called Perrigan?"

"Perrigan?" I repeated. "I don't think so; it's an uncommon name."

"It became very commonly known indeed," she assured me. "Doctor Perrigan was a biologist, and his concern was the extermination of rats—particularly the brown rat, which used to do a great deal of expensive damage.

"His approach to the problem was to find a disease which would attack them fatally. In order to produce it he took as his basis a virus infection often fatal to rabbits—or, rather, a group of virus infections that were highly selective, and also unstable since they were highly liable to mutation. Indeed, there was so much variation in the strains that when infection of rabbits in Australia was tried, it was only at the sixth attempt that it was successful; all the earlier strains died out as the rabbits developed immunity. It was tried in other places, too, though with indifferent success until a still more effective strain was started in France, and ran through the rabbit population of Europe.

"Well, taking some of these viruses as a basis, Perrigan induced new mutations by irradiation and other means, and succeeded in producing a variant that would attack rats. That was not enough, however, and he continued his work until he had a strain that had enough of its ancestral selectivity to attack only the brown rat, and with great virulence.

"In that way he settled the question of a long-standing pest, for there are no brown rats now. But something went amiss. It is still an open question whether the successful virus mutated again, or whether one of his earlier experimental viruses was accidentally liberated by escaped 'carrier' rats, but that's academic. The important thing is that somehow a strain capable of attacking human beings got loose, and that it was already widely disseminated before it was traced—also, that once it was free, it spread with devastating speed; too fast for any effective steps to be taken to check it.

"The majority of women were found to be immune; and of the ten percent or so whom it attacked over eight percent recovered. Among men, however, there was almost no immunity, and the few recoveries were only partial. A few men were preserved by the most elaborate precautions, but they could not be kept confined forever, and in the end the virus which had a remarkable capacity for dormancy, got them, too."

Inevitably several questions of professional interest occurred to me, but for an answer she shook her head.

"I'm afraid I can't help you there. Possibly the medical people will be willing to explain," she said, but her expression was doubtful.

I maneuvered myself into a sitting position on the side of the couch.

"I see," I said. "Just an accident—yes, I suppose one could scarcely think of it happening any other way."

"Unless," she remarked, "unless one were to look upon it as divine intervention."

"Isn't that a little impious?"

"I was thinking of the Death of the Firstborn," she said, reflectively.

There did not seem to be an immediate answer to that. Instead, I asked:

"Can you honestly tell me that you never have the feeling that you are living in a dreary kind of nightmare?"

"Never," she said. "There *was* a nightmare—but it's over now. Listen!"

The voices of the choir, reinforced now by an orchestra, reached us distantly out of the darkened garden. No, they were not dreary; they even sounded almost exultant—but then, poor things, how were they to understand...?

My attendants arrived and helped me to my feet. I thanked the old lady for her patience with me and her kindness. But she shook her head.

"My dear, it is I who am indebted to you. In a short time I have learned more about the conditioning of women in a mixed society than all my books have been able to show me in the rest of the my long life. I hope, my dear, that the doctors will find some way of enabling you to forget it and live happily here with us."

At the door I paused and turned, still helpfully shored up by my attendants.

"Laura," I said, using her name for the first time, "so many of your arguments are right—yet, over all, you're, oh, so *wrong*. Did you never read of lovers? Did you never, as a girl, sigh for a Romeo who would say: 'It is the east, and Laura is the sun'?"

"I think not. Though I have read the play. A pretty, idealized tale—I wonder how much heartbreak it has given to how many would-be Juliets? But I would set a question against yours, my dear Jane. Did you ever see Goya's cycle of pictures called 'The Horrors of War'?"

The pink car did not return me to the "Home." Our destination turned out to be a more austere and hospital-like building where I was fussed into bed in a room alone. In the morning, after my massive breakfast, three new doctors visited me. Their manner was more social than professional, and we chatted amiably for half an hour. They had evidently been fully informed on my conversation with the old lady, and they were not averse to answering my questions. Indeed, they found some amusement in many of them, though I found none, for there was nothing consolingly vague in what they told me—it all sounded too disturbingly practicable, once the technique had been worked out. At the end of that time, however, their mood changed. One of them, with an air of getting down to business, said:

"You will understand that you present us with a problem. Your fellow Mothers, of course, are scarcely susceptible to Reactionist disaffection—though you have in quite a short time managed to disgust and bewilder them considerably—but on others less stable your influence might be more serious. It is not just a matter of what you may say; your difference from the rest is implicit in your whole attitude. You cannot help that, and, frankly, we do not see how you, as a woman of education, could possibly adapt yourself to the placid, unthinking acceptance that is expected of a Mother. You would quickly feel frustrated beyond endurance. Furthermore, it is clear that the conditioning you have had under your system prevents you from feeling any goodwill towards ours."

I took that straight; simply as a judgment without bias. Moreover, I could not dispute it. The prospect of spending the rest of my life in pink, scented, soft-musicked illiteracy, interrupted, one gathered, only by the production of quadruplet daughters at regular intervals, would certainly have me violently unhinged in a very short time.

"And so—what?" I asked. "Can you reduce this great carcass to normal shape and size?"

She shook her head. "I imagine not—though I don't know that it has ever been attempted. But even if it were possible, you would be just as much of a misfit in the Doctorate—and far more of a liability as a Reactionist influence."

I could understand that, too.

"What, then?" I inquired.

She hesitated, then she said gently:

"The only practicable proposal we can make is that you should agree to a hypnotic treatment which will remove your memory."

As the meaning of that came home to me I had to fight off a rush of panic. After all, I told myself, they were being reasonable with me. I must do my best to respond sensibly. Nevertheless, some minutes must have passed before I answered, unsteadily.

"You are asking me to commit suicide. My mind is my memories: they are me. If I lose them I shall die, just as surely as if you were to kill my—this body."

They did not dispute that. How could they?

There is just one thing that makes my life worth living— knowing that you loved me, my sweet, sweet Donald. It is only in my memory that you live now. If you ever leave there you will die again—and forever.

"No!" I told them. "No! No!"

At intervals during the day small servitors staggered in under the weight of my meals. In between their visits I had only my thoughts to occupy me, and they were not good company.

"Frankly," one of the doctors had put it to me, not unsympathetically, "we can see no alternative. For years after it happened the annual figures of mental breakdowns were our greatest worry. Even though the women then could keep themselves fully occupied with the tremendous amount of work that had to be done, so many of them could not adjust. And we can't even offer you work."

I knew that it was a fair warning she was giving me—and I knew that, unless the hallucination which seemed to grow more real all the time could soon be induced to dissolve, I was trapped.

During the long day and the following night I tried my hardest to get back to the objectivity I had managed earlier, but I failed. The whole dialectic was too strong for me now; my senses too consciously aware of my surroundings; the air of consequence and coherence too convincingly persistent.

When they had let me have twenty-four hours to think it over, the same trio visited me again.

"I think," I told them, "that I understand now. What you are offering me is painless oblivion, in place of a breakdown followed by oblivion—and you see no other choice."

"We don't," admitted the spokeswoman, and the other two nodded. "But, of course, for the hypnosis we shall need your cooperation."

"I realize that," I told her, "and I also see now that in the circumstances it would be obstinately futile to withhold it. So I—I—yes, I'm willing to give it—but on one condition."

They looked at me questioningly.

"It is this," I explained, "that you will try one other course first. I want you to give me an injection of chuinjuatin. I want it in precisely the same strength as I had it before—I can tell you the dose.

"You see, whether this is an intense hallucination, or whether it is some kind of projection which makes it seem very similar, it must have something to do with that drug. I'm sure it must—nothing remotely like this has ever happened to me

before. So, I thought that if I could repeat the condition—
or, would you say, believe myself to be repeating the condition?—there may be just a chance ... I don't know. It may
be simply silly ... but even if nothing comes of it, it can't
make things worse in any way now, can it? So, if you will let
me try it?"

The three of them considered for some moments.

"I can see no reason why not ..." said one.

The spokeswoman nodded.

"I shouldn't think there'll be any difficulty with authoriza-
tion in the circumstances," she agreed. "If you want to try,
well, it's fair to let you, but—I'd not count on it too much. ..."

In the afternoon half a dozen small servitors arrived, bus-
tling round, making me and the room ready, with anxious
industry. Presently there came one more, scarcely tall enough
to see over the trolley of bottles, trays, and phials which she
pushed to my bedside.

The three doctors entered together. One of the little servitors began rolling up my sleeve. The doctor who had done
most of the talking looked at me, kindly, but seriously.

"This is a sheer gamble, you know that?" she said.

"I know. But it's my only chance. I'm willing to take it."

She nodded, picked up the syringe, and charged it while
the little servitor swabbed my monstrous arm. She approached the bedside, and hesitated.

"Go on," I told her. "What is there for me here, anyway?"

She nodded, and pressed in the needle.

Now, I have written the foregoing for a purpose. I shall
deposit it with my bank, where it will remain unread unless
it should be needed.

I have spoken of it to no one. The report on the effect of

chuinjuatin—the one that I made to Dr. Hellyer where I described my sensation as simply one of floating in space—was false. The foregoing was my true experience.

I concealed it because after I came round, when I found that I was back in my own body in my normal world, the experience haunted me as vividly as if it had been actuality. The details were too sharp, too vivid, for me to get them out of my mind. It overhung me all the time, like a threat. It would not leave me alone....

I did not dare to tell Dr. Hellyer how it worried me—he would have put me under treatment. If my other friends did not take it seriously enough to recommend treatment, too, then they would have laughed over it, and amused themselves at my expense interpreting the symbolism. So I kept it to myself.

As I went over parts of it again and again in detail, I grew angry with myself for not asking the old lady for more facts, things like dates, and details that could be verified. If, for instance, the thing should, by her account, have started two or three years ago, then the whole sense of threat would fall to pieces: it would all be discredited. But it had not occurred to me to ask that crucial question. And then, as I went on thinking about it, I remembered that there was one, just one, piece of information that I could check, and I made inquiries. I wish now that I had not, but I felt forced to....

So I have discovered that:

There *is* a Dr. Perrigan, he *is* a biologist, he does work with rabbits and rats.

He is quite well known in his field. He has published papers on pest control in a number of journals. It is no secret that he is evolving new strains of myxomatosis to attack rats; indeed, he has already developed a group of them and calls them mucosimorbus, though he has not yet succeeded in making them either stable or selective enough for general use.

But I had never heard of this man or his work until his name was mentioned by the old lady in my "hallucination."

I have given a great deal of thought to this whole matter. What sort of experience is it that I have recorded above? If it should be a kind of prevision of an inevitable, predestined future, then nothing anyone could do would change it. But this does not seem to me to make sense; it is what has happened, and is happening now, that determines the future. Therefore, there must be a great number of *possible* futures, each a possible consequence of what is being done now. It seems to me that under chuinjuatin I saw *one* of those futures.

It was, I think, a warning of what *may* happen—unless it is prevented.

The whole idea is so repulsive and misconceived, it amounts to such a monstrous aberration of the normal course, that failure to heed the warning would be neglect of duty to one's kind.

I shall, therefore, on my own responsibility and without taking any other person into my confidence, do my best to ensure that such a state as I have described *cannot* come about.

Should it happen that any other person is unjustly accused of doing, or of assisting me to do, what I intend to do, this document must stand in his defence. That is why I have written it.

It is my own unaided decision that Dr. Perrigan must not be permitted to continue his work.

(Signed) JANE WATERLEIGH.

The solicitor stared at the signature for some moments; then e nodded.

"And so," he said, "she then took her car and drove over ɔ Perrigan's—with this tragic result.

"From the little I do know of her, I'd say that she probably id her best to persuade him to give up his work—though he can scarcely have expected any success with that. It is ifficult to imagine a man who would be willing to give up he work of years on account of what must sound to him like sort of gipsy's warning. So, clearly, she went prepared to ll back on direct action, if necessary. It looks as if the police re quite right when they suppose her to have shot him deberately; but not so right when they suppose that she burnt he place down to hide evidence of the crime. The statement nakes it pretty obvious that her main intention in doing that ⱱas to wipe out Perrigan's work."

He shook his head. "Poor girl! There's a clear conviction of uty in her last page or two: the sort of simplified clarity that rives martyrs on, regardless of consequences. She has never enied that she did it. What she wouldn't tell the police is ⱨy she did it."

He paused again, before he added: "Anyway, thank goodess for this document. It ought at least to save her life. I hould be very surprised indeed if a plea of insanity could il, backed up by this." He tapped the pile of manuscript ⱱith his finger. "It's a lucky thing she put off her intention of ⱥking it to her bank."

Dr. Hellyer's face was lined and worried.

"I blame myself most bitterly for the whole thing," he said. I never ought to have let her try the damned drug in the rst place, but I thought she was over the shock of her husand's death. She was trying to keep her time fully occupied, and she was anxious to volunteer. You've met her enough to know how purposeful she can be. She saw it as a chance to contribute something to medical knowledge—which it was of course. But I ought to have been more careful, and I ought to have seen afterwards that there was something wrong. The real responsibility for this thing runs right back to me."

"H'm," said the solicitor. "Putting that forward as a main line of defense isn't going to do you a lot of good professionally you know, Hellyer."

"Possibly not. I can look after that when we come to it. The point is that I hold a responsibility for her as a member of my staff, if for no other reason. It can't be denied that, if I had refused her offer to take part in the experiment, this would not have happened. Therefore it seems to me that we ought to be able to argue a state of temporary insanity; that the balance of her mind was disturbed by the effects of the drug which I administered. And if we can get that as a verdict it will result in detention at a mental hospital for observation and treatment—perhaps quite a short spell of treatment."

"I can't say. We can certainly put it up to counsel and see what he thinks of it."

"It's valid, too," Hellyer persisted. "People like Jane don't do murder if they are in their right minds, not unless they're really in a corner, then they do it more cleverly. Certainly they don't murder perfect strangers. Clearly, the drug caused an hallucination sufficiently vivid to confuse her to a point where she was unable to make a proper distinction between the actual and the hypothetical. She got into a state where she believed the mirage was real, and acted accordingly."

"Yes. Yes, I suppose one might put it that way," agreed the solicitor. He looked down again at the pile of paper before him. "The whole account is, of course, unreasonable," he said "and yet it is pervaded throughout with such an air of reasonableness. I wonder..." He paused pensively, and went on: "This expendability of the male, Hellyer. She doesn't seem to find it so much incredible, as undesirable. That seems odd in itself to a layman who takes the natural order for granted, but would you, as a medical scientist, say it was—well, not impossible, in theory?"

Dr. Hellyer frowned.

"That's very much the kind of question one wants more notice of. It would be very rash to proclaim it *impossible*. Considering it purely as an abstract problem, I can see two or three lines of approach. ... Of course, if an utterly improbable situation were to arise calling for intensive research—research, that is, on the sort of scale they tackled the atom—well, who can tell...?" He shrugged.

The solicitor nodded again.

"That's just what I was getting at," he observed. "Basically it is only just such a little way off the beam; quite near enough to possibility to be faintly disturbing. Mind you, as far as the defense is concerned, her air of thorough conviction, taken in conjunction with the near plausibility of the thing, will probably help. But as far as I am concerned it is just that nearness that is enough to make me a trifle uneasy."

The doctor looked at him rather sharply.

"Oh, come! Really now! A hard-boiled solicitor, too! Don't tell me you're going in for fantasy-building. Anyway, if you are, you'll have to conjure up another one. If Jane, poor girl, has settled one thing, it is that there's no future in this particular fantasy. Perrigan's finished with, and all his work's gone up in smoke."

"H'm," said the solicitor again. "All the same, it would be more satisfactory if we knew of some way other than this"—

he tapped the pile of papers—"some other way in which she is likely to have acquired a knowledge of Perrigan and his work. There is, as far as one knows, *no* other way in which he can have come into her orbit at all—unless, perhaps, she takes an interest in veterinary subjects?"

"She doesn't. I'm sure of that," Hellyer told him, shaking his head.

"Well, that, then, remains one slightly disturbing aspect. And there is another. You'll think it foolish of me, I'm sure, and no doubt time will prove you right to do so—but I have to admit I'd be feeling easier in my mind if Jane had been just a bit more thorough in her inquiries before she went into action."

"Meaning—?" asked Dr. Hellyer, puzzled.

"Only that she does not seem to have found out that there is a son. But there is, you see. He appears to have taken quite a close interest in his father's work, and is determined that it shan't be wasted. In fact he has already announced that he will do his best to carry it on with the very few specimens that were saved from the fire. . . .

"Laudably filial, no doubt. All the same it does disturb me a little to find that he, also, happens to be D.Sc., a biochemist, and that, very naturally, his name, too, is Perrigan."

VINTAGE SEASON

by
Henry Kuttner and
C. L. Moore

The husband-and-wife writing team of Kuttner and Moore was one of the great collaborations of all time—indeed, it was impossible to tell who did what; even the authors claimed not to know. In "Vintage Season" (originally published as by "Lawrence O'Donnell") they explore the commercial possibilities of time travel and show us some of the most interesting tourists in all of literature.

Three people came up the walk to the old mansion just at dawn on a perfect May morning. Oliver Wilson in his pajamas watched them from an upper window through a haze of conflicting emotions, resentment predominant. He didn't want them there.

They were foreigners. He knew only that much about them. They had the curious name of Sancisco, and their first names scrawled in loops on the lease, appeared to be Omerie, Kleph, and Klia, though it was impossible as he looked down upon them to sort them out by signature. He hadn't even been sure whether they would be men or women, and he had expected something a little less cosmopolitan.

Oliver's heart sank a little as he watched them follow the taxi driver up the walk. He had hoped for less self-assurance

225

in his unwelcome tenants, because he meant to force them
out of the house if he could. It didn't look very promising
from here.

The man went first. He was tall and dark, and he wore his
clothes and carried his body with that peculiar arrogant assurance that comes from perfect confidence in every phase of
one's being. The two women were laughing as they followed
him. Their voices were light and sweet, and their faces were
beautiful, each in its own exotic way, but the first thing Oliver
thought of when he looked at them was: Expensive!

It was not only that patina of perfection that seemed to
dwell in every line of their incredibly flawless garments. There
are degrees of wealth beyond which wealth itself ceases to
have significance. Oliver had seen before, on rare occasions,
something like this assurance that the earth turning beneath
their well-shod feet turned only to their whim.

It puzzled him a little in this case, because he had the
feeling as the three came up the walk that the beautiful clothing they wore so confidently was not clothing they were accustomed to. There was a curious air of condescension in the
way they moved. Like women in costume. They minced a
little on their delicate high heels, held out an arm to stare at
the cut of a sleeve, twisted now and then inside their garments
as if the clothing sat strangely on them, as if they were accustomed to something entirely different.

And there was an elegance about the way the garments
fitted them which even to Oliver looked strikingly unusual.
Only an actress on the screen, who can stop time and the film
to adjust every disarrayed fold so that she looks perpetually
perfect, might appear thus elegantly clad. But let these women
move as they liked, and each fold of their clothing followed

perfectly with the movement and fell perfectly into place again. One might almost suspect the garments were not cut of ordinary cloth, or that they were cut according to some unknown, subtle scheme, with many artful hidden seams placed by a tailor incredibly skilled at his trade.

They seemed excited. They talked in high, clear, very sweet voices, looking up at the perfect blue and transparent sky in which dawn was still frankly pink. They looked at the trees on the lawn, the leaves translucently green with an under color of golden newness, the edges crimped from constriction in the recent bud.

Happily and with excitement in their voices they called to the man, and when he answered his own voice blended so perfectly in cadence with theirs that it sounded like three people singing together. Their voices, like their clothing, seemed to have an elegance far beyond the ordinary, to be under a control such as Oliver Wilson had never dreamed of before this morning.

The taxi driver brought up the luggage, which was of a beautiful pale stuff that did not look quite like leather, and had curves in it so subtle it seemed square until you saw how two or three pieces of it fitted together, when carried, into a perfectly balanced block. It was scuffed, as if from much use. And though there was a great deal of it, the taxi man did not seem to find his burden heavy. Oliver saw him look down at it now and then and heft the weight incredulously.

One of the women had very black hair and skin like cream and smoke-blue eyes heavy-lidded with the weight of her lashes. It was the other woman Oliver's gaze followed as she came up the walk. Her hair was a clear, pale red, and her face had a softness that he thought would be like velvet to touch. She was tanned to a warm amber darker than her hair.

Just as they reached the porch steps the fair woman lifted her head and looked up. She gazed straight into Oliver's eyes and he saw that hers were very blue, and just a little amused, as if she had known he was there all along. Also they were frankly admiring.

Feeling a bit dizzy, Oliver hurried back to his room to dress.

"We are here on a vacation," the dark man said, accepting the keys. "We will not wish to be disturbed, as I made clear in our correspondence. You have engaged a cook and house-maid for us, I understand? We will expect you to move your own belongings out of the house, then, and..."

"Wait," Oliver said uncomfortably. "Something's come up, I—" He hesitated, not sure just how to present it. These were such increasingly odd people. Even their speech was odd. They spoke so distinctly, not slurring any of the words into contractions. English seemed as familiar to them as a native tongue, but they all spoke as trained singers sing, with perfect breath control and voice placement.

And there was a coldness in the man's voice, as if some gulf lay between him and Oliver, so deep no feeling of human contact could bridge it.

"I wonder," Oliver said, "if I could find you better living quarters somewhere else in town. There's a place across the street that..."

The dark woman said, "Oh, no!" in a lightly horrified voice, and all three of them laughed. It was cool, distant laughter that did not include Oliver.

The dark man said, "We chose this house carefully, Mr. Wilson. We would not be interested in living anywhere else."

Oliver said desperately, "I don't see why. It isn't even a modern house. I have two others in much better condition. Even across the street you'd have a fine view of the city. Here there isn't anything. The other houses cut off the view, and..."

"We engaged rooms here, Mr. Wilson," the man said with finality. "We expect to use them. Now will you make arrangements to leave as soon as possible."

Oliver said, "No," and looked stubborn. "That isn't in the lease. You can live here until next month, since you paid for it, but you can't put me out. I'm staying."

The man opened his mouth to say something. He looked coldly at Oliver and closed it again. The feeling of aloofness was chill between them. There was a moment's silence. Then the man said, "Very well. Be kind enough to stay out of our way."

It was a little odd that he didn't inquire into Oliver's motives. Oliver was not yet sure enough of the man to explain. He couldn't very well say, "Since the lease was signed, I've been offered three times what the house is worth if I'll sell it before the end of May." He couldn't say, "I want the money, and I'm going to use my own nuisance-value to annoy you until you're willing to move out." After all, there seemed no reason why they shouldn't. After seeing them, there seemed doubly no reason, for it was clear they must be accustomed to surroundings infinitely better than this timeworn old house.

It was very strange, the value this house had so suddenly acquired. There was no reason at all why two groups of semi-anonymous people should be so eager to possess it for the month of May.

In silence Oliver showed his tenants upstairs to the three big bedrooms across the front of the house. He was intensely conscious of the red-haired woman and the way she watched him with a sort of obviously covert interest, quite warmly, and with a curious undertone to her interest that he could not quite place. It was familiar, but elusive. He thought how pleasant it would be to talk to her alone, if only to try to capture that elusive attitude and put a name to it.

Afterwards he went down to the telephone and called his fiancée.

Sue's voice squeaked a little with excitement over the wire.

"Oliver, so early? Why, it's hardly six yet. Did you tell them what I said? Are they going to go?"

"Can't tell yet. I doubt it. After all, Sue, I did take their money, you know."

"Oliver, they've got to go! You've got to do something!"

"I'm trying, Sue. But I don't like it."

"Well, there isn't any reason why they shouldn't stay somewhere else. And we're going to need that money. You'll just have to think of something, Oliver."

Oliver met his own worried eyes in the mirror above the telephone and scowled at himself. His straw-colored hair was tangled and there was a shining stubble on his pleasant, tanned face. He was sorry the red-haired woman had first seen him in his untidy condition. Then his conscience smote him at the sound of Sue's determined voice and he said:

"I'll try, darling. I'll try. But I did take their money."

They had, in fact, paid a great deal of money, considerably more than the rooms were worth even in that year of high prices and high wages. The country was just moving into one of those fabulous eras which are later referred to as the Gay Forties or the Golden Sixties—a pleasant period of national euphoria. It was a stimulating time to be alive—while it lasted.

"All right," Oliver said resignedly. "I'll do my best."

* * *

But he was conscious, as the next few days went by, that he was not doing his best. There were several reasons for that. From the beginning the idea of making himself a nuisance to his tenants had been Sue's, not Oliver's. And if Oliver had been a little determined the whole project would never have got under way. Reason was on Sue's side, but...

For one thing, the tenants were so fascinating. All they said and did had a queer sort of inversion to it, as if a mirror had been held up to ordinary living and in the reflection showed strange variations from the norm. Their minds worked on a different basic premise, Oliver thought, from his own. They seemed to derive covert amusement from the most unamusing things; they patronized, they were aloof with a quality of cold detachment which did not prevent them from laughing inexplicably far too often for Oliver's comfort.

He saw them occasionally, on their way to and from their rooms. They were polite and distant, not, he suspected, from anger at his presence but from sheer indifference.

Most of the day they spent out of the house. The perfect May weather held unbroken and they seemed to give themselves up wholeheartedly to admiration of it, entirely confident that the warm, pale-gold sunshine and the scented air would not be interrupted by rain or cold. They were so sure of it that Oliver felt uneasy.

They took only one meal a day in the house, a late dinner. And their reactions to the meal were unpredictable. Laughter greeted some of the dishes, and a sort of delicate disgust others. No one would touch the salad, for instance. And the fish seemed to cause a wave of queer embarrassment around the table.

They dressed elaborately for each dinner. The man—his

name was Omerie—looked extremely handsome in his dinner clothes, but he seemed a little sulky and Oliver twice heard the women laughing because he had to wear black. Oliver entertained a sudden vision, for no reason, of the man in garments as bright and subtly cut as the women's, and it seemed somehow very right for him. He wore even the dark clothing with a certain flamboyance, as if cloth-of-gold would be more normal for him.

When they were in the house at other mealtimes, they ate in their rooms. They must have brought a great deal of food with them, from whatever mysterious place they had come. Oliver wondered with increasing curiosity where it might be. Delicious odors drifted into the hall sometimes, at odd hours, from their closed doors. Oliver could not identify them, but almost always they smelled irresistible. A few times the food smell was rather shockingly unpleasant, almost nauseating. It takes a connoisseur, Oliver reflected, to appreciate the decadent. And these people, most certainly, were connoissuers.

Why they lived so contentedly in this huge ramshackle old house was a question that disturbed his dreams at night. Or why they refused to move. He caught some fascinating glimpses into their rooms, which appeared to have been changed almost completely by additions he could not have defined very clearly from the brief sights he had of them. The feeling of luxury which his first glance at them had evoked was confirmed by the richness of the hangings they had apparently brought with them, the half-glimpsed ornaments, the pictures on the walls, even the whiffs of exotic perfume that floated from half-open doors.

He saw the women go by him in the halls, moving softly through the brown dimness in their gowns so uncannily perfect in fit, so lushly rich, so glowingly colored they seemed unreal. That poise born of confidence in the subservience of the world gave them an imperious aloofness, but more than once Oliver, meeting the blue gaze of the woman with the red hair and the soft, tanned skin, thought he saw quickened interest. She smiled at him in the dimness and went by in a haze of fragrance and a halo of incredible richness, and the warmth of the smile lingered after she had gone.

He knew she did not mean this aloofness to last between them. From the very first he was sure of that. When the time came she would make the opportunity to be alone with him. The thought was confusing and tremendously exciting. There was nothing he could do but wait, knowing she would see him when it suited her.

On the third day he lunched with Sue in a little downtown restaurant overlooking the great sweep of the metropolis across the river far below. Sue had shining brown curls and brown eyes, and her chin was a bit more prominent than is strictly accordant with beauty. From childhood Sue had known what she wanted and how to get it, and it seemed to Oliver just now that she had never wanted anything quite so much as the sale of this house.

"It's such a marvelous offer for the old mausoleum," she said, breaking into a roll with a gesture of violence. "We'll never have a chance like that again, and prices are so high we'll need the money to start housekeeping. Surely you can do *something*, Oliver!"

"I'm trying," Oliver assured her uncomfortably.

"Have you heard anything more from that madwoman who wants to buy it?"

Oliver shook his head. "Her attorney phoned again yesterday. Nothing new. I wonder who she is."

"I don't think even the attorney knows. All this mystery—I don't like it, Oliver. Even those Sancisco people—What did they do today?"

Oliver laughed. "They spent about an hour this morning telephoning movie theaters in the city, checking up on a lot of third-rate films they want to see parts of."

"Parts of? But why?"

"I don't know. I think... oh, nothing. More coffee?"

The trouble was, he thought he did know. It was too unlikely a guess to tell Sue about, and without familiarity with the Sancisco oddities she would only think Oliver was losing his mind. But he had from their talk a definite impression that there was an actor in bit parts in all these films whose performances they mentioned with something very near to awe. They referred to him as Golconda, which didn't appear to be his name, so that Oliver had no way of guessing which obscure bit player it was they admired so deeply. Golconda might have been the name of a character he had once played—and with superlative skill, judging by the comments of the Sanciscos—but to Oliver it meant nothing at all.

"They do funny things," he said, stirring his coffee reflectively. "Yesterday Omerie—that's the man—came in with a book of poems published about five years ago, and all of them handled it like a first edition of Shakespeare. I never even heard of the author, but he seems to be a tin god in their country, wherever that is."

"You still don't know? Haven't they even dropped any hints?"

"We don't do much talking," Oliver reminded her with some irony.

"I know, but—Oh, well I guess it doesn't matter. Go on, what else do they do?"

"Well, this morning they were going to spend studying Golconda' and his great art, and this afternoon I think they're taking a trip up the river to some sort of shrine I never heard of. It isn't very far, wherever it is, because I know they're coming back for dinner. Some great man's birthplace, I think—they promised to take home souvenirs of the place if they could get any. They're typical tourists, all right—if I could only figure out what's behind the whole thing. It doesn't make sense."

"Nothing about that house makes sense any more. I do wish..."

She went on in a petulant voice, but Oliver ceased suddenly to hear her, because just outside the door, walking with imperial elegance on her high heels, a familiar figure passed. He did not see her face, but he thought he would know that poise, that richness of line and motion, anywhere on earth.

"Excuse me a minute," he muttered to Sue, and was out of his chair before she could speak. He made the door in half a dozen long strides, and the beautifully elegant passerby was only a few steps away when he got there. Then, with the words he had meant to speak already half uttered, he fell silent and stood there staring.

It was not the red-haired woman. it was not her dark companion. It was a stranger. He watched, speechless, while the lovely, imperious creature moved on through the crowd and vanished, moving with familiar poise and assurance and an equally familiar strangeness as if the beautiful and exquisitely fitted garments she wore were an exotic costume to her, as they had always seemed to the Sancisco women. Every other

woman on the street looked untidy and ill at ease beside her
Walking like a queen, she melted into the crowd and wa
gone.

She came from *their* country, Oliver told himself dizzily
So someone else nearby had mysterious tenants in this montl
of perfect May weather. Someone else was puzzling in vair
today over the strangeness of the people from the nameles
land.

In silence he went back to Sue.

The door stood invitingly ajar in the brown dimness of th
upper hall. Oliver's steps slowed as he drew near it, and hi
heart began to quicken correspondingly. It was the red-hairec
woman's room, and he thought the door was not open b
accident. Her name, he knew now, was Kleph.

The door creaked a little on its hinges and from within
very sweet voice said lazily, "Won't you come in?"

The room looked very different indeed. The big bed ha
been pushed back against the wall, and a cover thrown ove
it that brushed the floor all around looked like soft-haired fu
except that it was pale blue-green and sparkled as if ever
hair were tipped with invisible crystals. Three books lay ope
on the fur, and a very curious-looking magazine with faintl
luminous printing and a page of pictures that at first glanc
appeared three-dimensional. Also a tiny porcelain pipe en
crusted with porcelain flowers, and a thin wisp of smoke float
ing from the bowl.

Above the bed a broad picture hung, framing a square c
blue water so real Oliver had to look twice to be sure it wa
not rippling gently from left to right. From the ceiling swun
a crystal globe on a glass cord. It turned gently, the light fron

the windows making curved rectangles in its sides.

Under the center window a sort of chaise-longue stood which Oliver had not seen before. He could only assume it was at least partly pneumatic and had been brought in the luggage. There was a very rich-looking quilted cloth covering and hiding it, embossed all over in shining metallic patterns.

Kleph moved slowly from the door and sank upon the chaise-longue with a little sigh of content. The couch accommodated itself to her body with what looked like delightful comfort. Kleph wriggled a little and then smiled up at Oliver.

"Do come on in. Sit over there, where you can see out the window. I love your beautiful spring weather. You know, there never was a May like it in civilized times." She said that quite seriously, her blue eyes on Oliver's, and there was a hint of patronage in her voice, as if the weather had been arranged especially for her.

Oliver started across the room and then paused and looked down in amazement at the floor, which felt unstable. He had not noticed before that the carpet was pure white, unspotted, and sank about an inch under the pressure of the feet. He saw then that Kleph's feet were bare, or almost bare. She wore something like gossamer buskins of filmy net, fitting her feet exactly. The bare soles were pink as if they had been rouged, and the nails had a liquid gleam like tiny mirrors. He moved closer, and was not as surprised as he should have been to see that they really were tiny mirrors, painted with some lacquer that gave them reflecting surfaces.

"Do sit down," Kleph said again, waving a white-sleeved arm towards a chair by the window. She wore a garment that looked like short, soft down, loosely cut but following perfectly every motion she made. And there was something curiously

different about her very shape today. When Oliver saw her
in street clothes, she had the square-shouldered, slim-flanked
figure that all women strove for, but here in her lounging robe
she looked—well, different. There was an almost swanlike
slope to her shoulders today, a roundness and softness to her
body that looked unfamiliar and very appealing.

"Will you have some tea?" Kleph asked, and smiled charm-
ingly.

A low table beside her held a tray and several small covered
cups, lovely things with an inner glow like rose quartz, the
color shining deeply as if from within layer upon layer of
translucence. She took up one of the cups—there were no
saucers—and offered it to Oliver.

It felt fragile and thin as paper in his hand. He could not
see the contents because of the cup's cover, which seemed to
be one with the cup itself and left only a thin open crescent
at the rim. Steam rose from the opening.

Kleph took up a cup of her own and tilted it to her lips,
smiling at Oliver over the rim. She was very beautiful. The
pale red hair lay in shining loops against her head and the
corona of curls like a halo above her forehead might have been
pressed down like a wreath. Every hair kept order as perfectly
as if it had been painted on, though the breeze from the
window stirred now and then among the softly shining strands.

Oliver tried the tea. Its flavor was exquisite, very hot, and
the taste that lingered upon his tongue was like the scent of
flowers. It was an extremely feminine drink. He sipped again,
surprised to find how much he liked it.

The scent of flowers seemed to increase as he drank, swirl-
ing through his head like smoke. After the third sip there was

a faint buzzing in his ears. The bees among the flowers, perhaps, he thought incoherently—and sipped again.

Kleph watched him, smiling.

"The others will be out all afternoon," she told Oliver comfortably. "I thought it would give us a pleasant time to be acquainted."

Oliver was rather horrified to hear himself saying, "What makes you talk like that?" He had had no idea of asking the question; something seemed to have loosened his control over his own tongue.

Kleph's smile deepened. She tipped the cup to her lips and there was indulgence in her voice when she said, "What do you mean 'like that'?"

He waved his hand vaguely, noting with some surprise that at a glance it seemed to have six or seven fingers as it moved past his face.

"I don't know—precision, I guess. Why don't you say 'don't,' for instance?"

"In our country we are trained to speak with precision," Kleph explained. "Just as we are trained to move and dress and think with precision. Any slovenliness is trained out of us in childhood. With you, of course—" She was polite. "With you, this does not happen to be a national fetish. With us, we have time for the amenities. We like them."

Her voice had grown sweeter and sweeter as she spoke, until by now it was almost indistinguishable from the sweetness of the flower scent in Oliver's head, and the delicate flavor of the tea.

"What country do you come from?" he asked, and tilted the cup again to drink, mildly surprised to notice that it seemed inexhaustible.

Kleph's smile was definitely patronizing this time. It didn't irritate him. Nothing could irritate him just now. The whole room swam in a beautiful rosy glow as fragrant as the flowers.

"We must not speak of that, Mr. Wilson."

"But—" Oliver paused. After all, it was, of course, none of his business. "This is a vacation?" he asked vaguely.

"Call it a pilgrimage, perhaps."

"Pilgrimage?" Oliver was so interested that for an instant his mind came back into sharp focus. "To—what?"

"I should not have said that, Mr. Wilson. Please forget it. Do you like the tea?"

"Very much."

"You will have guessed by now that it is not only tea, but an euphoriac."

Oliver stared. "Euphoriac?"

Kleph made a descriptive circle in the air with one graceful hand, and laughed. "You do not feel the effects yet? Surely you do?"

"I feel," Oliver said, "the way I'd feel after four whiskies."

Kleph shuddered delicately. "We get our euphoria less painfully. And without the aftereffects your barbarous alcohol used to have." She bit her lip. "Sorry. I must be euphoric myself to speak so freely. Please forgive me. Shall we have some music?"

Kleph leaned backward on the chaise-longue and reached towards the wall beside her. The sleeve, falling away from her round tanned arm, left bare the inside of the wrist, and Oliver was startled to see there a long, rosy streak of fading scar. His inhibitions had dissolved in the fumes of the fragrant tea; he caught his breath and leaned forward to stare.

Kleph shook the sleeve back over the scar with a quick gesture. Color came into her face beneath the softly tinted tan and she would not meet Oliver's eyes. A queer shame seemed to have fallen upon her.

Oliver said tactlessly, "What is it? What's the matter?"

Still she would not look at him. Much later he understood that shame and knew she had reason for it. Now he listened blankly as she said:

"Nothing... nothing at all. A... an inoculation. All of us ...oh, never mind. Listen to the music."

This time she reached out with the other arm. She touched nothing, but when she had held her hand near the wall a sound breathed through the room. It was the sound of water, the sighing of waves receding upon long, sloped beaches. Oliver followed Kleph's gaze towards the picture of the blue water above the bed.

The waves there were moving. More than that, the point of vision moved. Slowly the seascape drifted past, moving with the waves, following them towards shore. Oliver watched, half hypnotized by a motion that seemed at the time quite acceptable and not in the least surprising.

The waves lifted and broke in creaming foam and ran seething up a sandy beach. Then through the sound of the water music began to breathe, and through the water itself a man's face dawned in the frame, smiling intimately into the room. He held an oddly archaic musical instrument, lute-shaped, its body striped light and dark like a melon and its long neck bent back over his shoulder. He was singing, and Oliver felt mildly astonished at the song. It was very familiar and very odd indeed. He groped through the unfamiliar rhythms and found at last a thread to catch the tune by it—it was "Make

Believe" from *Show Boat,* but certainly a showboat that had never steamed up the Mississippi.

"What's he doing to it?" he demanded after a few moments of outraged listening. "I never heard anything like it!"

Kleph laughed and stretched out her arm again. Enigmatically she said: "We call it kyling. Never mind. How do you like this?"

It was a comedian, a man in semiclown makeup, his eyes exaggerated so that they seemed to cover half his face. He stood by a broad glass pillar before a dark curtain and sang a gay, staccato song interspersed with patter that sounded impromptu, and all the while his left hand did an intricate, musical tattoo of the nailtips on the glass of the column. He strolled around and around it as he sang. The rhythms of his fingernails blended with the song and swung widely away into patterns of their own, and blended again without a break.

It was confusing to follow. The song made even less sense than the monologue, which had something to do with a lost slipper and was full of allusions which made Kleph smile, but were utterly unintelligible to Oliver. The man had a dry, brittle style that was not very amusing, though Kleph seemed fascinated. Oliver was interested to see in him an extension and a variation of that extreme smooth confidence which marked all three of the Sanciscos. Clearly a racial trait, he thought.

Other performances followed, some of them fragmentary as if lifted out of a completer version. One he knew. The obvious, stirring melody struck his recognition before the figures—marching men against a haze, a great banner rolling backward above them in the smoke, foreground figures striding gigantically and shouting in rhythm, "Forward, forward the lily banners go!"

The music was tinny, the images blurred and poorly colored, but there was a gusto about the performance that caught at Oliver's imagination. He stared, remembering the old film from long ago. Dennis King and a ragged chorus, singing "The Song of the Vagabonds" from—was it *Vagabond King*?

"A very old one," Kleph said apologetically. "But I like it."

The steam of the intoxicating tea swirled between Oliver and the picture. Music swelled and sank through the room and the fragrant fumes and his own euphoric brain. Nothing seemed strange. He had discovered how to drink the tea. Like nitrous oxide, the effect was not cumulative. When you reached a peak of euphoria, you could not increase the peak. It was best to wait for a slight dip in the effect of the stimulant before taking more.

Otherwise it had most of the effects of alcohol—everything after a while dissolved into a delightful fog through which all he saw was uniformly enchanting and partook of the qualities of a dream. He questioned nothing. Afterwards he was not certain how much of it he really had dreamed.

There was the dancing doll, for instance. He remembered it quite clearly, in sharp focus—a tiny, slender woman with a long-nosed, dark-eyed face and a pointed chin. She moved delicately across the white rug—knee-high, exquisite. Her features were as mobile as her body, and she danced lightly, with resounding strokes of her toes, each echoing like a bell. It was a formalized sort of dance, and she sang breathlessly in accompaniment, making amusing little grimaces. Certainly it was a portrait-doll, animated to mimic the original perfectly in voice and motion. Afterwards, Oliver knew he must have dreamed it.

What else happened he was quite unable to remember later. He knew Kleph had said some curious things, but they all

made sense at the time, and afterwards he couldn't remember
a word. He knew he had been offered little glittering candies
in a transparent dish, and that some of them had been delicious and one or two so bitter his tongue still curled the next
day when he recalled them, and one—Kleph sucked luxu-
riantly on the same kind—of a taste that was actively nauseating.

As for Kleph herself—he was frantically uncertain the next
day what had really happened. He thought he could remember the softness of her white-downed arms clasped at the back
of his neck, while she laughed up at him and exhaled into his
face the flowery fragrance of the tea. But beyond that he was
totally unable to recall anything for a while.

There was a brief interlude later, before the oblivion of
sleep. He was almost sure he remembered a moment when
the other two Sanciscos stood looking down at him, the man
scowling, the smoky-eyed woman smiling a derisive smile.

The man said, from a vast distance, "Kleph, you know this
is against every rule—" His voice began in a thin hum and
soared in fantastic flight beyond the range of hearing. Oliver
thought he remembered the dark woman's laughter, thin and
distant too, and the hum of her voice like bees in flight.

"Kleph, Kleph, you silly little fool, can we never trust you
out of sight?"

Kleph's voice then said something that seemed to make no
sense. "What does it matter, *here?*"

The man answered in that buzzing, faraway hum. "The
matter of giving your bond before you leave, not to interfere.
You know you signed the rules..."

Kleph's voice, nearer and more intelligible: "But here the
difference is... it does not matter *here!* You both know that.
How could it matter?"

Oliver felt the downy brush of her sleeve against his cheek, but he saw nothing except the slow, smokelike ebb and flow of darkness past his eyes. He heard the voices wrangle musically from far away, and he heard them cease.

When he woke the next morning, alone in his own room, he woke with the memory of Kleph's eyes upon him very sorrowfully, her lovely tanned face looking down on him with the red hair falling fragrantly on each side of it and sadness and compassion in her eyes. He thought he had probably dreamed that. There was no reason why anyone should look at him with such sadness.

Sue telephoned that day.

"Oliver, the people who want to buy the house are here. That madwoman and her husband. Shall I bring them over?"

Oliver's mind all day had been hazy with the vague, bewildering memories of yesterday. Kleph's face kept floating before him, blotting out the room. He said, "What? I . . . oh, well, bring them if you want to. I don't see what good it'll do."

"Oliver, what's wrong with you? We agreed we needed the money, didn't we? I don't see how you can think of passing up such a wonderful bargain without even a struggle. We could get married and buy our own house right away, and you know we'll never get such an offer again for that old trash heap. Wake up, Oliver!"

Oliver made an effort. "I know, Sue—I know. But—"

"Oliver, you've got to think of something!" Her voice was imperious.

He knew she was right. Kleph or no Kleph, the bargain shouldn't be ignored if there was any way at all of getting the tenants out. He wondered again what made the place so suddenly priceless to so many people. And what the last week in May had to do with the value of the house.

A sudden sharp curiosity pierced even the vagueness of his mind today. May's last week was so important that the whole sale of the house stood or fell upon occupancy by then. Why? *Why?*

"What's going to happen next week?" he asked rhetorically of the telephone. "Why can't they wait till these people leave? I'd knock a couple of thousand off the price if they'd..."

"You would not, Oliver Wilson! I can buy all our refrigeration units with that extra money. You'll just have to work out some way to give possession by next week, and that's that. You hear me?"

"Keep your shirt on," Oliver said practically. "I'm only human, but I'll try."

"I'm bringing the people over right away," Sue told him. "While the Sanciscos are still out. Now you put your mind to work and think of something, Oliver." She paused, and her voice was reflective when she spoke again. "They're... awfully odd people, darling."

"Odd?"

"You'll see."

It was an elderly woman and a very young man who trailed Sue up the walk. Oliver knew immediately what had struck Sue about them. He was somehow not at all surprised to see that both wore their clothing with the familiar air of elegant self-consciousness he had come to know so well. They, too, looked around them at the beautiful, sunny afternoon with conscious enjoyment and an air of faint condescension. He knew before he heard them speak how musical their voices would be and how meticulously they would pronounce each word.

There was no doubt about it. The people of Kleph's mysterious country were arriving here in force—for something. For the last week of May? He shrugged mentally; there was no way of guessing—yet. One thing only was sure: all of them must come from that nameless land where people controlled their voices like singers and their garments like actors who could stop the reel of time itself to adjust every disordered fold.

The elderly woman took full charge of the conversation from the start. They stood together on the rickety, unpainted porch, and Sue had no chance even for introductions.

"Young man, I am Madame Hollia. This is my husband." Her voice had an underrunning current of harshness, which was perhaps age. And her face looked almost corseted, the loose flesh coerced into something like firmness by some invisible method Oliver could not guess at. The makeup was so skillful he could not be certain it was makeup at all, but he had a definite feeling that she was much older than she looked. It would have taken a lifetime of command to put so much authority into the harsh, deep musically controlled voice.

The young man said nothing. He was very handsome. His type, apparently, was one that does not change much no matter in what culture or country it may occur. He wore beautifully tailored garments and carried in one gloved hand a box of red leather, about the size and shape of a book.

Madame Hollia went on: "I understand your problem about the house. You wish to sell to me, but are legally bound by your lease with Omerie and his friends. Is that right?"

Oliver nodded. "But..."

"Let me finish. If Omerie can be forced to vacate before next week, you will accept our offer. Right? Very well. Hara!" She nodded to the young man beside her. He jumped to instant attention, bowed slightly, said, "Yes, Hollia," and slipped a gloved hand into his coat.

Madame Hollia took the little object offered on his palm, her gesture as she reached for it almost imperial, as if royal robes swept from her outstretched arm.

"Here," she said, "is something that may help us. My dear—" She held it out to Sue—"if you can hide this somewhere about the house, I believe your unwelcome tenants will not trouble you much longer."

Sue took the thing curiously. It looked like a tiny silver box, no more than an inch square, indented at the top and with no line to show it could be opened.

"Wait a minute," Oliver broke in uneasily. "What is it?"

"Nothing that will harm anyone, I assure you."

"Then what—?"

Madame Hollia's imperious gesture at one sweep silenced him and commanded Sue forward. "Go on, my dear. Hurry, before Omerie comes back. I can assure you there is no danger to anyone."

Oliver broke in determinedly. "Madame Hollia, I'll have to know what your plans are. I..."

"Oh, Oliver, please!" Sue's finger closed over the silver cube. "Don't worry about it. I'm sure Madame Hollia knows best. Don't you *want* to get those people out?"

"Of course I do. But I don't want the house blown up or..."

Madame Hollia's deep laughter was indulgent. "Nothing so crude, I promise you, Mr. Wilson. Remember, we want the house! Hurry, my dear."

Sue nodded and slipped hastily past Oliver into the hall.
Outnumbered, he subsided uneasily. The young man, Hara,
tapped a negligent foot and admired the sunlight as they waited.
It was an afternoon as perfect as all of May had been, translucent gold, balmy with an edge of chill lingering in the air
to point up a perfect contrast with the summer to come. Hara
looked around him confidently, like a man paying just tribute
to a stage set provided wholly for himself. He even glanced
up at a drone from above and followed the course of a big
transcontinental plane half dissolved in golden haze high in
the sun. "Quaint," he murmured in a gratified voice.

Sue came back and slipped her hand through Oliver's arm,
squeezing excitedly. "There," she said. "How long will it take,
Madame Hollia?"

"That will depend, my dear. Not very long. Now, Mr. Wilson, one word with you. You live here also, I understand?
For your own comfort, take my advice and..."

Somewhere within the house a door slammed and a clear
high voice rang wordlessly up a rippling scale. Then there
was the sound of feet on the stairs, and a single line of song,
"*Come hider, love, to me—*"

Hara started, almost dropping the red leather box he held.

"Kleph!" he said in a whisper. "Or Klia. I know they both
just came on from Canterbury. But I thought..."

"Huh." Madame Hollia's features composed themselves into
an imperious blank. She breathed triumphantly through her
nose, drew back upon herself and turned an imposing façade
to the door.

Kleph wore the same softly downy robe Oliver had seen
before, except that today it was not white, but a pale, clear

blue that gave her tan an apricot flush. She was smiling.

"Why, Hollia!" Her tone was at its most musical. "I thought I recognized voices from home. How nice to see you. No one knew you were coming to the—" She broke off and glanced at Oliver and then away again. "Hara, too," she said. "What a pleasant surprise."

Sue said flatly, "When did *you* get back?"

Kleph smiled at her. "You must be the little Miss Johnson. Why, I did not go out at all. I was tired of sightseeing. I have been napping in my room."

Sue drew in her breath in something that just escaped a disbelieving sniff. A look flashed between the two women, and for an instant held—and that instant was timeless. It was an extraordinary pause in which a great deal of wordless interplay took place in the space of a second.

Oliver saw the quality of Kleph's smile at Sue, that same look of quiet confidence he had noticed so often about all of these strange people. He saw Sue's quick inventory of the other woman, and he saw how Sue squared her shoulders and stood up straight, smoothing down her summer frock over her flat hips so that for an instant she stood posed consciously, looking down on Kleph. It was deliberate. Bewildered, he glanced again at Kleph.

Kleph's shoulders sloped softly, her robe was belted to a tiny waist and hung in deep folds over frankly rounded hips. Sue's was the fashionable figure—but Sue was the first to surrender.

Kleph's smile did not falter. But in the silence there was an abrupt reversal of values, based on no more than the measureless quality of Kleph's confidence in herself, the quiet, assured smile. It was suddenly made very clear that fashion

not a constant. Kleph's curious, out-of-mode curves without
arning became the norm, and Sue was a queer, angular, half-
asculine creature beside her.

Oliver had no idea how it was done. Somehow the authority
ssed in a breath from one woman to the other. Beauty is
most wholly a matter of fashion; what is beautiful today
ould have been grotesque a couple of generations ago and
ll be grotesque a hundred years ahead. It will be worse
an grotesque; it will be outmoded and therefore faintly
diculous.

Sue was that. Kleph had only to exert her authority to make
clear to everyone on the porch. Kleph was a beauty, sud-
nly and very convincingly, beautiful in the accepted mode,
d Sue was amusingly old-fashioned, an anachronism in her
he, square-shouldered slimness. She did not belong. She
us grotesque among these strangely immaculate people.

Sue's collapse was complete. But pride sustained her, and
wilderment. Probably she never did grasp entirely what
is wrong. She gave Kleph one glance of burning resentment
d when her eyes came back to Oliver there was suspicion
them, and mistrust.

Looking backward later, Oliver thought that in that mo-
ent, for the first time clearly, he began to suspect the truth.
it he had no time to ponder it, for after the brief instant of
mity the three people from—elsewhere—began to speak
at once, as if in a belated attempt to cover something they
l not want noticed.

Kleph said, "This beautiful weather—" and Madame Hollia
d, "So fortunate to have this house—" and Hara, holding
the red leather box, said loudest of all, "Cenbe sent you
s, Kleph. His latest."

Kleph put out both hands for it eagerly, the eiderdow
sleeves falling back from her rounded arms. Oliver had a qui
glimpse of that mysterious scar before the sleeve fell bac
and it seemed to him that there was the faintest trace of
similar scar vanishing into Hara's cuff as he let his own ar
drop.

"Cenbe!" Kleph cried, her voice high and sweet and d
lighted. "How wonderful! What period?"

"From November 1664," Hara said, "London, of cours
though I think there may be some counterpoint from the 13
November. He hasn't finished—of course." He glanced a
most nervously at Oliver and Sue. "A wonderful example
he said quickly. "Marvelous. If you have the taste for it,
course."

Madame Hollia shuddered with ponderous delicacy. "Th
man!" she said. "Fascinating, of course—a great man. But
so *advanced!*"

"It takes a connoisseur to appreciate Cenbe's work fully
Kleph said in a slightly tart voice, "We all admit that."

"Oh yes, we all bow to Cenbe," Hollia conceded. "I confe
the man terrifies me a little, my dear. Do we expect him
join us?"

"I suppose so," Kleph said. "If his—work—is not yet fi
ished, then of course. You know Cenbe's tastes."

Hollia and Hara laughed together. "I know when to lo
for him, then," Hollia said. She glanced at the staring Oliv
and the subdued but angry Sue, and with a commanding effc
brought the subject back into line.

"So fortunate, my dear Kleph, to have this house," s
declared heavily. "I saw a tridimensional of it—afterwards
and it was still quite perfect. Such a fortunate coincidenc

Would you consider parting with your lease, for a consideration? Say, a coronation seat at . . ."

"Nothing could buy us, Hollia," Kleph told her gaily, clasping the red box to her bosom.

Hollia gave her a cool stare. "You may change your mind, my dear Kleph," she said pontifically. "There is still time. You can always reach us through Mr. Wilson here. We have rooms up the street in the Montgomery House—nothing like yours, of course, but they will do. For us, they will do."

Oliver blinked. The Montgomery House was the most expensive hotel in town. Compared to this collapsing old ruin, it was a palace. There was no understanding these people. Their values seemed to have suffered a complete reversal.

Madame Hollia moved majestically towards the steps.

"Very pleasant to see you, my dear," she said over one well-padded shoulder. "Enjoy your stay. My regards to Omerie and Klia. Mr. Wilson—" she nodded towards the walk. "A word with you."

Oliver followed her down towards the street. Madame Hollia paused halfway there and touched his arm.

"One word of advice," she said huskily. "You say you sleep here? Move out, young man. Move out before tonight."

Oliver was searching in a half-desultory fashion for the hiding place Sue had found for the mysterious silver cube, when the first sounds from above began to drift down the stairwell towards him. Kleph had closed her door, but the house was old, and strange qualities in the noise overhead seemed to seep through the woodwork like an almost visible stain.

It was music, in a way. But much more than music. And it was a terrible sound, the sounds of calamity and of all human reaction to calamity, everything from hysteria to heartbreak, from irrational joy to rationalized acceptance.

The calamity was—single. The music did not attempt to correlate all human sorrows; it focused sharply upon one and followed the ramifications out and out. Oliver recognized these basics to the sounds in a very brief moment. They were essentials, and they seemed to beat into his brain with the first strains of the music which was so much more than music.

But when he lifted his head to listen he lost all grasp upon the meaning of the noise and it was sheer medley and confusion. To think of it was to blur it hopelessly in the mind, and he could not recapture that first instant of unreasoning acceptance.

He went upstairs almost in a daze, hardly knowing what he was doing. He pushed Kleph's door open. He looked inside . . .

What he saw there he could not afterwards remember except in a blurring as vague as the blurred ideas the music roused in his brain. Half the room had vanished behind a mist, and the mist was a three-dimensional screen upon which were projected—he had no words for them. He was not even sure if the projections were visual. The mist was spinning with motion and sound, but essentially it was neither sound nor motion that Oliver saw.

This was a work of art. Oliver knew no name for it. It transcended all art forms he knew, blended them, and out of the blend produced subtleties his mind could not begin to grasp. Basically, this was the attempt of a master composer to correlate every essential aspect of a vast human experience into something that could be conveyed in a few moments to every sense at once.

The shifting visions on the screen were not pictures in

themselves, but hints of pictures, subtly selected outlines that plucked at the mind and with one deft touch set whole chords ringing through the memory. Perhaps each beholder reacted differently, since it was in the eye and the mind of the beholder that the truth of the picture lay. No two would be aware of the same symphonic panorama, but each would see essentially the same terrible story unfold.

Every sense was touched by that deft and merciless genius. Color and shape and motion flickered in the screen, hinting much, evoking unbearable memories deep in the mind; odors floated from the screen and touched the heart of the beholder more poignantly than anything visual could do. The skin crawled sometimes as if to a tangible cold hand laid upon it. The tongue curled with remembered bitterness and remembered sweet.

It was outrageous. It violated the innermost privacies of a man's mind, called up secret things long ago walled off behind mental scar tissue, forced its terrible message upon the beholder relentlessly though the mind might threaten to crack beneath the stress of it.

And yet, in spite of all this vivid awareness, Oliver did not know what calamity the screen portrayed. That it was real, vast, overwhelmingly dreadful he could not doubt. That it had once happened was unmistakable. He caught flashing glimpses of human faces distorted with grief and disease and death— real faces, faces that had once lived and were seen now in the instant of dying. He saw men and woman in rich clothing superimposed in panorama upon reeling thousands of ragged folk, great throngs of them swept past the sight in an instant, and he saw that death made no distinction among them.

He saw lovely women laugh and shake their curls, and the

laughter shriek into hysteria and the hysteria into music. He saw one man's face, over and over—a long, dark saturnine face, deeply lined, sorrowful, the face of a powerful man wise in worldliness, urbane—and helpless. That face was for a while a recurring motif, always more tortured, more helpless than before.

The music broke off in the midst of a rising glide. The mist vanished and the room reappeared before him. The anguished dark face for an instant seemed to Oliver printed everywhere he looked, like after-vision on the eyelids. He knew that face. He had seen it before, not often, but he should know its name—"

"Oliver, Oliver—" Kleph's sweet voice came out of a fog at him. He was leaning dizzily against the doorpost looking down into her eyes. She, too, had that dazed blankness he must show on his own face. The power of the dreadful symphony still held them both. But even in this confused moment Oliver saw that Kleph had been enjoying the experience.

He felt sickened to the depths of his mind, dizzy with sickness and revulsion because of the superimposing of human miseries he had just beheld. But Kleph—only appreciation showed upon her face. To her it had been magnificence, and magnificence only.

Irrelevantly Oliver remembered the nauseating candies she had enjoyed, the nauseating odors of strange food that drifted sometimes through the hall from her room.

What was it she had said downstairs a little while ago? Connoisseur, that was it. Only a connoisseur could appreciate work as—as *advanced*—as the work of someone called Cenbe.

A whiff of intoxicating sweetness curled past Oliver's face.

Something cool and smooth was pressed into his hand.

"Oh, Oliver, I am so sorry," Kleph's voice murmured contritely. "Here, drink the euphoriac and you will feel better. Please drink!"

The familiar fragrance of the hot sweet tea was on his tongue before he knew he had complied. Its relaxing fumes floated up through his brain and in a moment or two the world felt stable around him again. The room was as it had always been. And Kleph...

Her eyes were very bright. Sympathy showed in them for him, but for herself she was still brimmed with the high elation of what she had just been experiencing.

"Come and sit down," she said gently, tugging at his arm. "I am so sorry—I should not have played that over, where you could hear it. I have no excuse, really. It was only that I forgot what the effect might be on one who had never heard Cenbe's symphonies before. I was so impatient to see what he had done with...with his new subject. I am so very sorry, Oliver!"

"What was it?" His voice sounded steadier than he had expected. The tea was responsible for that. He sipped again, glad of the consoling euphoria its fragrance brought.

"A...a composite interpretation of...oh, Oliver, you know I must not answer questions!"

"But—"

"No—drink your tea and forget what it was you saw. Think of other things. Here, we will have music—another kind of music, something gay..."

She reached for the wall beside the window, and as before, Oliver saw the broad framed picture of blue water above the bed ripple and grow pale. Through it another scene began to dawn like shapes rising beneath the surface of the sea.

He had a glimpse of a dark-curtained stage upon which a
man in a tight dark tunic and hose moved with a restless,
sidelong pace, his hands and face startlingly pale against the
black about him. He limped; he had a crooked back and he
spoke familiar lines. Oliver had seen John Barrymore once as
the crook-backed Richard, and it seemed vaguely outrageous
to him that any other actor should essay that difficult part.
This one he had never seen before, but the man had a fas-
cinatingly smooth manner and his interpretation of the Plan-
tagenet king was quite new and something Shakespeare
probably never dreamed of.

"No," Kleph said, "not this. Nothing gloomy." And she put
out her hand again. The nameless new Richard faded and
there was a swirl of changing pictures and changing voices,
all blurred together, before the scene steadied upon a stageful
of dancers in pastel ballet skirts, drifting effortlessly through
some complicated pattern of motion. The music that went
with it was light and effortless too. The room filled up with
the clear, floating melody.

Oliver set down his cup. He felt much surer of himself now,
and he thought the euphoriac had done all it could for him.
He didn't want to blur again mentally. There were things he
meant to learn about. Now. He considered how to begin.

Kleph was watching him. "That Hollia," she said suddenly.
"She wants to buy the house?"

Oliver nodded. "She's offering a lot of money. Sue's going
to be awfully disappointed if..." he hesitated. Perhaps, after
all, Sue would not be disappointed. He remembered the little
silver cube with the enigmatic function and he wondered if
he should mention it to Kleph. But the euphoriac had not

reached that level of his brain, and he remembered his duty to Sue and was silent.

Kleph shook her head, her eyes upon his warm with—was it sympathy?

"Believe me," she said, "you will not find that—important—after all. I promise you, Oliver."

He stared at her. "I wish you'd explain."

Kleph laughed on a note more sorrowful than amused. But it occurred to Oliver suddenly that there was no longer condescension in her voice. Imperceptibly that air of delicate amusement had vanished from her manner towards him. The cool detachment that still marked Omerie's attitude, and Klia's, was not in Kleph's any more. It was a subtlety he did not think she could assume. It had to come spontaneously or not at all. And for no reason he was willing to examine, it became suddenly very important to Oliver that Kleph should not condescend to him, that she should feel towards him as he felt towards her. He would not think of it.

He looked down at his cup, rose quartz, exhaling a thin plume of steam from its crescent-slit opening. This time, he thought, maybe he could make the tea work for him. For he remembered how it loosened the tongue, and there was a great deal he needed to know. The idea that had come to him on the porch in the instant of silent rivalry between Kleph and Sue seemed not too fantastic to entertain. But some answer there must be.

Kleph herself gave him the opening.

"I must not take too much euphoriac this afternoon," she said, smiling at him over her pink cup. "It will make me drowsy, and we are going out this evening with friends."

"More friends?" Oliver asked. "From your country?"

Kleph nodded. "Very dear friends we have expected all this week."

"I wish you'd tell me," Oliver said bluntly, "where it is you come from. It isn't from here. Your culture is too different from ours—even your names . . ." He broke off as Kleph shook her head.

"I wish I could tell you. But that is against all the rules. It is even against the rules for me to be here talking to you now."

She made a helpless gesture. "You must not ask me, Oliver." She leaned back on the chaise-longue, which adjusted itself luxuriously to the motion, and smiled very sweetly at him. "We must not talk about things like that. Forget it, listen to the music, enjoy yourself if you can." She closed her eyes and laid her head back against the cushions. Oliver saw the round tanned throat swell as she began to hum a tune. Eyes still closed, she sang again the words she had sung upon the stairs. *"Come hider, love, to me . . ."*

A memory clicked over suddenly in Oliver's mind. He had never heard the queer, lagging tune before, but he thought he knew the words. He remembered what Hollia's husband had said when he heard that line of song, and he leaned forward. She would not answer a direct question, but perhaps . . .

"Was the weather this warm in Canterbury?" he asked, and held his breath. Kleph hummed another line of the song and shook her head, eyes still closed.

"It was autumn there," she said. "But bright, wonderfully bright. Even their clothing, you know . . . everyone was singing that new song, and I can't get it out of my head." She sang another line, and the words were almost unintelligible—

English, yet not an English Oliver could understand.

He stood up. "Wait," he said. "I want to find something. Back in a minute."

She opened her eyes and smiled mistily at him, still humming. He went downstairs as fast as he could—the stairway swayed a little, though his head was nearly clear now—and into the library. The book he wanted was old and battered, interlined with the penciled notes of his college days. He did not remember very clearly where the passage he wanted was, but he thumbed fast through the columns and by sheer luck found it within a few minutes. Then he went back upstairs, feeling a strange emptiness in his stomach because of what he almost believed now.

"Kleph," he said firmly, "I know that song. I know the year it was new."

Her lids rose slowly; she looked at him through a mist of euphoriac. He was not sure she had understood. For a long moment she held him with her gaze. Then she put out one downy-sleeved arm and spread her tanned fingers towards him. She laughed deep in her throat.

"Come hider, love, to me," she said.

He crossed the room slowly, took her hand. The fingers closed warmly about his. She pulled him down so that he had to kneel beside her. Her other arm lifted. Again she laughed, very softly, and closed her eyes, lifting her face to his.

The kiss was warm and long. He caught something of her own euphoria from the fragrance of the tea breathed into his face. And he was startled at the end of the kiss, when the clasp of her arms loosened about his neck, to feel the sudden rush of her breath against his cheek. There were tears on her face, and the sound she made was a sob.

He held her off and looked down in amazement. She sobbed once more, caught a deep breath, and said, "Oh, Oliver, Oliver . . ." Then she shook her head and pulled free, turning away to hide her face. "I . . . I am sorry," she said unevenly. "Please forgive me. It does not matter . . . I *know* it does not matter . . . but—"

"What's wrong? What doesn't matter?"

"Nothing. Nothing . . . please forget it. Nothing at all." She got a handkerchief from the table and blew her nose, smiling at him with an effect of radiance through the tears.

Suddenly he was very angry. He had heard enough evasions and mystifying half-truths. He said roughly, "Do you think I'm crazy? I know enough now to—"

"Oliver, please!" She held up her own cup, steaming fragrantly. "Please, no more questions. Here, euphoria is what you need, Oliver. Euphoria, not answers."

"What year was it when you heard that song in Canterbury?" he demanded, pushing the cup aside.

She blinked at him, tears bright on her lashes. "Why . . . what year do you think?"

"I know," Oliver told her grimly. "I know the year that song was popular. I know you just came from Canterbury—Hollia's husband said so. It's May now, but it was autumn in Canterbury, and you just came from there, so lately the song you heard is still running through your head. Chaucer's Pardoner sang that song some time around the end of the fourteenth century. Did you see Chaucer, Kleph? What was it like in England that long ago?"

Kleph's eye fixed his for a silent moment. Then her shoulders drooped and her whole body went limp with resignation beneath the soft blue robe. "I am a fool," she said gently. "It must have been easy to trap me. You really believe—what you say?"

Oliver nodded.

She said in a low voice. "Few people do believe it. That is one of our maxims, when we travel. We are safe from much suspicion because people before The Travel began will not believe."

The emptiness in Oliver's stomach suddenly doubled in volume. For an instant the bottom dropped out of time itself and the universe was unsteady about him. He felt sick. He felt naked and helpless. There was a buzzing in his ears and the room dimmed before him.

He had not really believed—not until this instant. He had expected some rational explanation from her that would tidy all his wild half-thoughts and suspicions into something a man could accept as believable. Not this.

Kleph dabbed at her eyes with the pale-blue handkerchief and smiled tremulously.

"I know," she said. "It must be a terrible thing to accept. To have all your concepts turned upside down. We know it from childhood, of course, but for you... here, Oliver. The euphoriac will make it easier."

He took the cup, the faint stain of her lip rouge still on the crescent opening. He drank, feeling the dizzy sweetness spiral through his head, and his brain turned a little in his skull as the volatile fragrance took effect. With that turning, focus shifted and all his values with it.

He began to feel better. The flesh settled on his bones again, and the warm clothing of temporal assurance settled upon his flesh, and he was no longer naked and in the vortex of unstable time.

* * *

"The story is very simple, really," Kleph said. "We—travel. Our own time is not terribly far ahead of yours. No. I must not say how far. But we still remember your songs and poets and some of your great actors. We are a people of much leisure, and we cultivate the art of enjoying ourselves."

"This is a tour we are making—a tour of a year's seasons. Vintage seasons. That autumn in Canterbury was the most magnificent autumn our researchers could discover anywhere. We rode in a pilgrimage to the shrine—it was a wonderful experience, though the clothing was a little hard to manage.

"Now this month of May is almost over—the loveliest May in recorded times. A perfect May in a wonderful period. You have no way of knowing what a good, gay period you live in, Oliver. The very feeling in the air of the cities—that wonderful national confidence and happiness—everything going as smoothly as a dream. There were other Mays with fine weather, but each of them had a war or a famine, or something else wrong." She hesitated, grimaced, and went on rapidly. "In a few days we are to meet at a coronation in Rome," she said. "I think the year will be 800—Christmastime. We..."

"But why," Oliver interrupted, "did you insist on this house? Why do the others want to get it away from you?"

Kleph stared at him. He saw the tears rising again in small bright crescents that gathered above her lower lids. He saw the look of obstinacy that came upon her soft, tanned face. She shook her head.

"You must not ask me that." She held out the steaming cup. "Here, drink and forget what I have said. I can tell you no more. No more at all."

* * *

When he woke, for a little while he had no idea where he was. He did not remember leaving Kleph or coming to his own room. He didn't care, just then. For he woke to a sense of overwhelming terror.

The dark was full of it. His brain rocked on waves of fear and pain. He lay motionless, too frightened to stir, some atavistic memory warning him to lie quiet until he knew from which direction the danger threatened. Reasonless panic broke over him in a tidal flow; his head ached with its violence and the dark throbbed to the same rhythms.

A knock sounded at the door. Omerie's deep voice said, "Wilson! Wilson, are you awake?"

Oliver tried twice before he had breath to answer. "Y-yes—what is it?"

The knob rattled. Omerie's dim figure groped for the light switch and the room sprang into visibility. Omerie's face was drawn with strain, and he held one hand to his head as if it ached in rhythm with Oliver's.

It was in that moment, before Omerie spoke again, that Oliver remembered Hollia's warning. "Move out, young man—move out before tonight." Wildly he wondered what threatened them all in this dark house that throbbed with the rhythms of pure terror.

Omerie in an angry voice answered the unspoken question.

"Someone has planted a subsonic in the house, Wilson. Kleph thinks you may know where it is."

"S-subsonic?"

"Call it a gadget," Omerie interpreted impatiently. "Probably a small metal box that—"

Oliver said, "Oh," in a tone that must have told Omerie everything.

"Where is it?" he demanded. "Quick. Let's get this over."

"I don't know." With an effort Oliver controlled the chattering of his teeth. "Y-you mean all this—all this is just from the little box?"

"Of course. Now tell me how to find it before we all go crazy."

Oliver got shakily out of bed, groping for his robe with nerveless hands. "I s-suppose she hid it somewhere downstairs," he said. "S-she wasn't gone long."

Omerie got the story out of him in a few brief questions. He clicked his teeth in exasperation when Oliver had finished it.

"That stupid Hollia—"

"Omerie!" Kleph's plaintive voice wailed from the hall. "Please hurry, Omerie! This is too much to stand! Oh, Omerie, please!"

Oliver stood up abruptly. Then a redoubled wave of the inexplicable pain seemed to explode in his skull at the motion, and he clutched the bedpost and reeled.

"Go find the thing yourself," he heard himself saying dizzily. "I can't even walk—"

Omerie's own temper was drawn wire-tight by the pressure in the room. He seized Oliver's shoulder and shook him, saying in a tight voice, "You let it in—now help us get it out, or—"

"It's a gadget out of your world, not mine!" Oliver said furiously.

And then it seemed to him there was a sudden coldness and silence in the room. Even the pain and the senseless terror paused for a moment. Omerie's pale, cold eyes fixed upon Oliver a stare so chill he could almost feel the ice in it.

"What do you know about our—world?" Omerie demanded.

Oliver did not speak a word. He did not need to; his face must have betrayed what he knew. He was beyond concealment in the stress of nighttime terror he still could not understand.

Omerie bared his white teeth and said three perfectly unintelligible words. Then he stepped to the door and snapped, "Kleph!"

Oliver could see the two women huddled together in the hall, shaking violently with involuntary waves of that strange, synthetic terror. Klia, in a luminous green gown, was rigid with control, but Kleph made no effort whatever at repression. Her downy robe had turned soft gold tonight; she shivered in it and the tears ran down her face unchecked.

"Kleph," Omerie said in a dangerous voice, "you were euphoric again yesterday?"

Kleph darted a scared glance at Oliver and nodded guiltily.

"You talked too much." It was a complete indictment in one sentence. "You know the rules. You will not be allowed to travel again if anyone reports this to the authorities."

Kleph's lovely creamy face creased suddenly into impenitent dimples.

"I know it was wrong. I am very sorry—but you will not stop me if Cenbe says no."

Klia flung out her arms in a gesture of helpless anger. Omerie shrugged. "In this case, as it happens, no great harm is done," he said, giving Oliver an unfathomable glance. "But it might have been serious. Next time perhaps it will be. I must have a talk with Cenbe."

"We must find the subsonic first of all," Klia reminded them, shivering. "If Kleph is afraid to help, she can go out for a while. I confess I am very sick of Kleph's company just now."

"We could give up the house!" Kleph cried wildly. "Let Hollia have it! How can you stand this long enough to hunt—"

"Give up the house?" Klia echoed. "You must be mad! With all our invitations out?"

"There will be no need for that," Omerie said. "We can find it if we all hunt. You feel able to help?" He looked at Oliver.

With an effort Oliver controlled his own senseless panic as the waves of it swept through the room. "Yes," he said. "But what about me? What are you going to do?"

"That should be obvious," Omerie said, his pale eyes in the dark face regarding Oliver impassively. "Keep you in the house until we go. We can certainly do no less. You understand that. And there is no reason for us to do more, as it happens. Silence is all we promised when we signed our travel papers."

"But—" Oliver groped for the fallacy in that reasoning. It was no use. He could not think clearly. Panic surged insanely through his mind from the very air around him. "All right," he said. "Let's hunt."

It was dawn before they found the box, tucked inside the ripped seam of a sofa cushion. Omerie took it upstairs without a word. Five minutes later the pressure in the air abruptly dropped and peace fell blissfully upon the house.

"They will try again," Omerie said to Oliver at the door of the back bedroom. "We must watch for that. As for you, must see that you remain in the house until Friday. For your own comfort, I advise you to let me know if Hollia offers any further tricks. I confess I am not quite sure how to enforce your staying indoors. I could use methods that would make you very uncomfortable. I would prefer to accept your word on it."

Oliver hesitated. The relaxing of pressure upon his brain had left him exhausted and stupid, and he was not at all sure what to say.

Omerie went on after a moment. "It was partly our fault for not ensuring that we had the house to ourselves," he said. "Living here with us, you could scarcely help suspecting. Shall we say that in return for your promise, I reimburse you in part for losing the sale price on this house?"

Oliver thought that over. It would pacify Sue a little. And it meant only two days indoors. Besides, what good would escaping do? What could he say to outsiders that would not lead him straight to a padded cell?

"All right," he said wearily. "I promise."

By Friday morning there was still no sign from Hollia. Sue telephoned at noon. Oliver knew the crackle of her voice over the wire when Kleph took the call. Even the crackle sounded hysterical; Sue saw her bargain slipping hopelessly through her grasping little fingers.

Kleph's voice was soothing. "I am sorry," she said many times, in the intervals when the voice paused. "I am truly sorry. Believe me, you will find it does not matter. I know. I am sorry—"

She turned from the phone at last. "The girl says Hollia has given up," she told the others.

"Not Hollia," Klia said firmly.

Omerie shrugged. "We have very little time left. If she intends anything more, it will be tonight. We must watch for it."

"Oh, not tonight!" Kleph's voice was horrified: "Not even Hollia would do that."

"Hollia, my dear, in her own way is quite as unscrupulous as you are," Omerie told her with a smile.

"But—would she spoil things for us just because she can't be here?"

"What do you think?" Klia demanded.

Oliver ceased to listen. There was no making sense out of their talk, but he knew that by tonight whatever the secret was must surely come into the open at last. He was willing to wait and see.

For two days excitement had been building up in the house and the three who shared it with him. Even the servants felt it and were nervous and unsure of themselves. Oliver had given up asking questions—it only embarrassed his tenants—and watched.

All the chairs in the house were collected in the three front bedrooms. The furniture was rearranged to make room for them, and dozens of covered cups had been set out on trays. Oliver recognized Kleph's rose quartz set among the rest. No steam rose from the tin crescent openings, but the cups were full. Oliver lifted one and felt a heavy liquid move within it, like something half solid, sluggishly.

Guests were obviously expected, but the regular dinner hour of nine came and went, and no one had yet arrived. Dinner was finished; the servants went home. The Sanciscos went to their rooms to dress, amid a feeling of mounting tension.

Oliver stepped out on the porch after dinner, trying in vain to guess what it was that had wrought such a pitch of expectancy in the house. There was a quarter moon swimming in haze on the horizon, but the stars which had made every night of May thus far a dazzling translucency were very dim tonight. Clouds had begun to gather at sundown, and the undimmed weather of the whole month seemed ready to break at last.

Behind Oliver the door opened a little, and closed. He caught Kleph's fragrance before he turned, and a faint whiff of the fragrance of the euphoriac she was much too fond of drinking. She came to his side and slipped a hand into his, looking up into his face in the darkness.

"Oliver," she said very softly. "Promise me one thing. Promise me not to leave the house tonight."

"I've already promised that," he said a little irritably.

"I know. But tonight—I have a very particular reason for wanting you indoors tonight." She leaned her head against his shoulder for a moment, and despite himself his irritation softened. He had not seen Kleph alone since that last night of her revelations; he supposed he never would be alone with her again for more than a few minutes at a time. But he knew he would not forget those two bewildering evenings. He knew too, now, that she was very weak and foolish—but she was still Kleph and he had held her in his arms, and was not likely ever to forget it.

"You might be—hurt—if you went out tonight," she was saying in a muffled voice. "I know it will not matter, in the end, but—remember you promised, Oliver."

She was gone again, and the door had closed behind her, before he could voice the futile questions in his mind.

The guests began to arrive just before midnight. From the head of the stairs Oliver saw them coming in by twos and threes, and was astonished at how many of these people from the future must have gathered here in the past weeks. He could see quite clearly now how they differed from the norm in his own period. Their physical elegance was what one noticed first—perfect grooming, meticulous manners, meticulously controlled voices. But because they were all idle, all, in a way, sensation-hunters, there was a certain shrillness underlying their voices, especially when heard all together. Petulance and self-indulgence showed beneath the good manners. And tonight, an all-pervasive excitement.

By one o'clock everyone had gathered in the front rooms. The teacups had begun to steam, apparently of themselves, around midnight, and the house was full of the faint, thin fragrance that induced a sort of euphoria all through the rooms, breathed in with the perfume of the tea.

It made Oliver feel light and drowsy. He was determined to sit up as long as the others did, but he must have dozed off in his own room, by the window, an unopened book in his lap.

For when it happened he was not sure for a few minutes whether or not it was a dream.

The vast, incredible crash was louder than sound. He felt the whole house shake under him, felt rather than heard the timbers grind upon one another like broken bones, while he was still in the borderland of sleep. When he woke fully he was on the floor among the shattered fragments of the window.

How long or short a time he had lain there he did not know. The world was still stunned with that tremendous noise, or his ears still deaf from it, for there was no sound anywhere.

He was halfway down the hall towards the front rooms when sound began to return from outside. It was a low, indescribable rumble at first, prickled with countless tiny distant screams. Oliver's eardrums ached from the terrible impact of the vast unheard noise, but the numbness was wearing off and he heard before he saw it the first voices of the stricken city.

The door to Kleph's room resisted him for a moment. The house had settled a little from the violence of the—the explosion?—and the frame was out of line. When he got the door open he could only stand blinking stupidly into the darkness within. All the lights were out, but there was a breathless sort of whispering going on by many voices.

The chairs were drawn around the broad front windows so that everyone could see out; the air swam with the fragrance of euphoria. There was light enough here from outside for Oliver to see that a few onlookers still had their hands to their ears, but all were craning eagerly forward to see.

Through a dreamlike haze Oliver saw the city spread out with impossible distinctness below the window. He knew quite well that a row of houses across the street blocked the view— yet he was looking over the city now, and he could see it in a limitless panorama from here to the horizon. The houses between had vanished.

On the far skyline fire was already a solid mass, painting the low clouds crimson. That sulphurous light reflecting back from the sky upon the city made clear the rows upon rows of flattened houses with flame beginning to lick up among them, and farther out the formless rubble of what had been houses a few minutes ago and was now nothing at all.

The city had begun to be vocal. The noise of the flames rose loudest, but you could hear a rumble of human voices like the beat of surf a long way off, and staccato noises of screaming made a sort of pattern that came and went continuously through the web of sound. Threading it in undulating waves the shrieks of sirens knit the web together into a terrible symphony that had, in its way, a strange, inhuman beauty.

Briefly through Oliver's stunned incredulity went the memory of that other symphony Kleph had played here one day, another catastrophe retold in terms of music and moving shapes.

He said hoarsely: "Kleph—"

The tableau by the window broke. Every head turned, and Oliver saw the faces of strangers staring at him, some few in embarrassment avoiding his eyes, but most seeking them out with that avid, inhuman curiosity which is common to a type in all crowds at accident scenes. But these people were here by design, audience at a vast disaster timed almost for their coming.

Kleph got up unsteadily, her velvet dinner gown tripping her as she rose. She set down a cup and swayed a little as she came towards the door, saying, "Oliver . . . Oliver—" in a sweet, uncertain voice. She was drunk, he saw, and wrought up by the catastrophe to a pitch of stimulation in which she was not very sure what she was doing.

Oliver heard himself saying in a thin voice not his own, "W-what was it, Kleph? What happened? What—" But *happened* seemed so inadequate a word for the incredible panorama below that he had to choke back hysterical laughter upon the struggling questions, and broke off entirely, trying to control the shaking that had seized his body.

Kleph made an unsteady stoop and seized a steaming cup. She came to him, swaying, holding it out—her panacea for all ills.

"Here, drink it, Oliver—we are all quite safe here, quite safe." She thrust the cup to his lips and he gulped automatically, grateful for the fumes that began their slow, coiling surcease in his brain with the first swallow.

"It was a meteor," Kleph was saying. "Quite a small meteor,

really. We are perfectly safe here. This house was never touched."

Out of some cell of the unconscious Oliver heard himself saying incoherently, "Sue? Is Sue—" he could not finish.

Kleph thrust the cup at him again. "I think she may be safe—for a while. Please, Oliver—forget about all that and drink."

"But you *knew!*" Realization of that came belatedly to his stunned brain. "You could have given warning, or—"

"How could we change the past?" Kleph asked. "We knew— but could we stop the meteor? Or warn the city? Before we come we must give our word never to interfere—"

Their voices had risen imperceptibly to be audible above the rising volume of sound from below. The city was roaring now, with flames and cries and the crash of falling buildings. Light in the room turned lurid and pulsed upon the walls and ceiling in red light and redder dark.

Downstairs a door slammed. Someone laughed. It was high, hoarse, angry laughter. Then from the crowd in the room someone gasped and there was a chorus of dismayed cries. Oliver tried to focus upon the window and the terrible panorama beyond, and found he could not.

It took several seconds of determined blinking to prove that more than his own vision was at fault. Kleph whimpered softly and moved against him. His arms closed about her automatically, and he was grateful for the warm, solid flesh against him. This much at least he could touch and be sure of, though everything else that was happening might be a dream. Her perfume and the heady perfume of the tea rose together in his head, and for an instant, holding her in this embrace that must certainly be the last time he ever held her, he did not care that something had gone terribly wrong with the very air of the room.

It was blindness—not continuous, but a series of swift, widening ripples between which he could catch glimpses of the other faces in the room, strained and astonished in the flickering light from the city.

The ripples came faster. There was only a blink of sight between them now, and the blinks grew briefer and briefer, the intervals of darkness more broad.

From downstairs the laughter rose again up the stairwell. Oliver thought he knew the voice. He opened his mouth to speak, but a door nearby slammed open before he could find his tongue, and Omerie shouted down the stairs.

"Hollia?" he roared above the roaring of the city. "Hollia, is that you?"

She laughed again, triumphantly. "I warned you!" her hoarse, harsh voice called. "Now come out in the street with the rest of us if you want to see any more!"

"Hollia!" Omerie shouted desperately. "Stop this or—"

The laughter was derisive. "What will you do, Omerie? This time I hid it too well—come down in the street if you want to watch the rest."

There was angry silence in the house. Oliver could feel Kleph's quick, excited breathing light upon his cheek, feel the soft motions of her body in his arms. He tried consciously to make the moment last, stretch it out to infinity. Everything had happened too swiftly to impress very clearly on his mind anything except what he could touch and hold. He held her in an embrace made consciously light, though he wanted to clasp her in a tight, despairing grip, because he was sure this was the last embrace they would ever share.

The eye-straining blinks of light and blindness went on. From far away below the roar of the burning city rolled on, threaded together by the long, looped cadences of the sirens that linked all sounds into one.

Then in the bewildering dark another voice sounded from the hall downstairs. A man's voice, very deep, very melodious, saying:

"What is this? What are you doing here? Hollia—is that you?"

Oliver felt Kleph stiffen in his arms. She caught her breath, but she said nothing in the instant while heavy feet began to mount the stairs, coming up with a solid, confident tread that shook the old house to each step.

Then Kleph thrust herself hard out of Oliver's arms. He heard her high, sweet, excited voice crying, "Cenbe! Cenbe!" and she ran to meet the newcomer through the waves of dark and light that swept the shaken house.

Oliver staggered a little and felt a chair seat catching the back of his legs. He sank into it and lifted to his lips the cup he still held. Its steam was warm and moist in his face, though he could scarcely make out the shape of the rim.

He lifted it with both hands and drank.

When he opened his eyes it was quite dark in the room. Also it was silent except for a thin, melodious humming almost below the threshold of sound. Oliver struggled with the memory of a monstrous nightmare. He put it resolutely out of his mind and sat up, feeling an unfamiliar bed creak and sway under him.

This was Kleph's room. But no—Kleph's no longer. Her

shining hangings were gone from the walls, her white resilient rug, her pictures. The room looked as it had looked before she came, except for one thing.

In the far corner was a table—a block of translucent stuff— out of which light poured softly. A man sat on a low stool before it, leaning forward, his heavy shoulders outlined against the glow. He wore earphones and he was making quick, erratic notes upon a pad on his knee, swaying a little as if to the tune of unheard music.

The curtains were drawn, but from beyond them came a distant, muffled roaring that Oliver remembered from his nightmare. He put a hand to his face, aware of a feverish warmth and a dipping of the room before his eyes. His head ached, and there was a deep malaise in every limb and nerve.

As the bed creaked, the man in the corner turned, sliding the earphones down like a collar. He had a strong, sensitive face above a dark beard, trimmed short. Oliver had never seen him before, but he had that air Oliver knew so well by now, of remoteness which was the knowledge of time itself lying like a gulf between them.

When he spoke his deep voice was impersonally kind.

"You had too much euphoriac, Wilson," he said, aloofly sympathetic. "You slept a long while."

"How long?" Oliver's throat felt sticky when he spoke.

The man did not answer. Oliver shook his head experimentally. He said, "I thought Kleph said you don't get hangovers from—" Then another thought interrupted the first, and he said quickly, "Where is Kleph?" He looked confusedly towards the door.

"They should be in Rome by now. Watching Charlemagne's coronation at St. Peter's on Christmas Day a thousand years from here."

That was not a thought Oliver could grasp clearly. His aching brain sheered away from it; he found thinking at all was strangely difficult. Staring at the man, he traced an idea painfully to its conclusion.

"So they've gone on—but you stayed behind? Why? You . . . you're Cenbe? I heard your—symphonia, Kleph called it."

"You heard part of it. I have not finished yet. I needed—this." Cenbe inclined his head towards the curtains beyond which the subdued roaring still went on.

"You needed—the meteor?" The knowledge worked painfully through his dulled brain until it seemed to strike some area still untouched by the aching, an area still alive to implication. "The *meteor?* But . . ."

There was a power implicit in Cenbe's raised hand that seemed to push Oliver down upon the bed again. Cenbe said patiently, "The worst of it is past now, for a while. Forget if you can. That was days ago. I said you were asleep for some time. I let you rest. I knew this house would be safe—from the fire at least."

"Then—something more's to come?" Oliver only mumbled his question. He was not sure he wanted an answer. He had been curious so long, and now that knowledge lay almost within reach, something about his brain seemed to refuse to listen. Perhaps this weariness, this feverish, dizzy feeling would pass as the effect of the euphoriac wore off.

Cenbe's voice ran on smoothly, soothingly, almost as if Cenbe too did not want him to think. It was easiest to lie here and listen.

"I am a composer," Cenbe was saying. "I happen to be interested in interpreting certain forms of disaster into my own terms. That is why I stayed on. The others were dilettantes. They came for the May weather and the spectacle. The aftermath—well, why should they wait for that? As for myself—I suppose I am a connoisseur. I find the aftermath rather fascinating. And I need it. I need to study it at first hand, for my own purposes."

His eyes dwelt upon Oliver for an instant very keenly, like a physician's eyes, impersonal and observing. Absently he reached for his stylus and the note pad. And as he moved, Oliver saw a familiar mark on the underside of the thick, tanned wrist.

"Kleph had that scar, too," he heard himself whisper. "And the others."

Cenbe nodded. "Inoculation. It was necessary, under the circumstances. We did not want disease to spread in our own time-world."

"Disease?"

Cenbe shrugged. "You would not recognize the name."

"But, if you can inoculate against disease—" Oliver thrust himself up on an aching arm. He had a half grasp upon a thought now which he did not want to let go. Effort seemed to make the ideas come more clearly through his mounting confusion. With enormous effort he went on.

"I'm getting it now," he said. "Wait. I've been trying to work this out. You can change history? You can! I know you can. Kleph said she had to promise not to interfere. You all had to promise. Does that mean you really could change your own past—our time?"

Cenbe laid down his pad again. He looked at Oliver thoughtfully, a dark, intent look under heavy brows. "Yes," he said. "Yes, the past can be changed, but not easily. And it changes the future, too, necessarily. The lines of probability are switched into new patterns—but it is extremely difficult, and it has never been allowed. The physiotemporal course tends to slide back to its norm, always. That is why it is so hard to force any alteration." He shrugged. "A theoretical science. We do not change history, Wilson. If we changed our past, our present would be altered, too. And our time-world is entirely to our liking. There may be a few malcontents there, but they are not allowed the privilege of temporal travel."

Oliver spoke louder against the roaring from beyond the windows. "But you've got the power! You could alter history, if you wanted to—wipe out all the pain and suffering and tragedy—"

"All of that passed away long ago," Cenbe said.

"Not—*now!* Not—*this!*"

Cenbe looked at him enigmatically for a while. Then—"This, too," he said.

And suddenly Oliver realized from across what distances Cenbe was watching him. A vast distance, as time is measured. Cenbe was a composer and a genius, and necessarily strongly empathic, but his psychic locus was very far away in time. The dying city outside, the whole world of *now* was not quite real to Cenbe, falling short of reality because of that basic variance in time. It was merely one of the building blocks that had gone to support the edifice on which Cenbe's culture stood in a misty, unknown, terrible future.

It seemed terrible to Oliver now. Even Kleph—all of them had been touched with a pettiness, the faculty that had enabled Hollia to concentrate on her malicious, small schemes to acquire a ringside seat while the meteor thundered in towards Earth's atmosphere. They were all dilettantes, Kleph and Omerie and the others. They toured time, but only as onlookers. Were they bored—sated—with their normal existence?

Not sated enough to wish change, basically. Their own time-world was a fulfilled womb, a perfection made manifest for their needs. They dared not change the past—they could not risk flawing their own present.

Revulsion shook him. Remembering the touch of Kleph's lips, he felt a sour sickness on his tongue. Alluring she had been: he knew that too well. But the aftermath—

There was something about this race from the future. He had felt it dimly at first, before Kleph's nearness had drowned caution and buffered his sensibilities. Time traveling purely as an escape mechanism seemed almost blasphemous. A race with such power—

Kleph—leaving him for the barbaric, splendid coronation at Rome a thousand years ago—*how had she seen him?* Not as a living, breathing man. He knew that, very certainly Kleph's race were spectators.

But he read more than casual interest in Cenbe's eyes now. There was an avidity there, a bright, fascinated probing. The man had replaced his earphones—he was different from the others. He was a connoisseur. After the vintage season came the aftermath—and Cenbe.

Cenbe watched and waited, light flickering softly in the translucent block before him, his fingers poised over the note pad. The ultimate connoisseur waited to savor the rarities that no nongourmet could appreciate.

Those thin, distant rhythms of sound that was almost music began to be audible again above the noises of the distant fire. Listening, remembering. Oliver could very nearly catch the pattern of the symphonia as he had heard it, all intermingled

ith the flash of changing faces and the rank upon rank of the
ying—

He lay back on the bed letting the room swirl away into
he darkness behind his closed and aching lids. The ache was
mplicit in every cell of his body, almost a second ego taking
ossession and driving him out of himself, a strong, sure ego
aking over as he himself let go.

Why, he wondered dully, should Kleph have lied? She had
aid there was no aftermath to the drink she had given him.
No aftermath—and yet this painful possession was strong
nough to edge him out of his own body.

Kleph had not lied. It was no aftermath to drink. He knew
nat—but the knowledge no longer touched his brain or his
ody. He lay still, giving them up to the power of the illness
which was aftermath to something far stronger than the strong-
st drink. The illness that had no name—yet.

Cenbe's new symphonia was a crowning triumph. It had its
remière from Antares hall, and the applause was an ovation.
History itself, of course, was the artist—opening with the
neteor that forecast the great plagues of the fourteenth cen-
ury and closing with the climax Cenbe had caught on the
areshold of modern times. But only Cenbe could have in-
erpreted it with such subtle power.

Critics spoke of the masterly way in which he had chosen
ne face of the Stuart king as a recurrent motif against the
nontage of emotion and sound and movement. But there were
:her faces, fading through the great sweep of the composi-
on, which helped to build up to the tremendous climax. One
ice in particular, one moment that the audience absorbed
·eedily. A moment in which one man's face loomed huge in
ne screen, every feature clear. Cenbe had never caught an

emotional crisis so effectively, the critics agreed. You coul
almost read the man's eyes.

After Cenbe had left, he lay motionless for a long while
He was thinking feverishly—

*I've got to find some way to tell people. If I'd known i
advance, maybe something could have been done. We'd hav
forced them to tell us how to change the probabilities. W
could have evacuated the city.*

If I could leave a message—

*Maybe not for today's people. But later. They visit all throug
time. If they could be recognized and caught somewhere, som
time, and made to change destiny—*

It wasn't easy to stand up. The room kept tilting. But h
managed it. He found pencil and paper and through the sway
ing of the shadows he wrote down what he could. Enough
Enough to warn, enough to save.

He put the sheets on the table, in plain sight, and weighte
them down before he stumbled back to bed through closin
darkness.

The house was dynamited six days later, part of the futil
attempt to halt the relentless spread of the Blue Death.